Paradise is Deadly
Gripping Tales from Florida's Gulf Coast

Edited by

Wendy Dingwall
Martha Reed
Barbara Ryan

Mystery and Horror, LCC
Clearwater, Florida

Paradise is Deadly

Gripping Tales from
Florida's Gulf Coast

ISBN: 978-1-949281-24-8

Editors
Wendy Dingwall
Martha Reed
Barbara Ryan

Cover by
Karen Phillips/PhillipsCovers.com

Paradise is Deadly
Gripping Tales from
Florida's Gulf Coast

TABLE OF CONTENTS

INTRODUCTION

Lisa Black

Florida is a state of contradictions.

We have oranges and alligators, spring breakers, and old money. One can live in a cracker shack without air conditioning or a 173-million-dollar mansion on the shores of the Gulf Coast. In a state that produces some of the worst natural disasters, one can also comb its swamps for some of the rarest, most delicate orchids on the planet. We have the oldest city in the United States, with new ones popping up as over eight hundred people move in per *day*. For fun, head to the swamp buggy races or the ballet, a tractor pull, or the Salvador Dali Museum—or the largest knot of amusement parks to be found. The only things that *don't* vary are the weather—there's hot, hotter, and hot & rainy—and the elevation, 345 feet at the state's highest point.

The murders, however, are a different story. No pun intended.

In Florida, our murders are uniformly un-uniform. Perhaps we add the variety to our crime that we lack in weather and feet-above-sea-level.

Over the years, the state has gotten a reputation for the bizarre, the inexplicable, the defies-explanation. I can attest to this from personal experience—I've been a forensic specialist for a big small town in southwest Florida for over twenty years. We had two unrelated grandsons-killing-grandpas cases within a week of each other. We had a teenager stab another teen upwards of 175 times. We've had two separate people murder a total stranger because they 'wanted to see how it feels.' We also had a man hit his neighbor with his cane and then try to evade arrest by speeding away on his motorized wheelchair. And that's just my relatively sleepy big little town.

And every few years, this tropical paradise itself tries to kill you with hurricanes, floods, sinkholes, and tornados.

We don't complain. At least we're not boring.

And so, the stories in *Paradise is Deadly* reflect that need for variety. They range from creepy to terrifying to old-school whodunit to just plain fun. Their plots revolve around archaeological digs, murder for hire, and the accurate pricing of second-hand designer purses. All use the details that make this state stand out from the other forty-nine: the weather, alligators, Florida Man, and of course, a skunk ape.

If you're from Florida, you'll understand. If not, enjoy!

And come visit—it's really a very safe place.

Most of the time, anyway.

A LONG-TERM PLAN

Jenny Ramaley

Charlotte pulled off the rural road and parked the old 'Jacob's Orange Groves' truck in a yard overflowing with cars. Music floated from the house, and tiny white lights draped around the porch twinkled in the dusk. The metal roof was new. So was the siding. Mrs. Flores had done a great job redoing the 1950s farmhouse. Wearing faded Carhartt gear from a canvas cap to her dusty work boots, the stocky young woman lifted a large wicker gift basket off the worn passenger seat and stepped into south-central Florida's heavy, humid air. Sunset colored the May sky with splotches of blue and purple, colors that made Charlotte think of bruises.

A brand-new Dodge Ram 2500 pickup slammed to a stop, slinging gravel at the edge of the tough zoysia grass and blaring twangy country music. Charlotte felt a stab of envy—not for the speakers or the fancy wheels, but for the heavy-duty HEMI V8 engine. One day she'd own a decent truck.

A woman in a Walmart sundress climbed out as the driver yelled, "I'll be back at nine o'clock. You better be ready." She stumbled when the truck roared away, almost dropping a pastel gift bag.

Charlotte wound her way through the cars. "You okay, Mandy?"

"I'm fine. You know Tommy. Always in a hurry."

Charlotte managed to not roll her eyes. Together, they walked toward the house, passing a bouquet of pink and blue balloons tied to the light post, the shorter woman strong and tan from working outdoors, the other one pale and delicate.

"How's everything? You busy at Yankovitch's?" Charlotte asked.

"We sure are. Hey, do you want a pen? He put our favorite motto on them." Mandy dug a ballpoint from her purse and read the slogan out loud: "Yankovitch Insurance: Because Everyone Needs a Long-Term Plan."

Charlotte laughed. "Good old Mr. Yankovitch. Boy, you didn't waste any time bugging that man for a job after he talked to us on Career Day."

"Second best decision I made in high school. Hard to believe it's been three years since graduation." Mandy winked at Charlotte. At the bottom porch step, she took a deep breath like she was steeling herself before heading into battle. "Ready? We better get inside and wish the future mother all the best."

They stepped into a house overflowing with baby decorations and stylish young women who called loud greetings to the newcomers.

Charlotte whispered, "Five bucks says they already spiked the punch bowl."

"I'm not taking that bet," Mandy said.

A giggling woman hooked her arm through Mandy's. "Hey, girl. When are we throwing a baby shower for you and Tommy? You've been married two years already."

Before Mandy could answer, the party's expectant star announced it was time to start the Diaper Game. The giggling woman pulled Mandy into the living room with the others.

Charlotte hung back, like always, not sure where to set her big basket until Mrs. Flores swooped to the rescue.

"What a lovely gift assortment." A touch of gray showed near the future grandmother's temples. The look suited her. "Jacob's has the best orange marmalade. And these baby bibs are adorable."

"Let me know if you like the lemon-scented candles. They're new this year at the store." Charlotte shoved her hands into her pockets. "Sorry I'm late, ma'am. We're busy getting our fruit shipments out."

"I'm so glad you made it." Mrs. Flores put her hand on Charlotte's arm. "I was sorry to hear about your father. I'd have attended the memorial service if one had been held. Did you get my condolence card?"

"Yes, thank you. Daddy made his wishes clear about not having a service or a visitation. He said he didn't want anyone crying over him. You know what he was like."

"Yes, we all knew what Jacob Grey was like." Stepping closer, she lowered her voice. "Are the rumors true? Did Jacob shortchange you in favor of your brothers?"

Charlotte kept her face a neutral mask, hiding the anger and hurt she felt. "I didn't know those details were public."

"You know what Arcadia's like. In a small town, everyone knows everything."

Not everything, thought Charlotte. She decided she'd rather get the truth out than have distorted rumors spreading like citrus blight. "Daddy left me the store, the packinghouse, and some scrubland around the buildings, which comes to one-fifth of the property. My brothers split all the grove land, two-fifths each."

"How nice. They can sit in their cushy office jobs in Fort Myers while you stay here, do all the work, and give them the lion's share of the profit."

"I guess that's one way of looking at it, ma'am. But it wasn't a surprise. Daddy set it up that way when I was still in high school."

"He sent both boys to college. Why didn't you get to go? You were one of my brightest math students."

"I wanted to go. I planned to double major in business and agriculture, but Daddy got sick after my brothers graduated. The money was needed for other things. It's never too late, though. I've signed up for two online courses during the off-season." Now that her father was finally gone.

"Good for you. When you came in with Mandy, I remembered the project you two did in my Personal Finance class." She chuckled. "How to open a shell company! That was very advanced work for high school seniors. I didn't tell anyone at the time, but I had to research the topic before I could grade your paper. Whatever you decide to do, whether it's staying to run the groves or not, I'm sure you'll be successful. Mandy too, unless that Neanderthal she married ruins her life." She motioned to a table covered with platters of food. "Be sure to get something to eat."

* * *

Stars dotted the dark sky as Charlotte stood alone on the porch. She dug into a plate piled with pasta salad and chicken wings while snippets of conversation floated from the open living room windows, a mixture of town talk and baby tips. A few minutes before nine o'clock, goodbyes were called to Mandy, who slipped through the front door and stood watching the empty road, arms clutched tight over her chest like she was cold.

Charlotte pulled a small tin from her pocket and handed it to Mandy. "This is a new healing salve made from our beehives. It's good for cuts or scrapes."

Mandy's hand flew to a small bandage on her forehead, barely visible beneath her bangs. "It's nothing. But thanks."

"I ran into Jada the other day. She said you're a regular at the walk-in clinic."

Headlights appeared in the distance. Mandy edged toward the steps. "I've gotten awful clumsy lately."

"People have noticed. I've noticed." Charlotte bumped the toe of her boot on the porch floor. "Mrs. Flores mentioned our senior project. We should kick start the rest of our plan soon."

Mandy never took her eyes off the road. "Not until the timing's perfect. We have to stick to the schedule, Char."

"Okay. Call me when you're ready." She also watched the oncoming headlights. "Has Tommy found any work lately? To pay for his big, new truck?"

"He says no one's hiring."

"Tell him to come see me. He's still on my books from earlier this year. Tell him he'll get paid as a Senior Supervisor, like before."

The big pickup screeched to a stop at the side of the road.

"I'll call as soon as I can. Promise." Mandy flew off the porch at a run. Before she got the passenger door closed, the truck roared away, leaving in its wake the soft night sounds of chirping crickets.

A linen curtain lifted and fell at the living room window. "She's gone," said one of the young women from inside. Charlotte turned her attention to a tasty Cuban sandwich, listening while voices from the party guests once again drifted outside.

"Can you believe Tommy Fox married Mousy Mandy? I mean, he's so handsome. What does he see in her?"

"Come on, Katelyn. Tommy's a good-looking idiot who can't hold down a job. He married Mandy because she brings home the cash."

"Roseanne's mom works for Mr. Yankovitch too. She said they get great benefits—medical, vision, a 401K, and life insurance, of course. I'd say marrying Mandy was about the smartest thing Tommy ever did."

"It's not the smartest thing Mandy ever did. Remember how he hit Angie Rodriguez after prom? He busted her lip open."

"I was there! I saw it happen. That wasn't the first time he hit Angie, but it was the first time we saw him do it in person."

"Maybe Mandy didn't know. She was two years younger."

"How could she not know? Everybody knew."

A wicked laugh rang out. "Maybe she's the smart one. I bet Tommy's worth the trouble if you know what I mean!" Much whooping followed before the crowd returned to oohing and aahing over baby clothes.

Charlotte's daddy used to hit her mama all the time, until one day, Mama up and disappeared, never to be heard from again. She hadn't left anything behind, not even a note for her only daughter. A year later, Charlotte found the sapphire ring Mama always wore at the edge of Daddy's dump pile. Jewelry wasn't a real goodbye, but it felt nice to have something that was her mother's. Charlotte set down her empty plate, still thinking about Mandy and the reports from the clinic. At least that sixteen-year-old girl from Clermont who'd brought charges against Tommy three months ago had dropped the complaint. After the girl's family pulled up stakes and left for Gainesville, two strange men showed up and beat the crap out of Tommy. The police never caught the two men, but she doubted they'd looked very hard. Busted ribs were no joke, but Tommy had milked his injuries and quit work right in the middle of orange-picking season.

Charlotte hoped Mandy knew what she was doing.

* * *

A week after the baby shower, the whole town heard that Mandy was back at the clinic, this time with a dislocated shoulder. Thankfully she didn't need surgery. Jada told Charlotte that she'd urged Mandy to file a police report this time and create a paper trail, but Mandy had refused, saying, "I can't ever leave. That's the most dangerous time for a woman. That's when they'll kill you."

Mandy began physical therapy the same day Charlotte conducted the last 'Jacob's Orange Groves' tour of the season. From an open-air trolley filled with visitors, she took great pride in driving past tidy rows of citrus trees, all thriving on land that had been in her family for decades. Charlotte and her crew demonstrated how they clamped a mechanical arm around a tree trunk and shook it until the oranges fell into a tarp below the branches. The funnel shape of the tarp—lots of the kids shouted that it looked like batwings—guided the fruit to a collection box hitched to the tractor. After a quick stop to explain the packing and shipping process, Charlotte showed the sunburned tourists the massive composting system she'd developed from her father's original dump pile. She described how the orange peels left from juicing were transformed over time into nutrient-rich soil that went back into the land to nourish the fruit trees, completing a full cycle of the citrus farming life. At the end of the tour, Charlotte steered the sweaty, red-faced group into her fruit and souvenir store, betting they were now ready to cool off with icy cones of orange sherbet. As the final stragglers plodded inside, Charlotte's battered cell phone buzzed.

As she listened to the caller, her heartbeat quickened. "My winter crew finishes today," Charlotte said in a low voice. "They're heading north to work the soybean fields in Ohio, so the timing should be good. Tell him to stop by tomorrow around five." After hanging up, she leaned against the wall, thinking while she watched the seasonal workers in the packinghouse. Some of the crew stacked empty crates on shelves while others swept the floor or wiped down the ancient conveyor belts – all the tasks that needed to be done at the end of the growing season before she locked the building until next fall.

Outside, an ancient woodchipper and a mini-Bobcat digger from 1996 sat parked near the building. Charlotte ran through the checklist of everything she wanted to do today. After the workers finished the cleanup, she'd shift her attention to the compost piles. She needed to move half of the biggest pile to an open area at the back of the lot. Yes, Tommy coming tomorrow was perfect timing.

* * *

The next night, a quarter moon glowed while Charlotte worked the Bobcat's controls, dumping a final scoop on top of a new compost pile. Dragging out a hose, she scrubbed the woodchipper, then rinsed herself off too. The cold water from the hose felt rejuvenating.

Wearing blue latex gloves and a faded Tampa Bay Lightning sweatshirt with the hood pulled up, she drove a Dodge Ram pickup miles away from her family's property to a secluded

7

spot she knew near the Peace River. She turned onto a rutted, two-strip dirt road bordered by thick, native foliage. Palm ferns and hanging tendrils of Spanish moss scratched the fancy paint job as she steered over the rough terrain. Gunning the powerful vehicle, she ran the wheels up and over a clump of sawgrass palmetto until the right tires left the ground.

She cut the engine and took a moment to breathe. Heat and humidity snaked in the open windows while her eyes adjusted to the dark. The shrill nocturnal chorus of cicadas and barking tree frogs rose around her. Leaving the key fob in the cup holder, Charlotte grabbed a stuffed garbage bag, shook a pair of jeans and a T-shirt onto the ground near a marshy pond, and tossed a pair of work boots near a sign that read: *Caution - Alligator Area*. She picked through the empty, crumpled beer cans littering the floor of the cab and tossed two outside. Glancing around, she checked for any signs of life in the night, but no animals or humans stirred. Still wearing blue latex gloves, she hefted a rusty man's bike from the back of the pickup, slung it over her shoulder, and picked her way to a rarely used trail, careful not to break any branches along the way.

A narrow dirt road waited at the end of the twisty path. Charlotte pushed her way past a clump of southern shield ferns, feeling pleased to see no headlights or taillights in either direction. She mounted the bike and began to pedal. Miles later, the lights of Arcadia shone on her left as she coasted into a low-rent apartment complex and slipped behind a dumpster. Leaning the bike against an abandoned plaid couch, she peeled off the baggy men's clothing and tossed everything into the trash, revealing her own clothes—bike shorts and a tank top. Without looking back, she trotted to the main road and began running at a steady pace, away from the lights of the complex and town.

A rusty pickup slowed beside her while she ran along State Route 760. Six men sat crowded into the crew cab. Juan, one of her favorite workers, called from the front passenger seat, "Where's your bike, *Señora Jefa*?"

Charlotte didn't break stride. "I'm training for a triathlon. Trying to improve my run times. You guys heading north now?"

"Si. Thanks for the sandwiches, boss lady. We'll see you next fall."

"Drive safe, guys."

A mile up the road, Charlotte turned onto a long driveway and jogged by the fruit store to the house where her father had died only a month ago. The shrubs and flowers she'd planted around the foundation helped detract from the siding's peeling paint. She'd get all that fixed now that no one was here to stop her.

Charlotte was finally free to make changes and do things the right way. And while she planned to do many things, she didn't plan to rush. There was plenty of time.

SEVEN YEARS LATER

Mandy practiced looking sad in the mirror. She slumped her shoulders and forced her lips to not turn upwards. Taking a deep breath, she opened the three-ring binder, where she had carefully cataloged every detail of Tommy's disappearance. The initial searches. The article the local paper ran when state troopers found the truck with his clothes. The day they dragged a section of the river. Interrogations of that poor girl's family in Gainesville. She remembered how efforts to find her husband soon faded to nothing despite her quiet, tearful protest. Even the investigator stopped dropping by after she refused a third invite to his favorite barbeque joint.

She snapped the binder shut. Ten years of her life had been spent focusing on Tommy Fox. That ended today.

* * *

At the office, Mandy sat across the desk from Mr. Yankovitch, who straightened a stack of legal documents sitting before him.

"Southern Guardian Insurance wired the money to your bank account this morning," he said. "I apologize for the long wait, but as you know, when there's no body, the insurer is not required to pay the policy until seven years have passed, although I verified your good character and told them what a capable, trustworthy employee you are. I explained that you signed up for such a large policy because your late mother always kept one for your dad as a safety measure. How she believed if they bought insurance, they'd never need it, but if she didn't keep paying the premium, your father would surely wreck his car and leave your family penniless."

"I can't believe you remember that story."

"Of course I do. When you got married, you said you wanted a million-dollar policy to keep your new husband safe and by your side forever. Well, even the best-laid plans …" His voice trailed off. "Luckily, you bought our office benefit contract two years and one month before Tommy's unfortunate event, so you exceeded the cut-off period by thirty days, thank goodness. The company has awarded you the full amount of the insurance policy, as they should."

"Thank you for your help, Mr. Yankovitch. The money will never replace Tommy, but it will be a big help." Yes, it would—and she'd earned every dime.

He cleared his throat. "Mandy, were you aware that a second policy had been taken on Tommy's life, a COLI?"

"A corporate policy?" Mandy asked although she knew exactly what a COLI was, having passed her insurance exam five years ago. "I'd forgotten about that. Tommy said something once about signing a life insurance policy at work, way back when we were first engaged. He said one of his employers bought policies for all their key employees, and Tommy had been hired as a supervisor. He worked on and off for several different companies. I'm surprised the coverage was still in effect."

"A shell company bought it through me, although I never met anyone in person. I wasn't at liberty to tell you about it, but I am curious who the owners are. Any ideas?"

She shrugged. "I don't have a clue. From everything I've read, shell companies are set up to keep the owners' identities confidential. But you're the expert on that, Mr. Yankovitch."

"Yes, but we don't sell many COLIs, and I'm getting rusty in my old age. Are you sure I can't talk you into staying? You've been my best-selling agent for three years. I'll sell you half the business. You've got the money now to invest in your future."

A plate glass window overlooked the office and the women who'd been her coworkers for a decade. Mandy hoped Mr. Yankovitch was able to keep the financial details private from the staff and out of the Arcadia gossip mill. She pasted on a sad smile. "Although I do appreciate the business offer, I've decided to relocate to Sarasota. It's time for a fresh start."

Mandy liked everything about Sarasota, from the downtown marina filled with shiny boats to the silky white sand of Siesta Beach. She didn't mention that she'd already rented downtown office space on Pineapple Avenue. She planned to stick with what she knew, and people were already calling her about buying insurance. Over time, maybe she'd expand into setting up shell companies.

After climbing in the cab of the Ram pickup, now seven years old and paid off, Mandy drove to the walk-in clinic. She left Jada with a fat envelope of cash to help Arcadia's battered women who didn't have a long-term plan, to be used at the nurse practitioner's discretion. Jada wished her all the best, then Mandy began the forty-two-mile drive to a Sarasota Lexus dealer where a silver IS 300 sat waiting for her trade-in.

* * *

Across town at Jacob's Orange Groves, Charlotte pulled a vibrating iPhone from her pocket, not surprised to see her brother's name displayed on the screen. Jacob Jr. was in a mood. His shouting voice assaulted her through the speaker: "What the hell did you do? We got a letter that said you sold your part of the business to some company we've never heard of! They just made us a lowball offer on our trees. We've never been so insulted in our lives."

Charlotte let him rant, glancing around her new, modern processing building built on the once scrubby land behind her store, using savvy small business loans and grants from the State of Florida and the U.S. Department of Agriculture. She watched as one of her brother's citrus-growing competitors backed a truckload of grapefruit to the unloading dock. Nearby, her renovated fruit store was packed with more tourists than ever, all of them jostling to order crates of Honeybell oranges to ship home to family and friends.

"What are we supposed to do with our crop now? Let the fruit drop and rot? What in blazes were you thinking?"

"I'm thinking that I need a change of scenery." Charlotte took a breath, drawing on years of experience controlling her emotions when dealing with entitled men. "The groves are twice as profitable for you than me. If you don't sell your trees, I'm sure the new corporate owner will make you a fair offer for your fruit, although now you'll have to use some of your profits to hire a grove overseer and pay them an actual salary."

"What're you implying, Charlotte? We've always treated you fair. You live in the house. You drive the company truck. You don't have kids to feed like us. You do just fine."

Charlotte didn't tell him she was doing better than fine. Climbing into her fully loaded Ford F-150 King Ranch pickup, she didn't share that her shell company had also purchased a Sarasota tropical landscaping company from a Parrothead who'd decided it was Margarita time. Overseeing the citrus operations and running a tropical plant business would certainly keep her busy, especially while she finished the last credits for her master's degree. She also chose not to mention that she and Mandy had already signed a sales agreement on a mid-century modern house in their new town, one with a backyard deck, a saltwater pool, and a pond where egrets and turtles liked to visit.

"I hear what you're saying, but my decision isn't about you," Charlotte told her brother. "It's about me having a long-term plan. A wise man once said everyone needs one of those."

ACCIDENTS HAPPEN

B.W.W. Roark

"Look woman, the bar is busy, and I don't have time to deal with you tonight. You can take your money-grubbing demands and go to…"

Sam's soon-to-be ex-wife hung up before he finished. He didn't care. His words were harsh, but that's how it was all the time with her. She had her problems too, but the whole divorce thing had become a competition of who could hurt who the worst.

He also lied. The cash register at Sam's Tavern was silent most of the evening. A line of storms rolled through a little before dinner time, keeping the crowd light. Not even Tuesday Trivia Games could fill the tables. The few that did come didn't linger over appetizers or dessert. With the frequent lightning threatening worse things to come, many took their money and went home. Sam understood, but he hated to see his profits walk out the door.

The diehards never left early, but in a few hours, the clock would chase them away too. The slow night not only meant no income but also no one to talk to. Sam loved hearing tall tales from his customers. He knew all the stories the regulars had to offer, but at this late hour, it didn't matter. They were in their own worlds. The only conversation they wanted was to get a refill of the free peanuts and, if he was lucky, order another drink.

Two stragglers were drunk, giggling in the corner. A stray was drinking alone off to one side. Another one was hanging onto the jukebox, plugging it with more money. For the seventh time, this old cracker made the machine crank out his favorite song, "Florida Man's Paradise." The phrase, Florida Man, had become synonymous with a laughable death of a foolish Floridian. Sam hated the song.

The music was competing with the increasing sound of thunder and wind. Sam was fine with that. He set his concentration on Nature's interference and busied himself drying already dry glasses. He didn't hear the door open. Turning around, he was startled to see a new face standing at his bar. It was a welcome surprise. Sam was starved for some conversation. He hoped this guy would want to chat and spend some money.

"Evening. What will it be?"

The man closed his umbrella, took off his gloves, and laid the rain-soaked items on the bar. The foul weather had pushed the temperatures into the low 60s. The rest of the country would call it balmy. South Floridians called it a cold snap. Still, gloves seemed like overkill.

"Royal Crown Whiskey, neat. From a fresh bottle."

"Don't usually do that, but this other one is almost empty anyway." Sam took a new bottle from under the counter and opened it. He poured a generous amount into the palm tree etched glass.

"This'll take the chill off your bones, mister."

The customer sniffed the precious liquid. He held the glass to the light and swirled the contents as if looking for something. It was not like a wine snob would examine his drink. It was more like he was making sure it wasn't poison. He let the glass do a brief drive-by past his nose as he inhaled. He took a sip but allowed the drink to go no further into his body. The man closed his eyes for a moment. He then forced the whiskey to swish through his mouth like a drugstore mouthwash. His face relaxed as if he was satisfied this was the genuine article. Finally, he swallowed.

Sam tried not to stare. "What brings you out in this weather?"

The customer took a deep breath and answered, "Anniversary of a passing." The rest went down in one gulp. He shook his head as if it was exactly what he needed. He slammed the glass on the bar and said, "Another."

"It's never easy to lose somebody." Sam gave him a refill. As a bartender, he had seen a lot of people come to forget their troubles, but this fellow was hard to read. He appeared more focused than depressed.

"It's not the death. It's the how," he said.

"What happened?"

"Spiny tail iguana."

"They look like harmless little dinosaurs."

For the first time, the man's eyes brightened. "They love plants, but they'll eat most anything if they are hungry; crabs, insects, even eggs."

"I didn't think they had teeth for that."

"They're hard to see from a distance, but those reptiles come into this world with 80 to 120 diamond-shaped teeth. The little buggers form a sharp edge like a chef's favorite serrated knife."

"That could sure do some damage, but how could it kill anyone?"

"Didn't kill directly. It was more of a catalyst."

"How do you mean?"

"Baby spiny tail found itself stuck in a toilet. When ol' Johnny-boy went to the bathroom in the middle of the night, he sat down. His fat bottom covered the hole. The terrified reptile leaped up and slammed those teeth into the only thing it could reach."

"His ass?"

"No, his dangling junk," he said with a chuckle.

"And that killed him? The bite?"

"If he had lived, infection and embarrassment probably would've done him in. But no, it wasn't the bloody bite." He said with a smile, "The whole thing scared him so much that he died of a heart attack." Down went the whiskey. He choked a bit on that one but laughed and said, "Another."

It wasn't funny. Sam blamed the alcohol.

"How in the world did an iguana get in his toilet?"

"Got to love Paradise. Police didn't investigate. Said they get calls all the time about toilet invaders: rats, snakes, possums, and, yep, iguanas. They assumed this little guy was looking for water and came in through the vent stack on the roof."

"That's so sad."

"The iguana's fine. Cops put a long stick in the toilet and waited for it to crawl out," he said.

"No, I mean sad about your friend."

His face lost its jovial expression. "Johnny was nobody's friend. He cheated in business and on his taxes. He even cheated on his wife." The man paused and added, "But no one cheats Paradise."

Sam wasn't sure how to respond to that, so he changed the subject. "How about a bite to eat? Kitchen's closed, but I've got some leftover hushpuppies I could warm up."

"Round balls of deep-fried cornmeal?" He threw his head back with a howl. "I'm not an iguana, but that sounds good. Got something I can dip them in? Ketchup?"

Sam understood the joke but wished he had suggested something else.

The leftovers heated up quickly in the microwave. "Careful, the plate's hot," Sam said as he set the hushpuppies in front of him.

"That's a bizarre way to die," Sam said. "Funny the news never reported it."

"It's easy for Paradise to kill Florida man. Occasionally reporters grab a story like this, but it's just too common."

"His heart attack and the bite sound like coincidence to me."

"It does, right?" he asked rhetorically. The corner of his mouth lifted in a sarcastic snicker on his face as he finished his drink. "Love that whiskey, but I got to pull myself together. My night's not over yet. Let me chase it with some strong black coffee."

Sam poured him a large cup.

"These hushpuppies sure hit the spot. Thanks. Always this dead around here?" he asked as he took a sip of coffee.

"The weather keeps folks away."

"You get lonely?" he asked.

That seemed too personal a question to answer. Sam just smiled and said, "Well, I do enjoy hearing a good story."

"Then you'll like this one. Happened a few weeks ago. I knew this guy that walked his dog down by the lake. Someone had spread muck along his usual walking path."

"Wait. What's muck?"

"Just about the richest soil you can find around the Everglades. Not good to build a house on, but great for a new lawn. In this case, someone had sprinkled it on top of the grass from the edge of the water to about ten feet up the steep incline. And one more thing to make this a perfect storm, someone had also been feeding the alligators."

"Isn't that illegal?" Sam asked.

The stranger seemed to be trying to hold back a chuckle. "The gators don't mind. Anyway, this guy walked his dog by the lake's edge. Thanks to the rain and the muck, the grass had turned into slippery mud. It was past twilight, and he couldn't see the ground texture had changed. The dog knew something was wrong and tried to pull away. He stepped forward to pull the pup along. As soon as he stepped onto wet ground, he fell."

"I see where this is going, and I don't want to hear about a dog torn up by those creatures."

"You have a soft spot for animals like me. Don't worry about Rover. The police said the guy must have dropped the leash when he started slipping. The dog leaped onto solid ground and ran off. But this fool couldn't get his footing. So, down he went on the super-slide to hell. The pup's owner splashed into a congregation of hungry gators looking for a snack." He laughed a little harder. "Damn, that was a good one."

"I grew up here. Every year you hear about a gator attack. Reptiles always win," Sam said.

"That's what the cops said too. Flooded with what they called real cases, they didn't investigate this one any further. They filed it as just another Florida Man death."

"I'm glad the dog got away, but I feel sorry for his family."

"He got what he deserved. He was a no-good shyster. I never knew a lawyer more crooked than him. As for his lucky widow, she raked in some nice life insurance money for that unfortunate accident." He put a stress on the last two words, like he believed there was more to this.

The more he talked, the more animated he became. Sam thought the caffeine and the alcohol mixture made him tell these unbelievable stories.

"This one just happened. It has Mother Nature at her finest. I knew this rich brute of a man, you know, a grade-A narcissist. His wife said he was a real shit. She was afraid of him. I found a safe place for her, the kids, and the cat to hide from him. Guess that pushed his crazy button. After they left, he got it in his head that the pool needed to be emptied and filled with lake water. Pool guy got fired when he refused."

"Why did he want lake water?"

"Somebody," he stretched the word out and winked, "Yes, somebody told him that lake water was healthier than chlorinated. So, he refilled it himself. Didn't take long for that mess to get really nasty, but he insisted on doing his daily laps."

"He sounds gullible."

"Add stupid, and you got a good picture of him. The slime was so thick police said they couldn't see the bottom of the pool. It was just a matter of time before hundreds of tiny amoebas splashed into his nose and took a short run into his brain for a feast." He laughed at his own joke. Sam felt uneasy but tried to play along.

"Glad the family and pet got away," was all Sam could think of saying.

He didn't want to hear another morbid tale. He tried to change the subject.

"By the way, my name's Sam. What's yours?"

"Infelix, Latin for unfortunate. It's the other people that have the bad luck, not me. I go by the nickname Felix which means lucky or happy."

"Sounds like a good change. What do you do for a living, Felix?" he asked.

"I do mostly contract work. Sometimes I get side jobs to support my profession, like yard work and pool maintenance. Tell me about yourself. You like being a bartender?"

"I inherited this tavern from my dad. It's all I've ever done. But yeah, I like it."

"Ever want to do anything else?"

"I like people and animals. Couldn't afford veterinarian school, so I just stayed in the family saloon business." He pointed to the large jar at the end of the bar. It had a hand-printed sign that read - Lost Pet Rescue. "That's as close as I can come to helping animals."

"You're a man after my own heart. Animals are the innocent ones in this world. Pour me a large coffee to go."

"I can call you a taxi," Sam offered.

"I parked down the way. Between this caffeine and the weather, I'll be plenty sober before I get there."

Felix seemed clear-headed, but it was odd to Sam that he didn't park out front. On a night like this, there were plenty of close spots.

"Don't worry. I got a cell. I'm not stupid like the infamous Florida Man. I'll get a taxi if I need it."

"Felix, you may be lucky, but you sure do know a lot of people that Florida has killed. You ever think of moving away?"

"That's just a few of the things that Paradise has used to end the lives of Florida residents."

"No more than anywhere else," Sam said.

"Hurricanes, tornados, floods, lightning, sharks, pythons, coral snakes, fires, disease-carrying mosquitoes, and sinkholes. No one thing is all that odd, but put it all together, and it's a hell of an interesting place to work."

"Lots of places are interesting. Why stay here?"

"Paradise and I are partners. I couldn't survive anywhere else."

Sam set the to-go cup on the bar.

"Bartender, you seem like a decent sort. Take my advice. That woman that wants to become your ex, either make up with her or give her the house and the car and walk away. You're in an unhealthy relationship that won't end well." He pulled out a couple bills. He slipped two under the hushpuppy plate and three in the jar. "I don't often meet good people in my business, but you're one of them."

He got off his stool and stood to a height, head, and shoulders above Sam. He put on his gloves and picked up his coffee. With his next words, his voice was filled with grit as it dropped a register. Sam couldn't tell if it was a threat or promise, but it didn't sound like a joke. "Remember, what's paradise for some can be an unforgiving executioner for others. Make some changes, Sam, or the latter will become yours." With a loud thud, he slapped the bar with a closed fist as if he were a judge with a gavel.

Sam jumped away from this odd customer. He was afraid that the "gavel" was going to be a fist in his face.

Before he could respond, Felix was gone.

A few minutes later, the bar door opened, and another late-night customer walked in. Sam was happy to see him, "How's it going, Hector? The usual?" This was one of the best detectives with the county police. A couple of days a week, he would take a late shift and work the streets. He said it kept him fresh.

"Yep, give me your strongest cup of Joe. Got a few more hours to go. I sure could use a midnight lunch too."

"Got lots of hot coffee, but I served my last hushpuppies. I could build you a BLT with some chips?"

"Perfect."

Sam poured the coffee. In a few minutes, he brought out the sandwich.

"Thanks. Hey, looks like someone left their umbrella. This weather is bad enough. I don't see how anyone would forget it."

"Belonged to the last guy here."

"He'll probably be back while you're trying to close," laughed Hector.

Sam dropped the glass he was holding.

"You okay?"

"Just a little rattled," said Sam. "Had this weird customer earlier. He was drinking and telling wild stories. Been such a slow night, I actually was enjoying his company. Left me a hefty tip."

"I'd say you were lucky he came in," the detective said.

"Lucky?" Sam responded with a huff. "Just as he was leaving, he started in on me about my wife and how I should treat her better. I never mentioned her or the divorce. He talked like he knew everything."

"Did he threaten you?"

"Kind of. Well, no. Whiskey turns people into know-it-alls. I'm sure it's nothing."

"Do you want to make an official report? Might want this on record just in case he does something."

"I'm overreacting. Tell me what's happening with you."

"Nothing much tonight. Seems this storm has kept the small-time crooks off the roads." Hector took a drink and added, "But the pros and the schizos work rain or shine."

"Those are the scary ones."

"And hard to catch. Got a case that's got me stumped. A guy had fired his maid without paying her. Weeks later, when she came to collect her money, the poor gal found him stone cold. His family had moved out a month before, and he had fired the lawn and pool maintenance guy. The pool was a real mess. Looked like somebody had filled it with lake water. Test came back that there was not a drop of chlorine or anything else that would have killed the bacteria."

"Drowned in the pool?" This sounded too familiar to Sam.

"Nope. Autopsy said it was the brain-eating amoeba. Those things tend to get kids and teens more often than grown-ass adults. We tested the water, and sure enough, it was full of all kinds of stuff that could hurt you, including those killers. If he had been swimming and diving in it, well, eventually, it would've got him."

"The guy must have been insane or stupid, but it doesn't sound like a murder," Sam said.

"Normally, we would file this as another Florida Man story, but that part of town has had a rash of poorly explained deaths."

"It's Florida, Hector. People die all the time," Sam said as he tried to ignore the coincidence.

"I know, but my cop instinct says there's a connection. A year ago, an old guy had a heart attack after being bitten by a trapped and irritated iguana. About four months ago, another fella slipped on some wet grass into the lake. It was as if the gators were waiting for him. Wasn't much left."

Sam felt a chill.

"All seemed like accidents, but something in my gut says they're related."

"How so?"

"Each victim had their own set of demons. Their families were glad to see them go. Each died in a way that you would say was just fate." Hector took a bite of his sandwich. "Maybe I'm reading too much into this."

"You think they were murdered?"

"I don't have much to go on. The yardman with the muck and the pool guy were the same person. Still trying to tie him to the iguana attack."

"That would take a really clever bastard to let Paradise get the blame." Sam's own words buzzed in his head like a siren.

Hector laughed, "It's funny you should say that. The pool guy went by the name of Felix Paradise."

The blood drained from Sam's face. "The umbrella. Damnit, he's telling me he's coming back!"

He grabbed his cell phone, ran into the kitchen, and called his wife. "Hey, honey, I been thinking about our divorce settlement. I've been a real prick. You put a lot of money into that house. It's yours. I won't fight you for it. You can keep the car and our joint bank account. And I'll cover the taxes and maintenance. If there is anything else I can do to make this easy for you, tell me."

"Homeowners insurance?" she asked as if to test him.

"No problem. I'll call the lawyer tomorrow and arrange it all."

"Is this some kind of joke? What's come over you?"

"You're a good woman, and you deserve better than me. Take it all, and let's part friends."

He hung up. He grabbed the trashcan and puked. He held onto the counter with his back up against the wall. He wiped his face with a nearby dishcloth. He slid down the wall to the floor.

Hector ran into the kitchen. He knelt down beside his friend. "Sam? Your voice carried into the bar. What's going on?"

"I'll be okay now." He put his head into his shaking hands. "Hector, tell everyone, bar's closed. Go home. Put the damn umbrella outside by the door. Then come back. I have a story to tell you."

Sam started laughing and crying at the same time. He began to mumble something over and over. Hector could barely hear him.

"I'm not yours tonight, you fucking Paradise bastard. Not tonight."

BOLITA AND BLUES

Sarah Glenn and Gwen Mayo

Ybor City, 1926

Bembe Duarte may have been a kid, but he owned the corner of Central Avenue and India Street. His straw boater was perched atop a head of hair so slick with wax that hurricane winds wouldn't displace a single lock. Bembe was busy hawking this evening's *bolita* draw to anyone with a bit of spare change for the lottery. He barely came up to my chest, but what he lacked in height, he made up for with his voice. "Big drawing tonight! A dime on the right number could bring you dollars!" Dust kicked up from the street covered his shoes.

Chickens pecked at me and flapped their wings in protest when I neared the curb. Their angry clucks were ignored by Bembe's patrons. I patted the kid on the shoulder. "Hey, Bembe! *Acere, que bola?*"

He jerked, almost losing his grip on the lottery ticket he was waving, then saw it was me. He returned my smile. "Workin' hard, *Senor* Aldama."

"Good man." I tossed a nickel. The lad snatched it out of the air and stuffed it into his vest. The boss, Charlie Wall, sometimes threw bags of change to the kids when profits were rich. I wasn't that flush, but giving a little pocket money to my *bolita* boys was a great way to build loyalty.

I gave pennies to most of the kids but saved my nickels for Bembe because I hoped my generosity would win me favor with his sister. If you saw Jaquinda, you'd understand. Club Tropical had posted her picture next to its entrance, advertising her as "Jackie Dart" for the benefit of the tourists. It was a beautiful photograph, but it didn't do justice to the singer. Lots of tourists came to Ybor City to see the cigar factory and enjoy a Spanish meal. The local blend of Italians, Sicilians, Germans, and Cubans was somehow more exotic than the poor working slobs in other cities. The more adventurous ones found their way to the clubs on Central Avenue.

The ones who discovered Club Tropical found the highlight of their trip. Jaquinda was stunning in her white gown and red heels, not that it mattered. It was her voice that melted hearts. When she sang the blues, grown men wept.

Bembe's voice brought me back to the moment. He was waving at a passerby.

"Your dreams can point the way to big *dinero*! One for the sun, *gato es cuartro*!"

I wasn't into the *charada*—dreams giving you the winning numbers—aspect of the game, but a sale was a sale.

One of my other kids ran up to Bembe and whispered in his ear. His expression changed entirely, and they ran off together. It must have been bad to make both leave their posts. I started to follow, but the pair had already disappeared into an alley.

A good excuse to visit his sister, I thought. When I reached Club Tropical, though, I saw that Jaquinda's sign had been covered with a cloth. Something was very wrong.

The staff inside were clearing the floors and tables of the previous evening's revels. The scents of cigar smoke and coffee were strong, but I could still pick up a trace of stale beer. No signs of a liquor raid by the authorities, not that one was likely. Ybor City was Charlie Wall's seat of power, and little happened without his knowledge or tacit approval.

I got the attention of the woman sweeping the floor. "Diega, where is Jaquinda?"

She straightened and adjusted the kerchief on her head. "Looking for Renzo with her mother, *Senor* Aldama. He didn't come home last night."

Renzo was Jaquinda's older brother, the man in the house since their father had died. No wonder Bembe had seemed afraid. He was expecting bad news. So was I; Renzo didn't waste money on women or drink. His mind was focused on the future.

When I left the club, I went to find the kid again, but a different boy was on his corner. All he could tell me was that Bembe had gone home to his mother. I headed for The Scrub.

The better parts of The Scrub were like the row houses where cigar workers lived, only smaller and lacking the luxuries of running water and electricity. There were no hallways; each room opened into the next. Here and there, scrub palms provided a place to hang the clotheslines and enough shade for a rickety chair or two.

I climbed the stoop of the Duarte home and knocked on the door. I saw a face come to the window—Bembe's. I tipped my hat, but he was already gone. After a few moments, he cracked the door open. He met my gaze and straightened to his maximum height, jutting out his pointy chin. I tried not to show my pity.

"I came to see if I could help," I said.

"It's too late for help." The boy's jaw worked while he tried to find more words, then Jaquinda was there. She wrapped an arm around her brother.

"Santiago, how kind of you to visit." My Christian name sounded delightful when she spoke it. The only other people who said *Santiago* were my mother and the police, and never for pleasant reasons. "Go back to Mama, Bembe. She needs you."

Once we were alone, she stepped out on the stoop and pulled the door shut behind her. Jaquinda was a stylish girl, but today she wore a simple black dress. I didn't need to be told that Renzo was dead, but she told me anyway. He'd been found, stabbed, in St. Petersburg. When she finished, she wiped her eyes with my handkerchief.

"They took him to Mercy Hospital, but it was too late. Why would he be selling *bolita* in St. Petersburg, so far from home?"

I frowned. "What makes you think he was selling *bolita?*"

"He took the pouch of tickets with him yesterday morning. He told Mama he would be home late and not to hold dinner. She sat up all night waiting for him." She pressed her knuckles to her lips. "Renzo always worked so hard."

I looked into her eyes, clear and dark as rum. "I will find the man who did this. He will pay."

It was a rash promise. Renzo's murder would be avenged, but the boss was a careful man.

* * *

My first stop was the El Dorado, the boss's casino. The walk over gave me plenty of time to consider how to convince the boss that we needed to hit Renzo's killer fast and hard. Those mugs across the bay had to be reminded that their whole operation wasn't worth two bits without Mr. Wall's nod. By my way of thinking, they had gone too far. We had to do something before other gangs got ideas.

The boss was at his usual table. He was deep into a discussion with Tito Rubio, his right-hand man, and Sal Borerro, my senior partner.

I hung back, out of earshot, and waited for them to finish their business.

Tito was the first to notice me. He waved me over. "Glad you're here. It saves me the trouble of looking for you. We've got a little job for you and Sal."

Once I sat down, the boss leaned forward, crinkling his seersucker suit. He said, "Renzo was running a special errand for me last night. Word is, some action's going on in the Deuces that shouldn't be. I sent him over there to conduct a little business while keeping his eyes and ears open."

"He must've got noticed," Sal said. "So, now we have a problem."

Wall drained his glass and set it aside. It was whisked away. "I need you two to find out who killed Renzo so we can send the proper person a message they won't forget. *Entiendes?*"

He leaned back in his chair and grinned as the waiter plopped the biggest porterhouse I'd ever seen in front of me.

Over lunch, we discussed the particulars of the St. Petersburg situation.

* * *

An hour later, Sal and I took a drive across the new Gandy Bridge. Most days, I admire the expanse of clear blue sky and deep blue water, but this wasn't most days. Not even the bald eagle swooping down to catch its lunch cheered me.

"The Deuces" is the term for the area around Mercy Hospital. Twenty-Second Street was the Burg's version of The Scrub. White folks didn't wander here, not even swarthy types like Italians or Cubans. Driving down a dirt road with more mules than cars was slow travel. Me and Sal stood out like bulldogs on bicycles. The hair on my scalp prickled under the constant gaze of folks along the street.

There was no helping that. My first task was to arrange for Renzo's body to be taken back to our side of the bay. Besides, someone in the emergency room might remember who brought him to the hospital. We needed to find a witness. There was a good chance that the guy who tried to help him saw what happened.

I left Sal to watch the car while I went inside to handle things. He should have been the one in charge, but he wasn't comfortable questioning colored people. Me, I grew up in Cuba. My brother and I had cousins in a dozen shades of brown.

At the front desk, a round-faced nurse with skin the color of coffee and a spotless white uniform was questioning a skinny boy not much older than Bembe. He was clutching his arm close to his chest. The boy's face took on the red hue of ripe sea grapes when his mother answered for him.

"Showin' off. That's how he did this, Miz Baker. Don't let that bashful look fool you. He was all "Momma look at me' half an hour ago. Just before the branch he was swingin' cracked. He didn't even have the good sense to let go. Fell all the way to the ground, still clutching that tree limb."

I waited until the boy was ushered away for an x-ray before approaching the nurse. "Excuse me, *Senora* Baker, I'm here about my friend Renzo Duarte. I was told he was brought in last night."

The nurse consulted a clipboard on her desk. "I'm so sorry. It was too late to help. Your friend was pronounced on arrival."

"I see. Can you tell me how to claim the body?"

"I'm sorry, sir, we've got no place to keep bodies here," she said. "I don't have enough beds for the living. Mr. Henderson receives our departed and holds them for their loved ones or for the county if there's no kin." She scribbled an address on a small scrap of paper. "Here's his address."

I thanked her graciously. "One more question *senora*, I would like to thank the man who brought Renzo to the hospital. Do you know where I could find him?"

She checked the clipboard again. "Marcellus Cole brought him in. He runs the general store down the street near the Sharpe construction site. If he's not there, perhaps someone could direct you."

* * *

The store was dwarfed by the construction sites on either side. St. Petersburg was booming, even in the Deuces. Inside, the aisles of dry goods were so close together that I had to walk sideways. There were a few other customers in the store, but they left quickly. I guess they could tell I was looking for someone, and they wanted no part of it.

The man behind the counter hailed me. "Good evening, sir. How may I assist you?" If he was afraid, there was no sign.

"Good evening, *senor*. I need to speak to Marcellus Cole."

He pointed one thick thumb at his chest. "You've found him."

"Excellent," I said. "I understand that you took a friend of mine to the hospital last night. I want to thank you."

If a face could close, his did. "I don't need thanking. It was the Christian thing to do," Cole said. He began wiping down the smooth wood of the counter, not that it needed it, and stopped looking at me.

"I appreciate your kindness. My friend was a good man, but he got himself into trouble now and then."

Cole nodded and kept wiping.

"Maybe you're worried that the trouble will settle on you," I said, "but I've come to take care of his final affairs. The trouble will pass you by; you have my word. Tell me what happened to Renzo."

The shopkeeper sighed and dropped the cloth. "I didn't see what happened to him. I heard a cry—I hope to never hear a cry like that again—and I poked my head out the front door there. A white man was dragging your friend to a pile of construction material across the street. He stacked some boards over him to hide him, I guess. After he left, I went out to see if the poor fellow was still alive. He was breathing, but that was about it."

"Did he say anything?" I asked.

"Just 'Mama.'"

"Did you recognize the man dragging him?"

"Not by name."

He wasn't looking at me again, and I could hear a trace of anger in his voice.

"But you knew him well enough to wish he'd leave the Deuces?"

Marcellus twisted the cleaning rag between meaty fists. "His kind isn't needed in any neighborhood. He supplies M."

My jaw tightened. I nodded to the shopkeeper and walked out without saying another word. The morphine trade made me ashamed of being Cuban. I didn't know who this mug was, but I knew how to find out.

Sal listened as I told him what I'd learned. As I reached for the starter, he caught me by the arm. "Don't go off on your own, Chago. We've gotta run this by the boss. He made a deal with the Cubans to stay out of the dope business."

"The deal's broken. They killed Renzo while he was selling *bolita*."

"Fine. The deal's broken. But we still need to give the boss a call before making a move on the Cubans."

It took us twenty minutes to get to a part of town where they had a pay phone. That was a luxury that wasn't available anywhere in The Deuces. I found a parking space at the curb of the Grand Vinoy. This time Sal left me in the car while he went in to jaw with the boss.

My loyalty was tested as I waited for him to return. I'd promised Jaquinda that I'd find the man who killed her brother. What would I do if the boss ordered us home? We were right on the streetcar route. I could catch one and be off before Sal returned. Sweat beaded on my forehead as I watched a streetcar round the corner. It took all my willpower to stay put.

I almost jumped out of my wingtips when Sal popped up behind me. "Mr. Rubio says the Cubans wouldn't have killed one of Charlie's men. They know better. Gotta be one of the Italians from Chicago. The boss wants a sit down with this guy," my partner said as he opened the car door and climbed in beside me. "We're to bring him to the casino alive."

He turned and gave me a wicked grin. "Mr. Rubio also said to tell you that the boss doesn't care what condition he's in so long as he can talk."

* * *

The Gangplank was the place to look for answers, not that anything stronger than booze was sold on the premises, but the rumrunners didn't limit their cargo to rum. The same tunnel that ran from the dock to the billiards room of the swank club brought new shipments of M into the Burg on a regular basis. I have a friend, a nice *senora* that enjoys a good party, who told me about its other use. When the joint's being raided, the staff uses the tunnel to make their escape. Most of the club's employees work for Walter Fuller, but one works for Johnny Torrio, a boss from Chicago.

Before we make the long trip to Boca Ciega on Ninth Avenue, I paid a visit to a sergeant in the St. Petersburg police who owes me a favor. Sal and I stashed our car near the Indian mounds near the Prada, found a hiding spot, and waited for the fun to start. Within the hour, the cops raided the place. The sheiks and shebas were scattering like cockroaches when you turn on the light. We stood quietly in the bushes by the secret exit until our mole came out of the hole carrying a ledger.

Gabriel Vacco didn't see me until I grabbed him by the collar. He was a little chubby but easy to hoist. I dragged him away from the exit and threw him into Sal's arms. "What's up, Gabe?"

Vacco struggled, but Sal already had him in a good arm lock. We relocated to our hiding place, out of view of any other escaping employees.

"Looks like we caught a fat rabbit," my partner said. "Out of the hole and into a *fricase de conejo.*"

"You ain't got the right to be here," Vacco said. "Hey, Fr—" he began to shout, and I struck him in the ear, hard. He yelped in pain.

"No one can hear you over the sirens," I said. "A friend of mine is dead. Renzo Duarte. Who did it?"

Our prisoner shook his head and winced. "It don't matter who. He came into our territory selling his lottery tickets."

"You have no territory here. From the Gulf to the Atlantic Central, Florida belongs to Mr. Wall," I said. "You killed one of our men. Mr. Wall doesn't tolerate that kind of disrespect."

"Your guy shoulda stayed across the Bay. We ain't afraid of Tito Rubio or Charlie Wall."

"They're not here. I am." I took my hat off and set it on the bushes. The jacket was next, neatly folded like my mama taught me. Then I picked up my Louisville Slugger. "And you're here, Gabe."

It didn't take long to get a name: Tommy Lazzari. I'd met him before if you consider trading buckshot a form of greeting. The last time I shot at him was during a fracas at a hotel up north in Homosassa. It was time to end our short acquaintance.

We turned Vacco loose once he told us where to find Lazzari. He believed me when I told him that I'd come back for him if he tipped Lazzari off. Vacco limped away. We went to retrieve the car. I wiped my bat clean, then returned it to the back seat. I locked the ledger in the trunk.

Sal and I didn't talk on the way to Tommy Lazzari's place. My mind was full of ideas that would leave him in a condition to satisfy the boss but also leave a lasting impression of what happened to guys who hurt my girl. A lot of possibilities were discarded *en route*, but by the time we reached his place, I was leaning towards playing baseball with his kneecaps.

"Nice digs," Sal said, slowing the car to a stop by a lush, well-clipped lawn.

It wasn't what I'd expected. Tommy had a sweet bungalow flanked by massive live oaks within walking distance of the waterfront. A rat like him didn't deserve this kind of setup when a man like Renzo worked hard and hurt no one, but couldn't afford more than a place in The Scrub.

Sal pulled his shotgun from under the seat and motioned for me to go to the back door.

He didn't look pleased when I loosened the holster of my revolver, then retrieved my bat.

I didn't care what he thought. If the boss let Tommy live, he wasn't going to leave the meeting unscathed. Tommy was going to remember me with every step he took for the rest of his life.

The back door opened as I came around the side of the house. Tommy was in his stocking feet with his shirt undone as he made a run for the Ford parked behind his house. He saw me and tried to pull his gun.

It was too late. I'd closed the gap between us, and the bat caught his gun arm with bone-splintering force.

He screamed as his knees buckled under him.

I wondered if that was the kind of scream Renzo made as this rat took his life. I remembered what Marcellus Cole had said.

Without thought, my body assumed a batting stance, the slugger ready to split his head.

Sal charged through the back doorway and stopped, taking the scene in. "Stop! Don't make me shoot you, Chago. Put the bat down," he ordered. "The boss wants him alive."

I stood there for a few seconds, torn between finishing Tommy and following orders. The distinctive sound of a shotgun being racked brought me to my senses.

* * *

A few days later, a fisherman found a body on the edge of the Hillsborough River. The authorities couldn't identify him; the gators had done their work. I didn't know the gory details, but I could tell Jaquinda that her brother had been avenged.

That should have been the end of it, but I kept wondering why Renzo was the guy Charlie Wall had sent. He didn't know how to defend himself against guys like Lazzari. He wasn't a soldier, just a cigar worker.

Finally, I headed back to the El Dorado and found the boss in his office, amusing himself with the ledger we'd brought back from the Gangplank.

He noticed me and grinned. "Good information here. Fuller's doing a brisk business with his club, and Vacco's been taking a slice of the pie. I wonder if Fuller knows." Then, he saw the serious expression on my face. "What's up? Some new trouble?"

"Everything's jake, sir. I'm just wondering; why Renzo? No offense, but I would have been happy to do the job for you."

Wall snorted and closed the ledger. "I couldn't afford to lose you on something like that, Chago. You would have stood out—and he didn't."

I nodded and said nothing. The wheels kept grinding in my head, though. Emile or Clevon would have been a better choice. Neither would have drawn attention. Each knew how to handle himself in a knife fight.

The boss must have heard those wheels because he was looking at me. "You still have questions?"

"No sir, no questions."

"I'll tell you since you're close to the family. Renzo came to me because he wanted me to give him a stake."

"A stake?"

"Renzo wanted to get his family out of The Scrub," the boss said. "I can't blame him; it's not the safest place for a body to live. He wanted to head north, perhaps to New York. He thought Jackie would be a hit there, and he wanted the kid, Bembe, to go to school instead of working. He wanted a job worth the money, so I tossed him one."

"And now his family has no man to protect them."

"I like the kid," Wall said. "He works hard, and he's sharp, counts better than my guys do. More importantly, he understands that *La Charada* system the players like. I'm thinking Tito should bring him along, help him move up the ladder as he grows." He stopped, seeing the flicker on my face that I couldn't keep hidden. "Don't ever play poker, kid. Education isn't going to take him far by itself, and, as I see it, his prospects are better with me. As for the mother, I'll see that she's taken care of. Renzo was working for me when he died."

His words were bitter to the ear, but this was a bitter world. "What about Jaquinda?" I asked.

"She's old enough to make her own decisions," the boss said. "She might do well in New York, but she's doing pretty good here. And hey, I think someone in this room might want to give her motivation to stay in Ybor City." He winked at me.

BIG FEET

Teresa Michael

Ellie cowered on the passenger floor of Josh's three-quarter-ton pickup truck. Something had run its nails along the door panels and crept about outside. Her hands shook as she turned on her phone's video and angled it upward, hoping to catch a glimpse of whoever or whatever lurked about. The truck rocked back and forth, and a slight shriek escaped her lips before she clamped her hands over her mouth. She fumbled with the phone. It fell on the seat as she folded herself further onto the floor, becoming as small as possible.

Why did I agree to go python hunting? I should've waited at the Blue Pelican with Roger and Michelle or just gone home!

Ellie met Josh two months ago at a little bar in Goodland, Florida. Her girlfriend from Chicago visited. They'd booked a room at the Marriott on Marco Island with plans to enjoy the coast's sun, sand, and dive bars. They'd walked into a little hole in the wall, and he sat at the bar with his shaggy sun-bleached hair, tanned biceps, and Ivy League smile. She and Josh had been together ever since.

Josh, a corporate dropout, fishing guide, and part-time python hunter, had asked her, and she'd finally agreed, to accompany him on a snake hunt. The fishing trip was fun, so why not? She'd try almost anything once.

"It's mostly driving around." He'd flashed that smile with a twinkle in his gray-blue eyes. "We can hang out and then go back to my place. Watch the moonlight over the water."

That part sounded nice.

They'd driven miles down a dark, gravel road with cypress trees and thick growth on either side until Josh jerked the truck onto the grassy shoulder. The light from the half-moon filtered through the clouds, covering the area with shifting gray shadows.

"I saw something." Josh surveyed the area through his high-power monocular. "Stay in the truck. I'll only be a few minutes."

Famous last freaking words.

She should have asked him to define "a few." He'd been gone at least twenty. A muggy, humid night, he'd left the truck running with the air conditioning on as a respite from the mosquitos. She was hungry and had struggled with the cooler in the backseat. After getting out of the truck, she jerked the lid open and rummaged through the water bottles. She found a small bag of chocolate-covered nut candies and ripped it open, grateful for Josh's sweet tooth. Leaning against the door, she popped one into her mouth. The night air felt close and heavy like it wrapped her in a cocoon. As she swatted at a buzzing mosquito, she heard a rustling noise. Then it crescendoed into what sounded like a dump truck slamming through the dense undergrowth.

She knew alligators and feral hogs lived there, along with snakes and other creatures that could harm or maim. A grunt. She dropped the candies in a rush to climb into the truck. Locking the doors, she'd slipped onto the floor and folded herself into a fetal position.

She sniffed and gagged at the smell of rotting garbage wafting into the truck.

A shuffling, and a grunt, were followed by dead silence. Thinking it was gone, she raised her head. A loud bang and a scrape of metal in the truck's bed caused her to jump.

"Josh?" She remembered the large crate labeled *Dangerous Reptiles.* Maybe he caught something.

Josh pulled open the driver's door and froze. "Sorry, El … why are you curled up on the floor?"

Ellie slid onto the seat—eyes wide. "Didn't you see it? There's something out there. Something big."

"I didn't see anything."

She turned to face him. "It was there. I heard it."

"The Everglades can have scary sounds."

"There was someone, or … some *thing* by the window."

"Someone was outside the truck?"

"Yes. Right. Out. There." She pointed over her shoulder.

He stepped out of the truck, his lip twitched, trying not to smile. Ellie watched him walk around the truck, then disappear out of sight as he squatted. A moment later, he stood, holding the torn candy wrapper. "It must have been ET."

She rolled down the window. "Different candy and a lot bigger."

Using the flashlight on his phone, he crouched down for a closer look. "ET with enormous feet." He took pictures of two large, faintly visible footprints in the sand at the edge of the unpaved road. For comparison, he put his foot next to the footprint and snapped another photo.

She leaned out the window. "It smelled like month-old trash."

Josh stood over the footprints. "I think you had a skunk ape encounter."

She wrinkled her nose. "What's a skunk ape?"

Josh jogged around the front of the truck and hopped in. "It's like a Bigfoot. Local folklore."

"Sasquatch?"

"Yeah, but it's smelly and lives in the Everglades." He raised a shoulder in a half-shrug. "They're supposed to be harmless unless you're a rabbit, cat, or another small mammal. There's a research place down on the Trail in Ochopee. I can take you—if you want."

She hesitated. "Maybe."

"They have a gift shop."

Ellie rolled her eyes.

"There's one more thing?" There was that twitchy lip again.

"What's that?"

"Besides rabbits, dogs, and cats, I hear they like cute blondes. They have this radar. They hone in and go straight for them."

"You . . ." She punched him playfully on the arm.

"Ouch." He rubbed his arm and mused, "That explains it."

Ellie gave him a narrow-eyed gaze. "Explains what?"

"Why the skunk ape has come out of the deeper woods. He's looking for food. Those pythons are invasive and eat rabbits and other small game. That's why it's legal to hunt the snakes."

As he maneuvered a U-turn, Ellie rolled up the window and kept a keen eye out for unusual movements. They were almost to Josh's house when she realized she'd forgotten to ask him if he'd seen any pythons.

* * *

The next morning, Ellie watched the sun rise over the water from Josh's lanai. He lived in the Ten Thousand Islands area, where his house was half surrounded by water. Unable to go back to sleep after a bad dream, she'd made coffee and snuggled in the cool spring morning air wearing Josh's thick terrycloth robe.

No more late-night python hunting for me.

Behind her, the sliding door opened. "You're an early riser."

"I couldn't go back to sleep and didn't want to wake you."

"Bad dream?"

She wrinkled her nose. "Sort of."

He slid onto the chair beside her, setting his coffee on the table. "I'm sorry you were scared." He kissed her cheek. "And thanks for making the coffee."

Before she could respond, the doorbell rang.

"Awfully early for visitors." He rose to answer the bell.

Through the open lanai door, Ellie heard him say, "Detective Owens, you're out early on a Sunday morning."

Ellie stepped inside as Josh entered from the hallway, followed by the detective, who was mid-to-late-forties, tall, and broad-shouldered. He wore a black polo shirt, khaki cargo pants, and a gun on his hip.

"I have some questions for you," the detective said.

"About what?"

"Let's have a seat and discuss it."

"All right," Josh said. "Would you like a cup of coffee?"

"No thanks." When he saw Ellie, he raised his eyebrows and nodded. "Good morning. I'm Detective Jake Owens."

As Josh gestured toward the dining room table, Detective Owens asked, "Were you out python hunting last night?"

"Yes, for a short while." Josh sat at the head of the table. "We didn't catch anything."

Ellie slid into the seat next to Josh.

"What about Roger Larsen?" The detective pulled out the chair opposite Ellie. "Did you see him last night?"

Josh's eyes narrowed. "We left him at the Blue Pelican Bar with a woman. What's this about?"

Directing his gaze on Ellie, the detective asked, "Were you with Josh last night?"

"Yes."

"The whole time?"

Ellie's head jerked toward Josh. "N-No. He saw something and told me to stay in the truck."

"I thought I saw a snake," Josh said. "I wanted to check it out, so I asked her to stay in the truck."

"Did you? Stay in the truck?"

Ellie's eye's widened. "I . . . uh . . . got out of the truck because I couldn't open the cooler in the backseat. The lid was stuck."

"Did you see anything?"

"Yes, there was something out there. Something big and smelly."

"When I came back," Josh said, "she was crouched on the floor in a fetal position, half scared to death."

"What did you see?"

She straightened. "I don't know."

Josh leaned forward. "I think she had a skunk ape encounter."

Detective Owens chuckled. "That's a new one."

"Wait, I might have a picture on my phone." Ellie retrieved her phone from the robe's pocket, brought up the video application, and pressed play.

"It's mighty dark there, young lady," he said.

She replayed it and froze the screen. "Look at the face in the window." She pointed to the screen. "Here are his beady eyes and hair all over his face."

The detective took the phone and manipulated the photo. "Looks like someone in a gorilla mask." He directed an accusatory stare at Josh.

Josh called up the photos on his phone and showed him the footprint picture.

"If it wasn't a skunk ape, it was a big, stinky, crazy person walking barefoot in the Glades."

The detective set Ellie's phone on the table. "Send me those photos. From both phones."

"What does this have to do with Roger?" Josh asked.

"A fisherman found him dead early this morning."

Ellie gasped.

Josh's eyes widened. "What did you say?"

"I'm sorry. Roger is dead. They beat him with a baseball bat or a pipe. Did he have any enemies or a disagreement with someone?"

Josh shook his head. "No, Roger was a *nice* guy. Everybody liked him. After a long day on the water, he was the first guy to offer a cold beer. Roger was great with boat motors, and he'd help anybody. He knew all the good places to fish."

The detective nodded and scribbled something in a small notebook he'd pulled from his back pocket. "I want you to take me to where you parked last night, and let's see how close you were to where they found Roger's body."

"Uh . . . all right," Josh said. "Let me take Ellie home, and I'll meet you."

"No, sir. The young lady is coming with us."

"Are we suspects?" Ellie asked.

"Interested parties." The detective gestured toward Ellie. "You'd better get some clothes on."

Hugging the robe tighter, she rose and headed toward the bedroom to change.

Detective Owens said, "Wait. Who is this woman from the bar you mentioned, and how can I reach her?"

Ellie stopped and met the detective's gaze. "Her name is Michelle. We only met her last night. Roger introduced her as an old friend."

Josh stood. "The bartender might know how to reach her. He knows everyone around here." He slipped his arm around Ellie's waist. "We'll be right out."

* * *

Forty minutes later, Josh pulled into the same spot they'd stopped the night before. On the drive, he'd told her not to worry—it was probably routine. She knew he was trying to reassure her, but her father was a cop, and she knew they were more than interested parties. They were persons of interest. She thought about calling her dad. He'd know what to do.

The detective pulled his car behind Josh's truck. Ellie watched as he strode over to them and opened the passenger door.

He pointed to a long scratch from the tailgate to the door. "Looks like someone keyed your truck."

"Whatever was outside my window last night did that." Ellie shivered despite the heat. "It was like fingernails on a chalkboard."

Josh joined them, and the detective asked, "Is this where you stopped?"

Josh nodded. "About." He looked around and soon found what he was looking for. "Here. The footprints are still somewhat visible."

"Uh-huh. Not much there."

"Where was Roger?" Josh asked.

Detective Owens gestured further up the road and beckoned for them to follow. A Sheriff's Office Crime Scene van was parked next to a trail. The van's doors were open, and a young man worked inside. Detective Owens waved and gestured toward the path that disappeared into the dense forest.

Ellie looked around before following them into the thicket. "Are there alligators in there?"

Detective Owens gave her a sidelong glance. "City girl, huh?" He sighed. "There are probably alligators in most canals and ponds. This path leads to a canal where people like to fish."

"Watch for snakes," Josh said.

Ellie grabbed his arm. He smiled and took her hand.

The path opened into a small clearing. A woman in her late thirties wearing a ball cap and an expensive digital SLR camera around her neck took photographs of the locations designated by numbered forensics tags. Yellow crime scene tape blocked the spot where Ellie assumed they had found Roger.

"Finishing up the photos," the forensics tech said. "You just missed the morgue van."

"Thanks, Terry," Detective Owens said. "Find anything significant?"

"There are big footprints here." She pointed to the number eight tag and a right-angled ruler beside the print she was photographing. "Looks like Bigfoot did it."

"I told you Ellie had a skunk ape encounter," Josh said. "He must have come back here after he left our truck."

"Now, Josh, I'd be laughed right out of the county if I try to pin this on the skunk ape," Detective Owens said. "According to the medical examiner, Roger was beaten with a bat or a pipe, and it wasn't by some mythical creature. A flesh and blood human did that."

The forensics tech flashed another picture of the footprints. "Detective, there's something in the footprint."

He crossed the small space in a few steps. "What is it?"

Josh followed the detective, and Ellie was close behind. "Looks like a piece of candy," Ellie said. "I dropped a bag of candy by the truck. He picked it up."

"I found the wrapper," Josh said. "It's in the truck."

The detective turned toward the forensic tech. "Terry, I'll collect the wrapper when we return to your vehicle. See if we can get any prints off it."

She gave him a quizzical look. "Jake, do you know how many people handle a candy wrapper?"

He gave her his "humor me" face.

"All right," Terry said. "But don't expect too much. I'll let you know if I get some big prints, though."

Ellie stifled a smile at the banter between the work colleagues.

Terry packed up her camera. "I'm done here. We're going to make casts of the footprints. Jerry's back at the van getting the supplies."

Ellie squatted to examine the first set of prints closest to where she stood outside the taped-off area. "These prints are more defined than the ones in the parking lot."

Terry crouched next to her. "The parking lot is hard-packed. The ground is softer here, so the impressions would be deeper and more visible." She pointed to smaller prints marked with evidence tags and said, "Those are the victim's prints. I matched them to the boots he wore. The Bigfoot prints obliterated any others that might have been here."

"Makes it difficult to determine who else was here," Ellie said as she stood.

"Tell me about it," Terry said.

"Hey," the detective called out. "I don't want to hear any more talk about a Bigfoot."

Terry rolled her eyes. "He's a good detective but not always a great sense of humor."

Ellie raised her shoulders, "Someone is dead. I can understand it."

Terry muttered, "Yeah," removed her cap, wiped her brow with her sleeve, picked up the scale, and returned to packing her equipment.

Since Josh and the detective were deep in conversation, Ellie walked about the crime scene perimeter. She remembered her dad telling her he always walked the crime scene. He called it "walking the grid." The edge of the path rolled into a ditch. Though there was no running water, the ground was murkier than where Roger's body had been found. She saw another large footprint in the ditch, larger than the ones around the crime scene. She bent down, her knee on the cool ground. This print was much deeper than the others. A puddle of water had formed where the ball of the foot would have been.

"Did you see this?" Ellie called. "There's another print over here."

Detective Owen's head jerked in her direction. "*Another* print?"

"Yes, and this one is bigger than the others."

Josh rushed to her side and gave her a hand up.

Terry looked at the distance between where the body was discovered and where Ellie found the print. "I hadn't expanded the scene further than where the responding officers roped off."

"Hey, what'd you find?" The young man from the forensics van joined them, carrying what looked like a bag of cement and a black equipment case. He stopped next to Terry and dropped his supplies.

Terry gestured toward the ditch. "More prints to cast."

"Man, this guy must weigh 400 pounds," the young man said. "And another one is further up the ditch. With this stride, he must be seven feet tall."

"Can you determine height and weight based on footprints?" Josh asked.

"Yeah," Jerry said. "Based on calculations of the print's length, width, and depth."

"And within a slight variation and margin of error," Terry added.

"Cool," Ellie said.

Detective Owens, Ellie, and Josh left the forensics experts to their work and returned to their vehicles. The detective collected the torn candy wrapper, careful not to touch it with his fingers, and placed it in an evidence bag.

"I need to find the woman Roger was with last night. Any ideas?" Detective Owens asked.

Josh glanced at Ellie and shrugged. "Talk to Alex, the bartender. He might know something."

"He introduced her as an old friend," Ellie said. "Perhaps they had some kind of past relationship. There was an awkwardness between them. Like they had unfinished business."

Josh nodded. "Now that you mention it, Roger seemed a little tense."

"Thanks. I'll be in touch." Detective Owens turned and walked to his car.

Ellie was quiet as they drove down the gravel road. The drive was different during the day. The birdcalls and other noises seemed louder, closer, and scarier in the dark. She thought about the three sets of prints—the victim's, the big prints near the crime scene, and the larger ones in the ditch near the path.

Where did her previous night's encounter fit into Roger's death?

After turning onto the paved road, Josh said, "I feel bad about Roger. He was a cool guy and a damn good fisherman."

Ellie turned to face him. "How'd he get out there?"

"What?"

"I didn't see another vehicle. Did you?"

"No, but he could have parked somewhere else and hiked in or . . ."

"Or he drove there with the killer, or the killer drove away in Roger's truck," Ellie said. "And where's his equipment?

You went into the woods with a flashlight, a knife on your belt, and that hooky thing, but there was no equipment. The officers would have left it at the scene for the forensic team to collect as evidence."

"That's no big deal. Roger probably thought he'd take a drive before going home. It's solitary and a good time to think."

"If that's the case, maybe he and Michelle had a disagreement. And again, where's his vehicle?"

He gave her a puzzled look. "Where are all these questions coming from?"

She looked away. "Did I mention that my dad's a homicide detective up in Tampa?"

He shook his head in disbelief. "We've been together for over two months, and you're just now telling me this?"

She stared straight ahead. "I rarely lead with that. The fact that my dad carries a gun puts guys off a bit."

He watched the road ahead. "Huh."

"Do you know where we can find the bartender? Perhaps he knows this Michelle and how to reach her. Are you in?"

"I'm in." He glanced over at her and held her gaze for a moment before returning his attention to the road. "And I'm not put off."

She flashed him a smile. "Good."

* * *

When Josh turned toward Goodland, she thought he was returning to the bar. She looked puzzled when he pulled into an apartment complex overlooking the water.

"Where are we?" she asked.

"Alex lives here." He pulled out his phone, scanned his contacts, and punched the call button. "Hey Alex, Josh here. Got a minute? . . . Yeah, well, got some bad news. Ellie and I are in the parking lot. Okay. See you in a minute?" He looked at Ellie. "On his way out. He'll be down in a minute."

Alex appeared at the front door, and they met him on

the sidewalk. He had a duffel bag and looked like he was headed to the gym.

"Hey, what's up? You just caught me. I'm going to work out before starting my shift."

"Did you hear about Roger?" Josh asked.

"No, what about Roger?"

"He was found dead this morning out in the Glades off that road where we go python hunting sometimes."

Alex's breath caught, and he stepped back. "We just saw him last night. What happened?"

Josh raised his hands, palms up. "Someone beat him with a bat or something like that. Do you know Jake Owens from the Sheriff's Office?"

Alex nodded affirmatively.

"He came to my house early this morning and told us."

Ellie stepped forward. "Do you know the woman Roger was with last night?"

Alex nodded. "Michelle? I've seen her before. I think they used to go out, but that was over a year ago. She got a traveling job and hasn't been around in a while."

"Did they have a bad breakup?" Ellie asked.

Alex shrugged. "I don't know. Maybe. You know Roger. He never was the monogamous type."

Josh agreed. "His relationships never lasted long. I just get used to one girl, and he's got another."

Ellie cocked her head in their direction. "If he cheated on Michelle—now that's a motive."

"We don't know if they had a relationship," Josh said. "It was always casual with Roger."

Ellie glanced between Josh and Alex. "At some point, things can change on either side and then it's no longer casual."

"That can happen," Alex said. "Based on my experience, anyway."

"Do you know where Michelle lives?" Ellie asked.

Alex shook his head. "No idea."

Ellie snapped her fingers. "That's a scenario. She's back in town and wants to get back together, but Roger's not into it. She gets mad, and things get out of hand."

"That's a gigantic leap," Josh said.

Alex pulled a water bottle from the side of the duffel. "But not far off from some of the conversation I heard." He flipped open the top and took a sip.

"Who left first?" Ellie asked.

"She did, and she wasn't happy either." Alex gestured toward the street. "Hey, I gotta go. Stop by later, and we'll drink one to Roger."

On the way out of town, they drove by the bar. In the far corner of the parking lot, crime scene tape encircled Roger's truck.

Josh slowed. "That's Detective Owens talking to the bar's owner."

"Now we know the whereabouts of Roger's truck," Ellie said. "Either he left with someone else, or whoever killed him drove the truck back here after closing time."

"Alex didn't say how soon Roger left after Michelle."

"We need to find her."

"But where do we look?"

Josh's stomach growled. "How about we go to the Island Café? If we hurry, we can still get breakfast."

* * *

Over a plate of pancakes and eggs, they discussed the morning's events and reviewed everything they knew about Roger. They planned to go back to Josh's and do some research on his computer, but Ellie grabbed Josh's arm before he started the truck.

She pointed to a couple across the parking lot. "Look, isn't that Michelle?"

He leaned forward. "Looks like her."

"Do you know that guy?"

"No. Never seen him before. It sure doesn't look like a pleasant conversation."

Despite rolling down the windows, they were too far away to hear clearly what the other couple said. Ellie watched as Michelle threw up her hands, screwed up her face, and argued with the man. "He looks at least ten years older than Michelle, so maybe he's a coworker. Maybe a brother or an uncle. He doesn't look old enough to be her father."

Josh raised a brow. "Lover?"

The man opened the passenger door of a white van and motioned for Michelle to get in. She glared at the man before she complied. He slammed the door, stomped to the driver's side, and quickly glanced around the parking lot before entering the van. As he drove by, they could see a red circus tent and clowns painted on the side of the van.

"Do you think they work for the circus?" Ellie asked.

"It's a logical assumption. Do you want me to follow them?"

"Hell, yeah."

Josh laughed and pulled onto the road a suitable distance behind the van. They followed them to the turnoff to Goodland.

Ellie gestured to the van in front of them. "If he's paying attention, he might be suspicious about this blue truck following them."

Josh smiled, a twinkle in his eye. "I'll just pull into the bar. Later, we can see where the van goes." Josh took the second left. The van continued. Josh slowed, and Ellie watched where it went.

"It turned left three more streets down," she said.

"There are only residences down that street."

"That must be where she's staying."

"We can check it out later. Let's go have that drink with Alex." Josh opened the door.

"You go ahead," Ellie said. "I'm going to take a little walk." She unlatched the glove compartment and removed his monocular.

"What are you up to?"

Surprised at the concern that crossed his handsome face, she patted his arm. "Don't worry. I'll just be a few minutes." She hopped out of the truck and stood in the open door. "I'm going to head them off at the pass and see what they're up to. This is a peninsula. They can't go far."

"If you're not back in twenty minutes, I'm coming after you."

* * *

She shut the door, turned, and continued on past the bar. One block down, she turned right but hit a dead end, so she turned left until she came to a right turn. She took that right, and two blocks over, she stopped behind a copse of palm trees and searched for the white circus van. She saw it midway down the block. Standing behind a palm tree, she pulled out the monocular. When she saw what Michelle and the man were unloading, she knew exactly how they staged the crime scene.

* * *

Josh was sitting at the bar drinking a beer when Ellie arrived at the Blue Pelican and slid onto the barstool next to him.

"Ellie, you'll never guess what Alex found out."

"What's that?"

Alex set a draft beer in front of her. "My boss knows Michelle. Remember that traveling job she got? Guess where?"

"Working in a circus."

The two men exchanged glances. "How did you know that?" asked Alex.

"I saw Michelle and her friend unloading the van." She took a sip. "I know how they did it."

"How?" The men asked in unison.

"I called Detective Owens, asked him to check something out, and let him know we'd be here."

Josh straightened. "You aren't going to make us wait, are you?"

Before Ellie could answer, Michelle walked up to the bar, plopped onto the seat next to Josh, and ordered a beer.

"Hey, y'all," Michelle said. "Have you seen Roger? I've been calling him all morning."

Ellie exchanged glances with Josh and Alex. "Haven't you heard?"

Wide-eyed, Michelle asked, "What?"

Josh placed his hand on Ellie's arm and said, "Perhaps we should wait for the detective to get here."

Michelle's dark eyes darted between them. "Detective? What for?"

A deep male voice called out from behind them. "Michelle Romano, please stand, turn around, and put your hands on the bar."

Detective Owens stood behind them, flanked by two uniformed sheriff's deputies.

Tears spilled down Michelle's cheeks. "What's this about?"

"Enough with those alligator tears." Detective Owens pointed at Michelle. "You're under arrest for first-degree murder and contaminating a crime scene."

Michelle placed her hands on the bar. "I didn't do it. I loved Roger and wanted us to get back together."

A female officer frisked Michelle as her tears continued to flow.

The detective cuffed her. "But your boyfriend didn't."

"Oh, my goodness," Ellie said. "She's acting all innocent like she doesn't know a thing about what happened to Roger."

Detective Owens turned Michelle around. "She's trying to establish an alibi."

Josh asked, "But how *did* she do it?"

The detective pushed her forward, "Didn't Ellie tell you? She's a stilt walker? They put Bigfoot's feet on the bottom of her stilts. She used them to alter the crime scene."

"But I didn't kill him," Michelle moaned. "I swear."

Detective Owens pushed her forward. "Tell it to the judge." As he passed Ellie, he said, "Thanks for the tip."

Josh drained his beer. "That only solves one mystery. They didn't explain the larger set of footprints in the ditch, the scratch on my truck, or what scared you last night."

Ellie winked. "I guess our work isn't done."

SMALL CRAFT ADVISORY

Jenna Kernan

"You saved my life, Austin. I mean it. Swear to God." Zach Williams sat on the live bait tank, staring sternward at his buddy, Austin Mercy, as they left the dock in Sarasota, Florida, amid a cloud of diesel smoke.

The single outboard motor buzzed like a chainsaw as Austin navigated the twenty-foot bay boat from the calm of the canal into the chop of the bay waters. Above them, a band of storm clouds hung low over the gray water.

"We shouldn't even be out here."

Zach knew that. It was why he wasn't here in his fifteen-foot skiff. The flat-bottomed boat handled the bay and could run in only eight inches of water, but it swamped in rough seas, and the tropical depression qualified. The small craft advisories were up. But he figured they'd be in and out before the storm got really kicking. The salt spray told a different story.

He lifted the open beer can to his mouth, wrinkling his nose at the stench of the rotten chicken necks that clung to his fingers. He'd promised to supply the bait, and he'd come through, even if he'd had to dumpster dive to do it.

"I don't know why you can't leave them until tomorrow," Austin griped.

"Because the last time I did that, they got raided, and I need the money." Zach crushed the empty can and dropped it into the live well, then returned to his seat.

"Quit those darn scratch-offs, and you could pay off your bond."

Leave it to good old Austin to bring up his arrest and the money he owed him in one sentence. After finding the boot on his truck, he'd tried to raise the cash to clear the fines. Instead, he got caught with his mitts in a commercial crab trap.

Stone crab claws sold for more than fifty-bucks a pound. Ten pounds and he'd make enough to pay Austin back. That left only attorney's fees, court costs, the fine, child support, gas for his truck, and every other damn thing.

But Austin was the reason he wasn't now sitting in jail. He owed him for that.

Trouble was, a recreational crabber permit included only five traps. He'd talked his friend into letting him use his name and address for five more. But they could only take two gallons a day and only if Austin was on the boat with him, which today took some convincing.

"Raiding that trap was stupid, I know." Stupid because he'd gotten caught by Florida Fish and Wildlife Conservation and charged with taking the contents of the owner's trap.

"You can't do stuff like that anymore."

"Yeah. I know. Thanks for posting the bond."

"Getting real tired of bailing you out."

As tired as he was of having to say thank you.

The pair had grown up together, and worked together out of high school a decade past, laying cable all over the county. Now Austin was his boss. This was not the perk he'd expected because Austin said, when he cut him slack, it ticked off the other guys.

Why should he care? Zach was his oldest friend. It was natural, wasn't it?

"I hear you."

"Do you? Because…" He stopped talking and pressed his lips tight, shaking his head.

Austin had always been in his corner. Until recently. Now he sensed a weariness that he recognized from wife number one. A kind of grimacing, begrudging tolerance.

Austin motioned with his chin, keeping his hands on the wheel. "Look at those idiots."

Zach wiped the gritty salt from his face and turned. Two young men on jet skis zipped out of the marina at full throttle. It was wake speed only in the bay and channel. But these two were young and, judging from their pale skin, tourists.

With their passing came the scent of coconut suntan lotion.

"They should stay in the bay," said Austin following the pair from Big Pass to the rolling waves of the Gulf of Mexico.

"We wouldn't have. How many times did we flip your dad's ski?"

Austin's brow remained furrowed as he watched them roar between the moored boats. Talk about the old days used to make him smile.

"Be rough out on the Gulf. Big waves mean big air."

"They'll get killed."

"That's what they said about us." Zach grinned.

Austin fixed his gaze on the channel. "Neither one has a life vest."

Despite the law, people went without them all the time, and shockingly, many who did so could not swim.

"Five bucks says they flip before we reach open water," Zach said.

Austin's frown deepened. "I don't bet anymore."

"It's only five bucks." Now they were both scowling.

"I nearly lost the house. The kids. Everything. I promised I'd quit."

Zach waved a dismissive hand. "Okay."

The boys buzzed past them, too close and still hollering like fools.

Austin ignored them, keeping the vessel in the center of the channel and reaching the Gulf twenty minutes later, where he turned north toward their first buoy.

To the south, Zach spotted familiar blue flashing lights.

"Police boats." He shaded his eyes. "Three of them. Wonder what's going on."

"Somebody caught in a riptide, maybe. Or swamped," Austin said, staring back in the direction of the activity. "That a cigar boat?"

"Yeah. A big one."

Beyond the marine drama, the outer bands of the tropical storm stretched gray fingers low over the water.

They continued north, running parallel to the coast. Zach lost sight of the marine patrol. The two on the jet skis were nowhere in sight, but before they reached the first trap, the pair appeared running seaward into the white caps, sailing skyward and crashing into the furrows.

"Grab the boat hook," Austin said, cutting the motor to idle.

Zach lifted the aluminum pole, easily hooked the rope beneath the first buoy, and hauled it aboard.

Each trap needed its own float, marked with the letter R to designate recreational crabbers. The plastic trap required the owner's address and now a registration number. A registration number on a crab trap! It was ridiculous.

When they were kids, they'd tie a string to a chicken bone and lower it off a bridge into the water. The crustaceans kept eating until they spotted you. Then they'd drop right into the net. Greedy buggers. That greed was what got them killed.

Zach dragged the trap aboard.

"Watch the gunnel, Zach. Geesh!"

They'd poured a thin layer of concrete into the bottom of each trap to ensure they sank. That made them heavy and hard to lift. But Austin didn't like scratches on his bay boat, so Zach lifted the darn thing into the cockpit.

"Zip tie is still there." Zach had added this precaution. It didn't always stop thieves, but it did alert him if someone had beaten him to the trap.

The two boys howled as they flew past, jetting toward shore, going airborne on a large swell. One of the pair landed with a slap and his motor cut.

"That one hurt," Austin said, smiling, seeming to enjoy other people's mistakes.

"Live and learn, I guess."

He didn't like the sullen glance Austin cast him. "Here's hoping," he replied.

Zach used a utility knife with a retractable blade to cut the trap's seal, slashing with more force than necessary and gouging the top before flipping back the lid. Inside were the pale, mangled remains of the chicken necks he'd added last night and several scuttling crabs. He used the calipers to verify the claws were long enough to harvest. Two qualified, and he snapped off a single claw from each. The crack of the crustacean's joint gave him a small zip of satisfaction. If Austin wasn't here, he'd take both claws. That wasn't strictly illegal, but it did eliminate any chance of the crab defending itself until it molted and the claws grew back. They could still feed themselves, but his friend disapproved.

"Two doorknobs," he muttered, referring to the pair of crabs already missing both claws. Clearly, not everyone had Austin's moral compass.

The second trap was better, yielding seven, one of which was slightly under size. Zach turned his back while measuring before snapping off the claw at the joint and flinging the crab overboard.

One jet ski roared past, splashing Zach as he secured the stinking bait into the trap. The peal of laughter told him the twerp had done that on purpose. His partner slowed to bob beside them.

"Hey, whatcha doin'?" the kid asked, straddling the seat of the vehicle. He had curly brown hair, green swim trunks, chicken arms, and blue ink on one shoulder.

"Get lost," Zach muttered.

"Crabbing," Austin answered.

"All of these floats are crab traps?" the kid said, glancing about at the Styrofoam spheres bobbing in the restless water.

"Yeah."

"And they're all private property," Zach added.

The kid glanced at him and directed his next question to the boat's captain.

"Filled with crabs?" he said, eyebrow quirked in apparent interest. "How much you get for them?"

"Well, if you're caught stealing from someone else's trap," Austin said, "You get arrested and charged up to five thousand dollars in fines."

"Plus, up to a year in jail," Zach added. That part he remembered his attorney telling him.

"*If* you get caught," the boy said. "And there's nobody out here but us and the marine patrol after that cigar boat. And we've got more horsepower than you, so… nobody."

Zach dropped the cage on the deck, turning. "Listen you little twerp…"

But he gunned the engine and took off after his buddy.

Zach watched him catch his friend, and the pair had a little talk as they bobbed like corks.

"They're going to raid these traps."

Austin pointed to the south. "No one out here because of that."

The low gray bands of storm clouds billowed closer, the vanguard of the tropical storm sweeping over the Gulf of Mexico from the Yucatan.

"Hope they flip. Then they'll be sorry there's no one out here."

"But us. Eight to go. Let's hurry. Try and beat the rain."

The water churned, and the rising wind blew the tops off the white caps that now splashed into the idling boat. If Zach had come in his skiff, he'd be scuttled.

The high whine of the jet ski engines ceased. He turned, seeing they'd cut their engines and bobbed in the waves as they hauled the rope on someone's trap.

Zach shouted. "Hey! You little shits. Get away from that trap."

One of the pair flipped him the bird. They sat on their jet skis with an open trap across a seat, stuffing crabs into a mesh sack.

"It's illegal to take the whole crab," he shouted. But the pair finished removing the living contents and roared away with their prize, bouncing over the waves like skipping stones.

Zach plunked back into his seat on the live bait tank.

"It's stealing?" Austin said. "Really?"

"That's different." Zach glanced back at the pair. He'd taken those crabs because he was desperate. They'd taken them for the thrill. His friend saw no difference.

Austin steered them to the next trap. "Motor sounds funny," he said.

Since it was his boat, the outboard motor wasn't Zach's problem, though it did seem to be straining.

Zach caught the first blast of cold air pushed by the approaching blue-black sheets of rain.

"Grab it," said Austin, bringing his attention back to the task at hand.

Zach leaned over the gunnel and captured the line, and tugged. This time he struggled to bring the trap to the surface.

"Heavy," he groaned.

"That's good. Right?"

Austin came to help, lifting the trap to the gunnel.

"What's that?"

Zach stared at the black duffle bag in their trap. "Someone is messing with us. They cut the zip tie." He touched the place where he'd secured the closure.

"What's that?" Austin stuck his finger in the circular hole in the trap where the tie had been. It looked like someone had used a drill to bore through the plastic. "Is that a bullet hole?"

Zach hesitated. He reached for the bag.

"Probably full of empty beer bottles."

"In a duffel?" Austin shook his head. They set the trap on the deck and opened the lid. Austin dragged out the pristine black canvas bag. "Hasn't been there long. No algae."

"Careful, Austin. You don't know what's in there."

People had found bundles of heroin, weed, and even body parts washed up on the beach. But he'd never heard of anyone putting something in a crab trap.

Austin drew the zipper around in the track and opened the bag to reveal neat stacks of soggy twenty-dollar bills. "It's money," he said, miffed.

"Holy hell. It's a lot of money!" shouted Zach.

Austin cut the engine causing the boat to rock like a carnival ride.

"Is it real?" Zach asked, squatting beside the open bag and snatching up a stack of bills. He fanned through the pile. "All twenties. Hundreds of them!"

Zach was out of breath as he handed the cash to Austin.

"Seems real," Austin replied, deadpan, as he returned the hoard to its original place.

"How much is it, ya think?"

Austin and Zach crouched on opposite sides of the open bag, staring in wonder.

"Count the number of bundles," Austin said.

Zach counted. "Thirty."

"A bundle usually has a thousand bills."

"Thirty thousand?" Zach exhaled the words.

"No. Twenties. So that's…" He closed his eyes for an instant, as he'd once done in elementary school when figuring. His eyes popped open. He sucked in a breath through flaring nostrils. "That's 600,000 dollars."

Zach beat his fists on the deck and sprang to his feet, making the boat rock dangerously.

Austin's expression of pure wonder hardened into the look of his supervisor displeased with his subordinate's work.

"What?" Zach asked.

"It's drug money."

"You don't know that."

"Who else would be out here with a duffel of cash?" He turned, looking over his shoulder toward the south. "The cigar boat. Those cops. This is what they had aboard."

"And they left it for us!"

The cold wind whistled past them. Austin shivered and glanced at the sky. They didn't have long before the sheets of rain reached them.

"Put it back," Austin said.

"Are you crazy?" Zach motioned with open hands at the bag. "It's ours."

"It's not ours."

Somehow, Zach managed to keep his voice level. "It was in our trap."

"You don't get it. Someone pulled up that trap, blasted a hole through your zip tie, and stuffed the bag inside. That someone will be back for it."

"And we'll be gone."

Austin shook his head.

"Oh, come on! You could pay off your truck. Take Stacey on a nice vacay to the Keys. She loves snorkeling. Right? Hell, take her to Cancun." Zach zipped the bag and hugged it to his chest as possibilities jumped like a silver tarpon on his hook. "I could take a trip to Vegas."

"Grab my radio. We're calling the police. The Marine patrol is out here. We just saw them."

"The hell you are." The anger leaked through. What was wrong with the guy? This was the windfall of a lifetime. A one in a zillion chance to get a first-class do-over, and he was not giving it back.

"You can't keep it," Austin said, making a declaration as if he were king instead of captain of a used fishing boat.

"I can," Zach said.

Austin pinched his lips and blew out a blast of hot air. "Whoever dumped that money will be back."

"So, let's go."

"And they'll find an empty trap."

"So?"

"You talked me into crabbing! That is one of *my* traps."

Oh, now he understood. Austin wanted to keep it all. Zach ducked his chin and glared, clutching the bag tighter.

"Half of it is mine, more than half because that trap wouldn't be here if not for me." He set his jaw, daring Austin to argue.

"You don't get it!" He pointed at the trap. "That's my registration number. My name and my home address are on that trap."

"But anyone could have robbed this trap," Zach said, desperation making his breath come fast. "Anyone."

"They'll know where I live. My house. My wife." He rose and pointed over the gunnel to the churning waves slapping the side. "Throw it back."

"Maybe they aren't coming. They could be dead or arrested or something. And maybe they didn't see the name or have time to write it down, you know?"

"And maybe they did. I would."

"I'm not leaving sixty thousand dollars out here."

"Six hundred thousand."

Correcting him. Always pointing out every single mistake. Zach stood, gripping the bag. He recognized that expression. Austin had his heels dug in. Well, so had he.

"We can empty the bag. Unzip it and put it back with a stack. Some loose bills. They'll think the bag opened, and the money washed out."

"Twenty bundles? And all but one bundle washed out of a two-and-a-half-inch hole?"

"Three holes."

Austin balled his fists. "I know how many escape rings are on a crab trap! But they're for small crabs, and last time I checked, dollar bills don't have legs!"

"It's possible."

"It's not." Austin looked away, shaking his head as if his friend were the stupidest man alive. "The bills are wider than the holes. Go on. Check."

He wouldn't. It would only prove Austin's point, so he changed tack.

"Someone else might have raided your trap before we even got here. Even those two idiots." He pointed toward the two boys and noticed them now, floating on the roiling surface, gazes pinned on him and Austin.

His friend followed the direction of his attention.

"Oh, great," Austin said.

Zach felt the cold stab of panic. "Did they see what we found?"

"How should I know?"

The pair accelerated away.

Zach's shoulders sagged, and Austin blew away a breath. But they kept their eyes on the pair, who turned, roaring straight for them.

A game of chicken. It was exactly the kind of thing Zach might have pulled when he was their age.

"Oh, God," said Austin, scrambling back to the helm and attempting to avoid a collision, but the one in green trunks swerved away. The two skis collided, sending a boy airborne as one craft skated over the other. The second rider dove clear, narrowly avoiding being crushed between the two sleds.

At the separation of driver from machine, the kill switch shut off the motor. This safety feature allowed the rider to climb back aboard. But both skis were now belly up, and the boys had vanished.

"Where are they?" Zach asked.

"One has got a hold of the jet ski. Where's the other?" Austin started the engine, clearly intending to make a rescue.

"Wait. You can't. They might see this!" Zach shook the bag as if Austin needed reminding. "They might already have seen it. Is that why they charged us?"

Austin ignored him, turning the wheel and bringing them about.

"We gotta get out of here. Like you said. Before they come back."

"You can't leave them. They'll drown."

"They're assholes."

"*We* were assholes. All boys that age are assholes. Doesn't mean they should die."

"Someone else can pick them up."

The first droplets of stinging rain arrived. The curtain of water obscured their view of the overturned watercrafts.

Austin stood at the helm, one hand on the wheel and the other on the throttle, sending them slow ahead. The rain and the outboard spoke for him and cut off any further arguments.

That was fine. Zach was through talking anyway.

The rain fell so hard and fast that Austin appeared only a gray outline at the helm.

Zach opened the live bait well and pushed the bag of money into the hold. He walked to the crab trap and lifted it as if to throw it over. Instead of releasing the box, he continued around and clobbered Austin on the back of his head.

Austin dropped.

The beating of the rain muffled the thud. The rain diluted the blood. Zach pulled back on the throttle, and the boat idled. He dragged his childhood friend to the gunnel, wrapped the trapline around his leg, and pushed both man and trap over the side.

For an instant, he thought Austin lifted his head, staring up at him as he sank from sight.

Zach wrapped his arms tight about him, shutting out the cold rain and the horror beating on his exposed skin with each raindrop.

What had he just done? Worse still, what would they do to him when they found out?

Panic drove him to the helm, where he played the story in his mind, speaking to the rising wind.

"Austin threw the trap back. Got tangled in the rope, and the trap dragged him over. Hit his head on the gunnel. I searched, but he was gone."

He nodded at this, continuing his practice. "The waves were threatening to swamp us. Swamp me. No, swamp the boat, so I made for shore to get help." Zach turned the wheel. Which way was shore? "I searched for a radio but didn't find one."

But there was one. He even knew where Austin kept it. The orange drybag.

Zach turned off the engine and searched the emergency bag holding the radio. Finding it, he tossed it over.

"No way to call for help," he said to himself. "And he wasn't wearing his life vest."

He stood there staring at the gray, churning water, grinning like a fool. His supervisor had left the building.

And all his problems were solved. He didn't need to convince or explain. He didn't need to apologize or beg. He didn't even need to split those lovely stacks of bills.

He could keep the money. All of it. He lifted his face to the rain and howled to the stormy sky. He was the luckiest man alive.

Zach moved to the helm and turned the key. The motor clicked but did not engage. Water sloshed at his feet. A glance over the gunnel confirmed the bilge was not pumping away the ankle-deep water.

An electric jolt of panic shot through him. He might sink.

His friend knew how to get this boat started.

Frantic, he glanced about for Austin, leaning over the side, then remembered what he had done. Zach dropped to the padded seat at the helm. Austin's seat.

If Austin had been breathing when he went over, he certainly wasn't now. He'd killed his best friend. "Shit!"

He recalled the jet skis. Austin said one rider was holding on to the upended sled. He could find him. Get that one to tow him in.

"But if he saw the money? What then?"

He glanced at the white belly of the overturned ski. Toss him the towline or take his watercraft? He knew how to right the jet ski. But the kid might be stronger than he looked. Even if he didn't see Austin go over, he'd notice Austin's absence. Had he heard them argue?

It would be harder to convince the police it was an accident if they'd overheard or, worse, seen Zach hit him. "Damn it." If he's seen, the boy wouldn't trust Zach to help him. He'd fight.

A thump brought him around. A hand appeared at the stern. The boy in the green shorts dragged himself aboard, spilling onto the deck.

"Get off my boat," Zach yelled. He couldn't keep from glancing at the live bait well.

"My friend is still out there."

"Get off, I said." Zach looked for a weapon. The only thing at hand was the aluminum pole. Not the weapon he would have hoped for since the boat hook had no sharp edges. He gripped the vinyl handle with both hands, like a broadsword, and advanced. The boy stood to face him.

"What's wrong with you? We need help. My friend. He's hurt." He took his eyes off Zach to motion toward the churning water.

In that momentary lapse, Zach ran at him, getting the cushioned tip squarely in the center of the intruder's chest. "Off!" he shouted. He'd come too far to lose now. He was sick of losing. Sick of being wrong and sick of people telling him what to do. This rangy little kid was not going to stop him from…

"I can get it started." He pointed at the engine. "I can fix it."

Zach narrowed his eyes. "Do it then."

"My friend."

"The motor first."

Zach took Austin's place as the boy went to work at the stern. He tipped the outboard motor to reveal fishing line tangled around the propeller. He let the boy work. Plenty of time to toss him overboard after the motor was running. With the monofilament removed and the propeller back in the water, he tried again. But the motor did not engage.

"Battery," said the boy moving to the battery case, fiddling with a red switch. "Try it now."

Zach twisted the key, and the motor started.

The boy stood and pointed. "He's over that way."

Zach gunned the engine and spun the wheel, sending the boy staggering. Zach charged him. But the kid sidestepped, and Zach sailed over the gunnel. The next moment, he was diving head-first into the Gulf.

* * *

Dustin took the helm. He'd grown up on his dad's boat on Long Island and knew his way about. He turned toward the upended jet skis. His parents were going to kill them. He'd taken the rented watercrafts without permission, then Frankie crashed into him. How bad was the damage?

He gripped his injured side with one hand, bracing against the stabbing pain. The wave of nausea receded. The way his ribs throbbed, he wasn't sure he could even tie a tow line to the skis.

He cast a quick glance about the restless water for the killer but saw nothing but the two upended skis. That man was nuts. Dangerous nuts. What had they been arguing over, the duffel bag?

His attacker had stashed the bag in the bow and killed the captain, leaving him and Frankie to drown. Sure, they'd charged the boat, but it was just for a laugh or had been until Frankie nearly killed them both.

With his ribs grinding with each breath, he'd never be able to right his watercraft. Best he could do was pick up his long-time friend and head in.

His friend still clung to the side of the inverted jet ski, head down, nearly in the water.

"Frankie!"

His friend lifted his head, revealing a huge purple goose-egg on his temple.

Dustin lifted the pole, gasping at the agony the task caused. "Grab it."

Frankie clasped hold. Dustin dragged him in and walked him to the stern. Each step sent another sharp jab of pain across his torso. The skin on his side was turning purple. The sight startled and sent a shaft of fear through him. He needed a doctor.

"Climb in. Can you?"

Frankie scrambled aboard. "Where's the jerk?" he said.

"Overboard. Charged me and missed."

"What? Oh, snap." Frankie searched the water. "Got what was coming to him." He thumped to his seat on the aft compartments. "Dizzy."

"Let's head in."

"I hear that," Frankie said and stood. "What was in the bag?"

"We'll check when we get in. Look," he pointed. "The next band is nearly on us."

Frankie ignored him and the storm. Instead, he opened the aft storage, searching. "Here it is."

Dustin had a bad feeling. "Careful, Frankie. You don't know what's in here."

"But I'm about to find out." He drew the zipper open. "It's money. A lot of money!" Frankie shuffled to the helm as they idled ahead of the storm.

"Is it real?" Dustin asked.

"I think so."

Dustin looked towards shore. "That's why police boats were chasing that cigar boat. It stopped about here. Remember?"

"I saw them toss something overboard," Frankie said. "Thought it was drugs."

Dustin lifted one of the bundles.

"They threw this in the water?" Frankie said. "Why would they do that?"

"Hiding it, maybe."

"Yeah. When the police board them, there's nothing incriminating."

"We have to call the cops," Dustin said. "That guy killed the other one over this, and he tried to kill me."

"But he didn't. They're gone. The cigar boat is gone. The cops are gone."

"So?"

"So, we can keep it."

Dustin gaped. Then shook his head.

"Don't be stupid. That's drug money. If I saw them, they saw us. You think they won't remember?" He glanced about, the storm suddenly the least of his worries. "They might be back any minute."

"Or they might be under arrest." Frankie gave him that charming grin, the one that had always gotten him into trouble. "Just tow in the jet skis, apologize to your dad. Get grounded until Christmas."

"You can't take that home on the plane."

"Then we'll ship it."

"Look at your head. You need to go to the hospital."

"I don't. Because if I do, they'll know I was out here."

"Well, *I* need to go." He showed Frankie the growing purple bruise. "My ribs are broken."

"So, hire a private nurse." He thrust out the bag. "With this."

Dustin shook his head. "No way. My parents will find out."

Frankie clutched the bag to his chest. "I'm not giving this back. Cops will just take it."

"Maybe we'll get a reward?"

"Cops don't give rewards! Owners give rewards. And besides, we have it all!"

"It's wrong."

"Dustin, your family has money. Mine doesn't. I'm begging you. This could change my life."

THE MALICE CHALLENGE

Cindy Martin

I flick off the lights in the shop, and an ear-splitting boom silences the choir of cicadas outside. Another intense Florida storm makes its presence known on Seaspray Isle. Watching from the darkened interior of Killer Pages Mystery Books, sheets of rain pelt the front bay window. Lightning flashes nearby, flooding the packed shelves where thousands of crime stories await new readers.

Thunder rattles the windows and vibrates the floor under my flip-flops while another burst of bright light blinds me for a few seconds like a brief spotlight. As I blink to regain my focus, a strikingly white face is smushed against the glass door. Clutching my chest, my body locks, forbidding any movement. My eyes zoom in on a shriveled old man standing in the rain. I tell myself, *he's not real.*

Oh, he's real all right. The parking lot lamp showers the eerie man with an ugly glow, bouncing off his shiny bald head and highlighting the crevices in his cheeks. My heartbeat drums wildly in my chest as I feel raw fear. I'm trapped like a goldfish in a bowl.

What does he want? He presses his face into the glass door just above the dangling sign that reads:

Cindy Martin

KILLER PAGES MYSTERY BOOKS
CLOSED
We're dying to see you tomorrow!

He's motionless, similar to those living statue performers you see at Mallory Square in Key West.

I'm creeped out. Scanning the sea of pages, I consider running through the twisty maze of bookshelves so I can escape out the back door. A sudden shiver ripples through my veins as harsh shadows dance among the darkened spines of stories. The pale-faced guy is persistent as the inky blackness of his eyes remains sharp and cold. Reminding myself to breathe, I choke out raspy puffs of air. Do I know this guy from somewhere? There is something familiar about him. I run through my social list: Katie's school, church, restaurants, neighborhood, beaches, dog park, my husband's work. Nothing clicks. I can't place him.

A quiet panic rises in my chest as the peculiar guy reaches into his slicker. The corners of his wrinkled lips twitch. *What if he has a gun?*

I should run out the back door, but I bet he would beat me there by the time I make my way through the maze of bookshelves.

Thunder crackles with a vengeance as I make a split decision to flee toward the register to grab my cell to call 911. On the way, I trip over the new mystery series display; books skitter and thud along the wooden floor, and my phone goes flying. Crawling. Scrambling. From all fours in the dim light, fumbling, my fingers grope for my phone, but I can't find it. Peeking over the counter, I check the door. The creep is still out there. Squinting hard, I see him hold up a small book.

Not a gun. A book. Feeling relieved it's not a pistol, I relax my hunched shoulders and try to catch my breath. This weirdo is probably another wannabe crazy author hoping to sell his book among the accomplished crime writers in our independent bookstore. Shaking my head in disbelief, I stand tall and confident and approach the door.

"Sorry. We're closed. Come back tomorrow."

Scowling, he returns the book into the drenched slicker, spins on his heels, and walks off into the deluge, disappearing between the sheets of rain.

"What in the world was that?" I pull down the shade.

Picking up the books I knocked over, I locate my phone and then collect my belongings before heading for the back door and the alley where I parked my car. My phone is in my left hand, prepared to hit Emergency. After twisting the key into the lock, I turn and spot a little book on the back patio table.

Lifting it up, my fingers glide over the smooth cover like one of those moleskin journals. Tilting it toward the parking lot light, I read:

Malice Challenge

Twisting my head left and right, I scour the parking lot for the terrifying man, but no one is there. I dump my phone into my tote, whip open my umbrella, and splash through ankle-deep puddles to my car. Plopping into the driver's seat, I toss the umbrella, book, and tote bag on the passenger seat. While eager to get home, I carefully navigate the slick island roads lined with whipping palm fronds. Glancing at the odd novel every so often, I wonder what it's about.

Pulling onto Seahorse Lane, I can hear Zoltan yipping over the uproar of the storm. The pet sitter forgot to turn the lights on, again. Grabbing my bag and, after some hesitation, the book, I dash inside.

My Doberman nearly knocks me over to shower me with sloppy kisses. "Sorry, buddy. Ooh, you were busy."

I stroke his silky fur and notice my pup lived up to being named after Dracula's dog. His fierce teeth have ripped through Katie's stuffed Snoopy. Hopefully, at 12 years old, my daughter won't be too upset over losing a childhood toy.

It feels strange to have the house to myself with Katie sleeping over at her best friend's and my husband, Dean, in Fort Lauderdale at a law enforcement conference. After showering off the grime of tonight's freaky experience, I get into my comfy nightshirt, slip under the covers, and open the mysterious book.

Instead of joining me on the bed, Zoltan breaks into a barking frenzy. His short black fur stands up, his pointy ears are flattened sideways like a bat, and he retreats from the bedroom to take up a command post position in the hallway.

"Zoltan, what's wrong? Okay, have it your way."

Cracking open the book, I can't believe my eyes.

This book belongs to Sabrina Weber

The nut job has my attention now. How does he know me? I flip again, expecting a copyright and publisher page, but instead, I see this:

Malice Challenge Rules

1. You have been chosen to participate in this secret challenge. You do not have a choice.
2. Do not show this book to anyone.
3. Do not tell anyone about it.
4. Do not destroy the book.
5. You have 48 hours to complete 4 evil acts.
6. Do not report this to law enforcement or any authority.
7. Do not ignore my texts.

On the next page "IMPORTANT" was stamped in big bold letters. Below this the nut job had written:

This is not a prank. This is not voluntary. I am watching you.

If you break any rule or decide not to participate, there will be dangerous consequences.

The Malice Challenge clock begins at midnight of
the day you receive this book.

I throw the book across the room. Zoltan jumps up,
going after it. Before he can get his fangs into the spine, I roll off
the bed and snatch it away, fearing he'll destroy it –breaking one
of the rules. After I toss the book into my nightstand drawer,
Zoltan returns to his lookout post just beyond the bedroom
door. Grabbing my phone, I Google "The Malice Challenge"
hoping to find out if this is a hoax. I spend hours going down
the rabbit hole and find nothing.

I hate to bug Dean at his conference, but I need to hear
his reaction. The clinking of glasses and a baseball game droning
in the background tells me he's at a bar with the guys. He walks
to a quieter spot and listens as I tell him about the encounter
with the creepy man and the Malice Challenge book. With
confidence, Dean tells me it's a prank and says he'll look at it
when he gets home. Grateful for his calm, I blow Zoltan a kiss
at his post near the door, and I collapse under the covers.

* * *

A beam of sunshine welcomes me as it slices through the
bedroom curtains pulling me out of my fog. Daylight chases my
midnight fears away. I shower, feed Zoltan, and at the last
minute, throw the odd book into my tote.

Watching my every move, my pup releases a low-pitch
moan that slithers from his throat.

"Okay. Okay. I'll get rid of the stupid book."

My cell dings and I look at the text message from a
number I don't recognize:

**Do not break the rules. Tick Tick Tick. 39
hours to go.**

How does he know my number? I look from my bed to the ceiling, the baseboards, the dresser, throwing novels off my bookshelf, searching desperately for a hidden camera. Nothing.

"Let's go!"

Grabbing Zoltan, my bag, and keys, I run for my car.

As I pull into Killer Pages Mystery Books, Lucy's bright red Jeep, she's named Redrum, is in the lot, and I relax a bit. Lucy's a perfect bookshop manager with her adoration for Stephen King and any story that prickles her skin. She loves horror. I do not. I'm grateful not to be alone.

"Hey, Dracula! Reporting for work?" Lucy says, petting my pup.

"It's Zoltan, Lucy. Hope you don't mind. I needed to bring him in after being left alone during that awful storm yesterday." Dropping my bag on the counter, it dumps over, spilling the contents.

Lucy spots the Malice Challenge book among my wallet, pens, and dog treats. She reaches for it.

"No, don't touch it!" Grabbing the book, I press it to my chest. My shrill warning triggers a bark fest.

Lucy shuffles backward, looking insulted.

"You can't see this," I say. "It's private."

"That's mysterious. Well, you're in the right place." Lucy waves her arms around the bookstore, a hoarder's paradise of novel-packed rows. Before I can stop her, she snatches the book from me and flips it open to the page of rules.

"Are you in some kind of cult?" Her steel blue eyes widen.

Letting out a mammoth breath, I pull her into an alcove in the store where we can hide. Whispering, I describe the creepy guy, the book, and Zoltan's growling intuition last night. "I can't tell anyone about this. He's watching me somehow. There's got to be cameras planted in my house."

Lucy flips another page. Her hand goes to her mouth, and in a muffled voice, she says, "It wants you to commit four crimes in 48 hours. You are *not* going to kill someone! Dean's a detective, for crying out loud." She hands me the book. "Stop this right now. You need to call him."

"I did last night. Dean's at a conference and says it's a prank, and he'll look at it when he gets home tomorrow. Lucy, I disagree. I think this challenge is real. The book says I can't tell anyone, and I've already said too much."

"Sabrina, you're dealing with a highly intelligent and twisted psycho. Problems don't just go away. You need to do something."

"I will. I need a minute to think." I nod and toss the book into my tote. Looking for a distraction, I busy myself by reshelving novels. After an hour, Lucy doesn't let up.

"Don't ignore this. I've known you for twenty years. I may be old, but I've been on this bouncing ball long enough to sniff out trouble."

"What do you say I grab us coffee?" I ask as I leash up my pup.

"Sounds great. Zoltan, knock some sense into this gal."

I plunge into the summer humidity. Cranking the air in my car, we drive to the Isle Beanery, where I order two coconut milk lattes. I take the slow island route back to the bookstore admiring the white sandy beaches of Florida's Gulf Coast, hoping to clear my mind and help me make a decision.

As we get closer to the bookstore, my spirits are higher, and I'm ready to ignore the challenge. Instead, Zoltan and I are greeted by what looks like a crime scene with a firetruck, paramedics, and a Seaspray Isle Police cruiser parked out front.

We run toward George, the hippie bookstore owner, who's talking to a uniformed officer. Spotting me, George adjusts his tie-dye shirt over his protruding belly, brushes his long frizzy hair out of his face, and gives me the report.

"I walked in. Lucy was lying on the floor, so I called 911. She's unconscious, but they say she'll be okay."

My stomach flips. I can't help but think that this is tied to the Malice Challenge. Lucy saw, touched, and talked about the book.

"What happened, George? She was fine an hour ago."

Paramedics push Lucy on a stretcher passed us. My sweat in the oppressive summer heat turns to chills as I look at her closed, blue-shadowed eyelids and pale lips.

Suddenly, my phone dings, and a message appears:

You broke rules 2 and 3.

My blood runs cold.

"You all right?" George asks, looking concerned. "You look like you saw a ghost. Why don't you go home? I'll manage today. We can check on Lucy at the hospital later."

I'm thankful George allows me to leave. Zoltan leaps into the passenger seat of my car, and I head to the house. I call Katie and feel better hearing her sweet voice, especially knowing she's home from school with the doors locked.

Fearing something might happen to my precious daughter, I speed, hoping none of Dean's patrols are nearby. He'd have a fit. I could imagine the headline: "Wife of Seaspray Isle's Detective pulled over."

My tires crunch along my shell driveway, and as I pull the evil book from my tote to read the first challenge, Zoltan goes berserk.

1. Vandalize property owned by someone who hurt you in the past. Spray paint the words EVIL and MALICE on their car.

Katie sprints out of the house with her long brown hair trailing behind her, and she greets the puppy first. Zoltan eagerly slathers her with kisses.

"What's wrong, Mom? Why are you home so early?" Katie comes around the car and wraps her arms around my shoulders. I love that she's still affectionate as a pre-teen.

"Miss Lucy fell at work and had to be taken to the hospital," I say, tossing the book into the tote and stepping into the sweltering afternoon sun.

"Is she okay?" She asks as we walk inside.

"She'll be fine. Do you mind going to Julie's house this afternoon so I can go visit Lucy?"

"Sure! Can I bring Zoltan?"

"Not today, honey. Grab your homework, and let's get going. I'll call Julie's mom on the way."

Dread takes over after I wave to Katie, Julie, and her mom and drive off. I pray the psycho who left the book stays away from my daughter. I must do this challenge to protect my family. *It's sick, really sick.*

There's only one person I can think of that truly hurt me in the past. Lauren Peterson. I recall the ruthlessly cruel acts she and her posse made me endure in high school: sticking nasty notes on my locker, telling any boy that expressed interest that I was a slut, flattening my tires, dumping chocolate milk and other food on me when the urge hit them in the cafeteria, and stealing my homework. Being shy and afraid, I never spoke up. It was four hard years of survival. Lauren, the ringleader, is now a Seaspray Isle Commissioner. I still avoid her at all costs.

The Malice Challenge book feels real now that Lucy got hurt. I don't know what I'd do if Katie or Dean were injured— or killed. Feeling sick to my stomach, I breeze through the Seaspray General Store, offering fake smiles to staff as I buy some groceries to disguise the purchase of a can of black spray paint.

Can I do this?

I drive by Lauren's beachfront house. Her sparkling silver Mercedes sits in the circular driveway.

I park down the street, sweating in my car, my temples throbbing. I can't do this. Fifteen minutes later, I'm back home, worried sick. Opening the door, the house feels eerily quiet.

"Zoltan?"

Searching room to room, there's no sign of my Doberman. The back window facing the canal is open. My cell dings.

The pup is fine. Complete Challenge 1.
Tick Tick Tick. 31 hours to go.

Panic spikes my blood pressure. I call Julie's mom and ask if my daughter can stay the night because Zoltan has escaped. She kindly offers to join the search, but I convince her she's helping more by watching the girls—and not telling Katie about the missing pup.

First Lucy, now Zoltan. This guy with the challenge means business. I don't have a choice—I've got to get the nerve to vandalize Lauren's car. Tossing a dark hoodie and the spray paint into a bag, I dash out the door lead-footing back to Lauren's neighborhood, where it's dark and quiet.

Parking on a side street, I take long strides until I reach her hibiscus hedge. Four cars are parked out front, but my target is her Mercedes. *Do it, Sabrina. Just do it.* Shaking the can, hoping no one hears the banging of the metal ball inside, I spray the words "EVIL" and "MALICE" on the smooth driver's side doors. Darting off like a bank robber, I head home, ditching the hoodie and paint can in my trunk. As I'm walking up the front porch, my phone glows with a message:

Good Girl. 3 more to go.

* * *

I wake up the next morning to a splitting headache with sharp pain needling my eyes. I miss Zoltan's kisses. Struggling, I convince myself to get out the door and follow through with the second challenge. Sipping my coffee, I read the instructions:

1.   Purchase a weapon locally at a store.

No gun. I decide on a butcher's knife, figuring it won't raise any eyebrows. After arriving at the only kitchen store on the island, I purchase an enormous knife telling the clerk I'm making steaks for an anniversary, like she cares.

Another text bleeps through while I slip the knife into the trunk.

2 down. 2 to go. Tick Tick Tick. 14 hours to go.

Is someone stalking me? The parking lot is jam-packed with cars and shoppers, but no one seems to be looking in my direction. I slump into the driver's seat, completely exhausted. Tears stream down my face as I try to make sense of this evil game. *Think. Who is the shriveled soul who left the book for me?*

Pulling out the book, I double-check the next tasks:

2. Injure the person who hurt you in the past. The same one you vandalized.
3. Confront and kill the person who hurt you in the past.

Am I going to do this?? *Injure and kill Lauren?*

Sure, I hated her years ago, but I can't kill her—or anyone. Why does this psycho want me to take revenge now? I push my palms together and pray for God's guidance. Glancing up, the digital clock reads 12:16, reminding me of today's daily devotion from Proverbs 12:16.

"Fools show their annoyance at once, but the prudent overlook an insult." God is telling me to overlook this challenge. What should I do?

Trembling as I arrive at work, Lucy greets me, showing off her bandaged head, knees, and elbows. She takes a long look at me and says, "You're a wreck. Have you been doing the challenge?"

I lie. "No, I'm just rattled. How are you feeling?"

"Luckily, no broken bones." She does a little dance. "I just tripped. So, you're *really* not doing the Malice Challenge?"

"Nope. Must be a hoax," I try to keep my poker face as I grab a stack of books out of a box. Walking to the darkest corner of the store, I tear a page out of a novel, pull a pen from my pocket, and write two words:

Call Dean

I place the folded note next to the register, hoping Lucy will see it tonight after my shift has ended. When I reach Katie's school car line to pick her up, she's not there. Panic strikes. They advise me to park while they look for her. My heart is about to burst. *He took Katie!*

My phone beeps. Thankfully, it's Katie's cell.

"Where are you?" I shout as a text bubble pops up.

You broke Rules 3 and 6.

"NOOOOOO!" My cell dings again.

**Katie is safe. DO NOT CALL POLICE.
Complete Challenge 3.**

The lunatic took my daughter! I break into a cold sweat as I fight the nausea. My sweet Katie. Please don't hurt her. Realizing I have to calm down because I look like a crazy woman, I lie to a staffer that I forgot Katie was walking home with her friend today.

Running back to my car, I plop into the driver's seat, trying to focus my jumbled thoughts. I want to call Dean, but I'm afraid what will happen to Katie. I've told two people too many, and I can't lose my daughter. My phone chimes again.

7 hours. 6 minutes.

Is he following me? Frantically, I plunge into the challenge. Scrolling my cell, I find Lauren Peterson's Facebook page and her schedule. She's busy campaigning for re-election.

Bingo. She's at town hall from 3:00-4:30 p.m.

I drive away with my hands slickly gripping the steering wheel. I can't believe I'm going to do this. *God, please forgive me.*

I park in a shady spot up the street from town hall. I watch Lauren's platinum head bounce into the building. Trembling, I wait for the meeting to end.

Lauren walks down the front steps and slides into a navy BMW, assuming her vandalized Mercedes is in the shop for repairs.

"Now or never, Sabrina." I inhale and exhale, not allowing my eyes to look away from the navy car. Flooring the gas, I tear out of the parking lot, heading straight for her. Jamming my sneaker to the floor, white knuckles on the steering wheel, my eyes are on the BMW. I aim for her with all the speed I can muscle as everything blurs. I hear the crunching sound of metal, screaming, exploding airbags, and then, blackness.

*** ***

Over constant beeping, a small voice whispers in my ear, "Just one more left, Sabrina." I will my eyes to open, but by the time they do, no one is there.

"Stop him!" I scream.

A nurse is at my side in seconds and says, "What's wrong? Stop who?"

"The man who was in my room."

"The doctor checked on you a while ago." The angelic nurse walks toward the hallway and looks both ways. "No one is there. You need rest after your awful accident."

I turn to the slapping of leather heels. Dean, dressed in his blue Seaspray Isle Police polo, rushes into my room.

"Honey, thank God you're alive." His warm hand engulfs mine. He gently kisses my forehead. "I left the conference as soon as I heard."

"My phone has been blowing up. Chief Merker said you rammed into Commissioner Peterson."

"No. No. No," I push my palm across his mouth.

Removing my hand, Dean says, "What is going on? In your trunk, officers confiscated a butcher's knife, a hoodie, black spray paint, and that book you told me about, Malice Challenge. Don't tell me you did those things?"

"I shouldn't talk about it." I look past his red, angry face. "I don't want you to get hurt. He's here in the hospital. Before you came in, the creep whispered in my ear."

Dean adjusts his gun belt and says, "Who? What creep?"

"The psycho who gave me the book," I say. "He's got Katie and Zoltan."

"What!" Our heads spin toward the hallway to the sound of slapping flip-flops beating a mile a minute. Lucy rushes into the room, huffing and puffing with red-rimmed eyes and her thick braid astray. She heaves and lets out a breath, "We found Katie and Zoltan." Another breath leaves her chapped lips, "Alive. The hospital allowed the pup in." Lucy shouts behind her, "George!"

Dean looks at me in disbelief. "Wait, our daughter was kidnapped, and you didn't tell me or report it?!"

"I couldn't!" I direct my attention to my scruffy boss waddling in with one hand holding Katie and the other on Zoltan's leash. George lets them go and flops into a chair. Katie leans her warm arms around me, sobbing. I hug her tight with my right arm around her, grateful she's safe. Zoltan wastes no time squeezing in between my daughter and me, slapping us with his long tongue.

Katie cries. "Zoltan and I were trapped in a shed by this mean bald man."

Hugging her like I'd never let her go, I say, "Did he hurt you?"

"No, but I was scared to death."

"What mean bald man?" Dean scrunches his brows and lips. "Why didn't you call me?"

"Find my phone. That book, the Malice Challenge, is real. Every time I didn't follow through, someone got hurt. You'll see the texts he sent me. I swear the house, my car, and maybe even the store is bugged with hidden cameras."

Dean pulls my phone from the hospital bag with my belongings and scrolls. "Whoa. This is insane."

Lucy slides in between us. "Good news Sabrina. Fortunately, you didn't complete all the challenges. Lauren is alive. In serious condition, but she will recover." She takes her lower lip and blows her bangs from her eyes. "We know who he is. Dr. Warrington, the island's oldest shrink. He did a number on you ..."

Interrupting her, I say, "Did you say, Dr. Warrington?"

"Yes. You know him?" Lucy asks.

"Oh gosh. That's why he looked a little familiar." I place my bandaged hands on my cheeks. "He looks completely different. He's wrinkled, no beard and hair, and skinny. Why didn't I put two and two together? This is all about revenge. Dr. Warrington was my psychologist when I was in high school. Lauren Peterson bullied me physically, mentally, and emotionally for four years. My parents sent me to him every week because his specialty was teenage psychology, everything from eating disorders to bullying."

Everyone in the room is staring at me, pity pouring from their eyes.

"Back then, he wanted me to confront her, but I couldn't. I had no friends, and he was the only one I could talk to. It was lonely on this island. Killer Pages, George, Lucy, and all the stories were my escape from reality."

Lucy nods and says, "I had no idea. I just thought of you as our resident teen bookworm."

Dean steps in and tenderly rubs his hand down my back, touching my skin between the little strings that keep my hospital gown closed. He says, "Sorry, sweetheart. You never told me."

"Wow, Mom, that's so sad. I hope that doesn't happen to me," Katie says.

"It won't. Schools pay more attention to bullying now. You know how to stand up for yourself." I slide my fingers along her soft cheek. Switching gears, I look at Lucy. "Where's Dr. Warrington now?"

George pulls himself up and pats Lucy on the back. "Detective Lucy is all over it."

"The day after you showed me the Malice Challenge book, I 'fall.'" Lucy uses air quotes. "At the time, I couldn't remember because of the concussion, but something nagged me.

Tonight, I found the note to call Dean, and I heard about your accident on the news. Then, I checked the surveillance video in the shop, and I saw a little man running out the back door. Rewinding to the night before. It's the same creep who was haunting you outside the shop."

All eyes are glued on Lucy. "George and I divided and conquered to track down this guy. Assuming he parked nearby, I went next door to the Seaspray Grill, and Charlie tells me some little bald guy has been parking there lately. We got a good camera view of his license plate, and my brother with the state did a favor."

"Look at you with connections," Dean says.

Lucy says, "We identified Dr. Joseph Warrington."

"Where is he now?" I ask impatiently. "It's midnight. My 48 hours are up."

"Let me finish. George and I found the doc's office. He wasn't there, so we wandered and heard barking. Following the sound in the dark, we approached a shed. George popped the padlock, and boom: Katie and Zoltan are free. We had no idea they were kidnapped!"

Dean sighs. "You didn't think to call 911? You broke the law like trespassing, breaking and entering…"

"We had no idea what we were dealing with," Lucy says.

"Again, no one thought to call the police? Look at all three of you taking on this psycho. One of you could have been hurt." Dean says as he pulls me in for a kiss and hugs Katie.

* * *

Two days later, I'm happy to be back at home and grateful for just a broken arm, cuts, and bruises. With a smile, I watch techs tear down teeny cameras in my house and car. It sounds like a stampede on the porch, but it's just Dean, Lucy, and George racing indoors.

"We got 'em!" Lucy shouts, wrapping her arms around me.

Dean nods, "Dr. Warrington is in custody, charged with attempted murder, conspiracy to commit murder, and kidnapping. Turns out we had two unsolved murders recently. The victims had their cars vandalized with guess what words?"

I mutter, "Evil and malice."

"Our squad connected the crimes through surveillance video to two different women. We pulled the ladies in for questioning and learned they were bullied as teens and received treatment from Warrington. They confessed to carrying out the Malice Challenge. Both of them. Like you, they were terrified for their families."

"Whoa! Did he say why he did it?"

Dean says, "He called it a social experiment. After 20 years, he wanted to see if bully victims would take revenge if forced to. Insane! As for the crimes the three of you committed, the State Attorney is negotiating reduced sentences to community service and to speak out against bullying. It'll be tough on the other women who killed their bullies. Glad you didn't take it that far."

"I'd like to start by visiting Lauren in the hospital so I can apologize," I say.

"Maybe she'll say sorry too." Lucy cheers.

"Let's go now."

Dean smiles as he helps me into his car.

ROSES AND OLEANDERS: A GARDENING TALE

Mary Ball

I pulled on garden gloves and walked out of my villa that beautiful morning to check on the roses. My heart filled with joy as a fluffy cloud drifted over the Gulf of Mexico below a bright blue sky. Birdsong filled the air. I shivered in memory of the Chicago apartment building covered in snow and ice that I had left. So happy I moved to the retirement village of Harmony on Florida's Gulf Coast.

My elation was short-lived.

The last thing I expected to find among the roses was Leonard Potter unconscious or, worse, dead. His bike lay a few feet from the garden, and it looked like he had veered from the road and flown into the garden. He landed among the bright red Mr. Lincolns and took out half of the soft pink American Beauties. They were the centerpiece that might win me first prize in *The Blooms of Harmony* village garden show. I felt ashamed of thinking about the prize with Leonard lying there needing help.

He wasn't moving. Was he alive or dead? My stomach felt queasy, and I wondered what I should do. I didn't want to touch him. Then I saw a beetle enter his mouth. I stifled a small cry before I screamed.

Next-door neighbor, Cassie Davidson, rushed to help. I stood frozen, one hand over my mouth, the other pointing at poor Leonard.

Cassie took one look before pulling out her cell phone and dialing 911.

"Is he alive?" I asked.

She ignored the sharp barbs from the American Beauties as she reached down and felt for a pulse before confirming that Mr. Leonard Potter was indeed deceased.

Two thoughts surprised me. First, I proved to be useless in an emergency. Not that it would matter to Leonard. And second, Cassie had a take-charge personality I hadn't seen before. I had thought of her as something of a ditz. Half the time, she forgets to brush her unruly red hair and whacks away like a mad woman when trimming her oleanders instead of careful pruning.

The garden club was one reason I retired to Harmony. I had read about Harmony's annual garden show in the *Gardener's Paradise* magazine, and Leonard Potter, the Master Gardener, was the show's driving force. On the cable show, *A Rose by Any Other Name*, Leonard demonstrated how to prune the canes from roses. He then toured the village of Harmony, showing off the beautiful floral displays in front of the villas. He sold me on the move.

I had wondered if Leonard would favor roses or oleanders. I suppose I could be considered a gardening snob, but anyone can grow oleanders. A magnificent rose garden takes a talented gardener, and roses are far superior. Cassie also belonged to *Harmony's Green Thumbs*, our local garden club, and she, like all the other members, hoped to win first prize in the show.

The morning Leonard died, gardening was not what we were thinking of as the sirens cut through the usual serenity of the village. Neighbors gathered, some walking their dogs, some interrupting their morning jog, and some in golf carts. They stood across the street, whispering and occasionally pointing in our direction.

* * *

The first responders rushed to Leonard after I pointed him out. The sheriff arrived with his green uniform rumpled like he might have been sleeping in his cruiser. He ignored Cassie and me while he talked with the emergency medical technicians. Next, a sheriff's deputy came and took pictures of the scene. After the two officers talked, the sheriff gave permission to remove the body from the garden. The EMTs lifted Leonard onto a gurney, covered him with a white sheet, and quickly loaded him into the ambulance. I noticed they paid no attention to my garden as they knocked down what was left of the American Beauties and broke canes off the pure white Madame Hardees. I silently cursed them for their careless disregard for my Beauties. After a second brief conversation with the sheriff, the EMTs drove off.

The sheriff approached me. "Did you discover the victim?"

"Yes, I found him," I said and then explained that I knew Leonard Potter casually from the garden club but hadn't seen him this week until this morning.

Cassie took over the conversation. "When she screamed, I came over and called 911."

"I'll need your information for the report," he said, scribbling our names and phone numbers in his battered leather notebook.

Then he noticed the bike.

"It's Leonard's," I explained.

"The front wheel is bent like he hit the curb too fast, causing the accident," the sheriff said. "He may have died of a heart attack. The medical examiner will check it out and sign the death certificate. I doubt he suffered."

"How can you tell?" I asked him.

"There are no signs that he struggled to get up. I believe his death was sudden."

I hadn't thought of that, but the sheriff was right. He looked like he had landed amongst the Mr. Lincolns and didn't move. He might have disturbed the Madame Hardees if he had thrashed around. With the EMTs, Leonard Potter, and the sheriff gone, I could see the damage wrought by his crash. I would have to replace about twelve rose bushes if I still planned to enter the garden show.

"I'm shocked," Cassie said. "We enjoyed tea together this morning. He mentioned how wonderful my jasmine smelled."

I rubbed Cassie's back and said, "I'm so sorry. You must feel terrible."

"He seemed to be feeling ill and said he had to get home." Cassie sobbed before continuing, "I should have gone with him."

"You couldn't have known," I said.

She wiped tears from her eyes. "Leonard told me he loved my tea. And he had such a finicky appetite. This morning, Trudy Simmons had given him some breakfast cookies, which he claimed were dry. And Janet Ryan stopped him to ask about the aphids on her hydrangeas and coaxed him into sampling her brownies. He said he was grateful the tea helped wash them down."

"Were the cookies and brownies that dry?"

"I don't know," Cassie said. "Trudy and Janet didn't send samples for me. I think they baked them just for him."

Had those three women competed for Mr. Potter's affection? Or worse, were they bribing the judge? Why hadn't I thought of that? *Gardner's Paradise* was going to publish a feature on the winner, and I'd dreamed of seeing my now lost Princess Annes in the magazine's glossy pages. "Will the garden show go on as planned?" I wondered, not realizing I had spoken out loud until Cassie answered.

"Oh, I'm sure, but replacing Leonard will be difficult."

"He liked my roses," I said, "he stopped by several times to give me hints on their care. I'll miss him."

Cassie nodded and said, "Well, there are members of the garden club who won't mind replacing him."

"I thought he was popular with all the gardeners of Harmony."

"Not everyone."

I got the impression from her tone that she wouldn't miss him as a judge. Did she have a complex friendship with him? I knew Cassie entered her garden in the show every year and has yet to even place, let alone win.

"It's my oleanders," Cassie said as she pointed to her garden featuring red, pink, and yellow oleanders. "He complained about my beautiful bushes and said they looked like overgrown weeds." She stifled a small sob.

I don't care for oleanders, but I gave Cassie's hand a soft squeeze and said, "Your oleanders are beautiful. They don't look like weeds at all." I hoped I sounded convincing.

"Leonard and I were friends," Cassie said. "He came to tea every Tuesday morning, but I didn't care for his gardening advice or his judging."

"I like your red and pink oleanders, but I don't care for the yellow ones." Yellow oleanders mixed with a garden of reds and soft pinks; is Cassie color blind?

Cassie frowned at me and then gave me a strange smile. "Leonard didn't like them either."

* * *

Two weeks after Leonard Potter's death, I attended a garden club meeting. The president, Trudy Simmons, had sent an email telling us that Cynthia Meijer had qualified as a Master Gardener. Trudy nominated Cynthia as the head judge of this year's garden show.

After a brief business meeting where Cynthia was accepted as the new judge, we enjoyed a collection of snacks. I baked blondies, Trudy supplied her cookies, Cassie provided the iced tea, and Janet gave us her brownies.

The centerpiece of the buffet was a large vase of wildflowers featuring Queen Anne's lace, black-eyed Susans, and blue asters. "I love wildflowers," Trudy said as we admired her display. "These don't all grow in Florida. I ordered the bouquet especially for this meeting. It's too early in the season for my wildflowers."

Cynthia Meijer arrived, and Trudy introduced and congratulated her on being appointed the show's judge. She looked over Trudy's wildflowers and gasped. "Trudy, that's not Queen Anne's lace—that's hemlock."

"No," Trudy said as she reached for the plant.

I was surprised when Cynthia knocked her hand away, "It can be poison even to the touch."

We all stood in shock, it was a beautiful plant, but Trudy agreed to use her garden gloves and destroy it.

After a few glasses of Trudy's box wine, the meeting became an impromptu memorial for Leonard. He had served the community as a Master Gardener for over fifteen years. "I can't imagine the garden show without him," Cassie said. "I was president of the club the year of his tenth anniversary serving as the judge, and had the pleasure of presenting him the Golden Trowel." She showed us the picture of Leonard beaming with pride as he held up the trowel, an award for his tireless service.

Trudy whispered, "She hoped that giving him the trowel would influence him to give her garden first prize."

The members of the Harmony Garden Club suffered from both fierce and petty competition. Trudy's wildflowers are out of control, Janet's foxgloves need to be ripped out, and Cassie's yellow oleanders are unruly. I considered myself above the fray. I'm a better gardener.

While we sampled the desserts, Janet said, "I like your rose display, even if some think it's a bit much."

The look on my face must have told her I was annoyed.

"Not me, of course," she said, "but some think roses can be boring."

Boring? Beautiful roses boring? Who would say such a thing?

"Mr. Potter liked my garden," I told her.

Trudy nodded and said, "I'm sure he did. Leonard was a floral snob." She had the grace not to add 'like you.' "He wasn't sophisticated enough to like wildflowers."

Janet joined in, "I miss Leonard."

"Do you?" Trudy asked, "Even though he said your foxglove looked sick."

"Well, Leonard was opinionated, but he helped me get rid of the aphids."

"You never even received an honorable mention from him," Trudy said.

"You were so proud of your honorable mention last winter," Janet said, the tones of her voice shrill.

"He wasn't fair. I deserved first place," Trudy said. "And your foxgloves are sick."

The two women glared at each other.

"Excuse me," I said. "I believe Cassie is ready to leave."

I had come with Cassie and hoped she would back up my excuse for getting away from these women before they broke out in a physical fight.

"I'm thrilled with our new judge," Cassie said as we rode home in her golf cart. "That woman knows her flowers, and she loves oleanders."

I could see Cassie's chances of winning the coveted first prize—as my hopes were dashed—when Cassie added, "She's not so fond of roses. She says they are overdone."

Cassie must have noticed my dismay because she added, "Oh, I'm sure she won't think that of yours. You do have a wonderful garden." Even as Cassie tried to encourage me, I noticed a smug look on her face as if to say her oleanders would get the recognition they deserved.

* * *

It wasn't until a week after Cynthia had toured the village that I began to suspect Mr. Leonard Potter's death was suspicious, even though the medical examiner had ruled his death was due to natural causes. I doubt they bothered with an autopsy. Leonard was a seventy-year-old man suffering from a biking accident, perhaps caused by heart failure.

I was talking to Janet and Trudy one afternoon. Trudy believed she had a great chance to win with her wildflower display that Cynthia adored. She said something that made me think his death might not be accidental. "Fortunately, Leonard went before the garden show."

Janet agreed. "Cynthia loves foxgloves. And mine are not sickly. I don't think Leonard deserved to be a Master Gardener, and frankly, I'm glad we've replaced him."

"He's been replaced because he died," I reminded Janet.

How the powerful had fallen. Only last month, these ladies couldn't say enough good things about and to Leonard. But now, two women I knew best in the Harmony Garden club were all too happy to see him replaced by their good friend, Cynthia. I had a crazy dangerous thought. Could Trudy have killed him with hemlock? I remembered the reaction of our new Master Gardener when she saw the plant.

Fortunately, Cassie did not seem to agree and continued to mourn the loss of Leonard even though he didn't like her oleanders. After one glass of wine too many, I sent Cassie a text with my suspicions. *I think Trudy may have poisoned Leonard. What if the cookie was laced with hemlock?*

I immediately regretted the text. Cassie must think I'm crazy. Would someone commit murder just to win a grand prize in a garden show? The thought was preposterous. And yet Leonard Potter had shown no sign of a weak heart before that morning.

Cassie immediately texted back, "I was thinking the same thing. Come for tea tomorrow morning, and we can plan how to investigate."

What a relief. Cassie didn't think I was crazy.

* * *

The following morning promised a wonderful day in the village of Harmony with blue skies, songbirds trilling their tunes, and a riot of colors from the flowers in front of the villas. I breathed in the warm scented air, smiled at a blue jay chasing away a sparrow, and headed over to Cassie's for a serious discussion of how Leonard might have died.

We sat beside her pool. She had a plate of cookies and brownies and a pot of tea. "Rosebud," she said as she poured me a cup and pointed to a beaker of warm honey. "Floral tea can be bitter. I recommend a couple of dollops of warm honey."

I nibbled on a brownie and tried the tea. The honey made the drink a little sweet for my taste, but I drank some and complimented Cassie's presentation.

"Try a ginger cookie," Cassie urged. "They're still warm."

"Umm, good," I told her, and I wasn't lying. The cookie tasted great but was a little dry.

"Did you agree with me that Trudy might have poisoned Leonard?"

"I'm positive Leonard was poisoned," Cassie said. "Have you called the sheriff with your suspicions?"

"No, do you think I should? I have no proof. But you did say Trudy gave him a cookie. It could have contained hemlock."

Cassie drummed her fingers on the table and looked lost in thought. She refilled my teacup. The cookie made me thirsty.

"Are you going to call them?" I asked her.

"Not sure we should. We can't prove anything."

"But she may be guilty?" I coughed from the dry cookie crumbs.

"Could Trudy have baked the hemlock into her cookies?" Cassie pointed to the one I held. "That's one of Trudy's."

I dropped the cookie, but Cassie picked one up and happily munched it.

"Sorry," I felt silly and picked up the cookie again. Once more, I sipped some tea to wash it down. I emptied my cup, but Cassie quickly refilled it.

"If you think about it," Cassie said, "Janet baked her brownies and gave one to Leonard, and she is elated that Cynthia is now the judge of the garden show. Cynthia loves foxgloves."

"So?" I asked.

"Foxglove, digitalis," Cassie said. "Digitalis can induce a heart attack."

"Is this," I pointed to the brownie.

"Yes," Cassie said.

My head felt strange, and I continued to cough. Cassie was mocking me. If she didn't think these two ladies tried to kill Leonard, she could have simply said so. She didn't need to get so dramatic. I took another sip of tea and resolved to go home. I started to get up, but the world tilted, and I slumped back into the chair. My stomach cramped, and I bent over in pain. I thought I might throw up, and I cried out for help.

I looked over at Cassie, who continued to study me. I tried to escape her steady gaze.

"Ask yourself," Cassie said, "what would work the best if you wanted to kill someone, hemlock in a cookie, digitalis in a brownie, or oleander leaves in tea?" Cassie's eyes seemed enormous as she peered at me. "It might help you figure it out if you knew yellow oleanders are the most poisonous of the oleanders."

I clutched my stomach and sobbed as she leaned closer to me. "I told you Leonard didn't like the yellow oleanders," she said, then laughed.

Three thoughts surprised me. First, Cassie is insane. Second, there were oleander leaves in the rosebud tea; thus, I solved the mystery of who killed Leonard Potter. And third, as the world turned black, I was dying.

A QUESTION OF TIME

Harold Emanuel

Deputy Skip Jordan and Medical Examiner Nancy Sykes were hard at work when Jodi Potter, Liberty County sheriff, entered the spacious hallway of Bradley Wayne's Hosford, Florida home.

Nancy, a fortyish woman with short curly salt and pepper hair, knelt beside Wayne's prone body. "No question, Sheriff, death by blunt force trauma." She pointed at a blood-stained sports trophy lying on the floor next to the fireplace.

"Estimated time of death?" the sheriff asked.

"I'd guess between six-thirty-five and six-thirty-six yesterday evening." Nancy grinned. "His watch smashed when he fell, stuck at six-thirty-six. Based on body temp, it had to be yesterday afternoon, not this morning."

Deputy Jordan, his baby face making him appear younger than his thirty years, stared at the broken watch as he placed it in the evidence bag. He turned to the sheriff. "This watch looks like the one you wear."

"It was from before your time, kid. I know most people wear digital watches now, but I still like the old-fashioned kind."

An officer peeked his head through the front door. "Sheriff, there's someone out front, says he's Mr. Wayne's attorney. Should I let him in?"

"Yes, but be sure he's wearing plastic gloves and shoe overlays. We don't want to contaminate the crime scene."

A tall, distinguished-looking gentleman wearing a tailored three-piece suit strode through the door and approached the body. "I'm Russell Brooks, Mr. Wayne's attorney."

The deputy approached the sheriff, holding a wallet in his hand. "Robbery doesn't appear to be the motive. He had over five hundred dollars in his wallet, and there's plenty of expensive items throughout the house to steal."

"I'd lay even money on greed being the motive," Brooks said.

The lawyer pointed toward a room adjoining the hallway. "The three people sitting in the living room," he spoke loud enough for all three to hear, "will share his estate's seven million dollars. His wife, Kelsey, and his nephew, Gary, will each inherit forty-five percent. His housekeeper, Doris, gets the other ten percent."

Gary, wearing a warmup suit and sweatband on his head, glared at Kelsey. "It had to be you. All you ever wanted was my uncle's money."

"That's a lie!" Kelsey's nostrils flared.

"Oh, really. Why else would an attractive twenty-five-year-old woman marry a seventy-two-year-old man?"

Kelsey cracked her open hand across Gary's face, leaving a large red welt, and wiped a tear from her cheek. "You bastard, Brad was the love of my life, my soul mate."

Gary rubbed his wounded cheek. "Love of your life, soul mate, really? You kept telling him you visited your sister every week. I suspect your sister wears pants."

Kelsey glared at Gary.

The sheriff withdrew a notebook from his jacket pocket. "We can resolve this quickly, Mrs. Wayne. Give me your sister's name, address, and telephone number. She'll be able to confirm that you spent time with her."

Kelsey slumped back into her chair, sighed, and pulled her skirt down over her well-formed legs. "I guess there's no reason to keep the secret any longer. You'll find out anyway. Yes, I am seeing someone. We were having dinner yesterday evening."

"And I'm sure your boyfriend will verify your alibi even if you weren't with him," Gary replied. "For three million dollars, he'll say anything."

"Sheriff, I can tell you where she was, or at least where her car was." Attorney Brooks then directed his question to Kelsey. "Where did you have dinner?"

"Garbarino's. It's a half hour from here."

Brooks pulled a smartphone from his jacket pocket and tapped a few keys. "Yup, that's where she was, or at least that's where her car was. Mr. Wayne suspected she was having an affair. He had me put a tracker on her car. It was parked at Garbarino's restaurant yesterday afternoon from six-fifteen until about eight."

"I'll check with the restaurant to verify Kelsey was there," Deputy Jordan said. "I'll have them download their video to me." In less than five minutes, he had his answer. "Sure enough, Sheriff. Video from both the parking lot and inside the restaurant show she was there from six-fifteen until just before eight."

"Now I see how you graduated with honors from that computer college," the sheriff said. "That eliminates Kelsey as a suspect."

Gary shook his fist at her. "Unless she hired someone."

"We'll get a subpoena for Mrs. Wayne's bank records," the sheriff replied. "If there are any unusual withdrawals, we'll find them."

The sheriff turned to the housekeeper. "Did you know you were in the will?"

Doris sat, shoulders hunched, staring at sweaty hands on her lap. "N … no. I once asked him what would happen to me when he died. I've worked for Mr. Wayne for forty-two years. I have no family. He never answered me."

"So, you never looked through his desk when you were cleaning?" Gary said. "I have a hard time believing that." He turned to the sheriff. "I'm sure she knew."

The sheriff faced Doris. "And where were you yesterday afternoon?"

"I was at the movies, the Princeton Theater."

"Do you have your ticket stub?"

"No. I bought my ticket online."

Deputy Jordan held his hand out. "Give me your phone. Your downloaded ticket will still display."

Doris handed her phone to the deputy, who punched in a few numbers and read the result. Using his own phone, he called the theater.

"This is Deputy Skip Jordan of the Liberty County Sheriff's Department. Can you verify the use of a downloaded ticket for me? . . .Yes, I have the confirmation number, 56G7742." He waited a few seconds. "Thank you." The deputy turned to the sheriff. "She was there. The theater manager confirms that her digital ticket was swiped at six-ten p.m."

Gary didn't wait to be asked. "At six-thirty last night, I was working out at a gym in Clarksville, which is a good thirty minutes from here. I coach basketball at Hosford High School. I know the time because I got on the stationary bike at about six-twenty. I had just begun to work up a sweat when the sports guy came on the TV. He always comes on at six-forty. He talked about our big game this Saturday against White Springs. I left the gym somewhere between eight-thirty and nine o'clock. I know they have surveillance cameras. You can check it out."

Kelsey turned toward Gary, her steel blue eyes glaring at him. "You seem to remember a lot of detail about last night, like you memorized and rehearsed it."

"I'll call the gym and get a copy of the tape," the deputy said.

"No need," the sheriff said. "Based on what we know, I can tell you who killed Bradley Wayne. Gary Swanson, you're under arrest for the murder of your uncle."

"What?" Gary jumped up from the couch to protest. The sheriff took the opportunity to pull Gary's arms behind his back and handcuffed him.

"But Mr. Swanson claims he was at the gym around six-twenty," Deputy Jordan said. "If we're able to confirm his alibi, he couldn't have killed his uncle at six-thirty-five."

Sheriff Potter smiled. "I'm pretty sure the gym video will verify that Gary was there when he said he was, but you're forgetting one thing, hotshot. Liberty County is in the Eastern Time Zone. Clarksville is in Calhoun County, one of ten Florida Panhandle counties in the Central Time Zone. The murder took place in Hosford, which is in Liberty County. Garbarino's restaurant and the theater are also in Liberty County. When Gary killed his uncle, it was five-thirty-six at the gym. That hour's difference gave him time to get into the video by six-twenty."

The sheriff led Gary to the patrol car. Wayne's body was taken to the county morgue, where Medical Examiner Sykes confirmed that Wayne was killed by blunt force trauma to his head. The Sheriff Department's lab pulled a partial fingerprint from the murder weapon, which matched the little finger on Gary's right hand. The GPS in Swanson's car showed he left his uncle's house at six forty-five the previous night and drove to the gym. Mr. Brooks distributed the estate per Mr. Wayne's will, with Gary's forty-five percent held until after the trial's outcome. When Gary was convicted, the court ruled that Kelsey would receive Gary's share.

DECEIT BY DESIGN

Mary Dutta

Kimberly smiled as the EMTs loaded Bernice onto a stretcher. She glanced around to see if anyone noticed, but the tourists were too absorbed in their fishbowl-sized frosted mojitos to pay attention to the commotion. Only one person seemed to be watching her, a blond woman in a vaguely nautical blue and white dress. She had probably wandered over from the cruise port. Well, now she would have a story to tell her cruise buddy at the all-you-can-eat buffet.

"I told Bernice she shouldn't be leading tours anymore," Elliot said, twisting his hands in distress. "It was too much."

Kimberly shrugged. "She didn't trust any of us to impress the financial sharks she's trying to land."

"Well, she certainly made an impression," he said, hopping back to avoid the emergency personnel rolling over his Prada loafers as they wheeled Bernice away.

The outing had started well enough. Art Deco Guild members and potential donors clustered together under a swaying palm tree on another perfect day on Miami's South Beach. Bernice had started the tour, walking backward and gesturing with her cane at the Art Deco hotels lining Ocean

Drive. But then, a bikini-clad woman taking a selfie with the Versace mansion struck a pose and collided with her, knocking Bernice to the ground. It would have been hilarious if it had not cut short the fundraising fishing expedition.

Did Kim dare hope for a broken hip? That would mean surgery, weeks of hospitalization, months of rehab, and, fingers crossed, a severely curtailed lifestyle. "I bet her seat on the board's going to be up for grabs." She did not realize she had said it out loud until she saw the disapproving look on Elliot's face. She got that look a lot.

She held up the tote bag she was gripping. "I'll drop Bernice's bag off at the hospital," she said, straining to portray herself as caring rather than conniving. But as the ambulance wailed down the street, all Kimberly heard was the sweet sound of opportunity.

Leaving Elliot to shepherd the VIPs away, Kim made her way to the Loomis Park Artisanal Market, where the Guild manned a booth every weekend. She did not expect to be thanked for her dedication or even noticed. She certainly didn't expect it to buy her a place on the Guild's board. Elliott didn't do a fraction of what she did, but Bernice was positively besotted with him, trotting him out to meet visiting experts and ensuring that his photo featured prominently on the guild website. Kimberly had been casting about for ways to promote her own interest in a board seat, succeeding so far only in annoying the current members with her efforts to raise her profile. Now the answer to her prayers seemed to have fallen into her lap, or more accurately, onto the sidewalk.

The market patrons showed more interest in hand-made jewelry and empanadas than in Art Deco design, leaving Kim free to search Bernice's bag unmolested. She set aside the rubber-banded pamphlets and laminated photos of South Beach hotels that had succumbed to the wrecking ball before preservationists had stepped in. She had hoped for a smartphone, but Bernice's ancient flip model could share no secrets. Her wallet yielded a driver's license showing her year of birth, confirming Kimberly's suspicions that the older woman routinely shaved a good decade off her age. Finally, she struck gold in an inner zipper pocket. A sheet labeled "Passwords." She probably could have figured them out even without the list since every password was a variation on PASSWORD, and every PIN was 1234.

"Hello." The blond woman who watched her earlier had appeared at the booth.

Kimberly swept Bernice's belongings back into the tote and shoved it under the counter. She fixed her best approximation of a welcoming smile on her face and hoped the woman would attribute her red cheeks to the Florida sun rather than annoyance at being caught snooping.

"I'm Lindsey," the woman said. "I just wanted to see how your friend was doing. I was there when she fell earlier."

What had this woman seen? Did she recognize the tote Kim had been searching as Bernice's? "Nice to meet you. I'm Kimberly." She feigned a friendly tone, then swapped it for an equally insincere one of concern. "Unfortunately, Bernice, the woman who fell, has a broken hip. Our guild president sent out an update. It'll be months before she can return."

Lindsey furrowed her brow in concern. Kimberly mirrored her expression, swallowing the grin that kept threatening to break out since she had gotten the news.

"That's too bad," Lindsey said. "And I'm sorry for your . . . guild, is it?"

Kimberly told her at great length about the Guild, and about the Art Deco movement, and about its history in Miami. If only the board could hear her, they would recognize that, unlike Elliot, she had a lot more to offer than just a pretty face and a fabulous wardrobe. Okay, he also had proven fundraising skills from working with Miami's big LGBTQ+ Winter Party Festival every year. And you couldn't read the society pages without finding a shot of him and his husband at the city's premier philanthropic events. Bernice obviously hoped the Art Deco Guild would bask in some of his reflected glow.

"One of the hotels has given the Guild a couple of rooms to use as a permanent installation," Kimberly said, "but …."

"But what?"

"Bernice has been doing the fundraising to build a collection. I don't know what's going to happen now." When Bernice hit the ground that morning, the donors had retreated like the ocean at low tide. Who knew if they would return?

"I doubt they'll be asking me to step in," Kim said. "Apparently, I'm not board material."

Lindsey looked confused but sympathetic. It would be nice to tell her all about Bernice. And Elliot. And the board members who excluded her, just like all the other members of every other organization Kimberly joined. And about how she had crossed over the causeway to South Beach for yet another fresh start that had failed to yield the recognition she deserved. Lindsey would probably be cruising off to the Caribbean soon anyway, and whatever secrets Kimberly shared would sail away with her.

But instead, Kim just handed her a pamphlet.

* * *

"Bernice is not dead." The guild president banged his gavel to cut Kimberly off. "And she's made her wishes clear."

Kim looked around the room. Only Elliot returned her gaze, the azure of his eyes emphasized by his pale blue guayabera. They all knew he was going to be elected to Bernice's board seat. Kimberly had tried to point out her own qualifications, but the president had not let her finish. "There's no campaigning for the position," he said. "We'll vote at the next meeting. I already have Bernice's proxy."

The guild members headed for lunch, all except Kim. She knew better than to wait for an invitation to join them. Not after how agitated she had gotten. Again.

She headed toward the ocean and wandered past the Beach Patrol Headquarters, silently pointing out its nautical Art Deco style to the imaginary tour group she never got to lead.

"Kimberly, is that you?"

Lindsey and another woman were approaching from the opposite direction. Today, Lindsey's thematic ensemble featured gold rope earrings and a blouse embroidered with anchors. She seemed happy to see Kim, a response she did not often evoke.

"This is Gloria," Lindsey said. "I was just telling her about you. Are you free for lunch by any chance?"

The three of them ducked into a Cuban restaurant. "I looked at that pamphlet you gave me," Lindsey said as they ate fried plantain chips, "and decided to check out the Wolfsonian Museum. They really do have a wonderful Art Deco collection."

Kimberly managed to stay quiet while Lindsey described the objects on display, even though she knew all about them. She had been practicing letting boring people finish their thoughts for years.

"So," Lindsey eventually said, "I turned to the woman next to me to comment on an ashtray, and she said she had one exactly like it. And that's how Gloria and I met."

Gloria took a long pull of her Hatuey beer and grimaced. "I have ashtrays, I have Lalique statues, I have Ruhlmann furniture. All sitting in a climate-controlled storage unit I'm paying through the nose for every month."

"And she has so many stories about Miami in the old days," Lindsey said. "Ollie Burgers and the Neptune Lounge. Just fascinating. Tell Kimberly about your grandparents."

"They met when my grandfather was stationed here for officer candidate school in World War II." Gloria pulled up a picture on her phone and shared it with Kim. "They're the ones who accumulated all the stuff I'm dealing with now. I'm sure Art Deco is fine, but it's totally not my taste. I'm in town just long enough to decide what to do with it."

"That's why I was talking about you," Lindsey said. "Your Art Deco Guild might be interested in a donation." She clapped her hands in apparent delight at her own cleverness. "Kim, maybe you could suggest it to them."

Kimberly could do that, of course, but then Elliot or Bernice or the president could steal all the credit. The better option was to present it to the guild as a fait accompli, a done deal that would surely win her a seat on the board. Failing to reward her extraordinary resourcefulness would not be a good look for the guild.

"Well, I'm already in talks with some people," Gloria said, "a design museum in Denver and another place in Nashville."

Kim felt her board seat slipping away.

"It was just an idea," Lindsey said. "Now, you have to tell Kimberly about that time your grandmother met Frank Sinatra and the Rat Pack."

Gloria launched into the story, but Kim's mind was racing down a different track—how to ensure that Gloria's donation went to the Art Deco Guild rather than one of the pushy museums already trying to steal it out from under them. She had not come up with a solution by the time the server came to clear their table.

"Are you feeling okay?" Lindsey asked, looking sympathetic again. "You didn't eat very much."

"Not hungry, I guess," Kim said. "Maybe we can do this again another time. Where is this collection? Can we go see it?"

"I'm afraid not." Gloria checked her diamond watch. "I've got an appointment. The rest of my day is shot."

Kim pulled out her phone, determined to reel this deal in. "Why don't I get both of your numbers? We can meet later."

The three women exchanged contact information and went their separate ways, Lindsey and Gloria heading in opposite directions. Kimberly watched them go, hoping her dreams weren't leaving with them.

* * *

The following Saturday, Kim arrived to relieve Elliot at the Guild's booth at the market in the park. Today he wore a coral shirt and linen shorts and smelled even better than he looked. He seemed in a particularly good mood. Presumably, because the board would be installing him in a *pro forma* vote at its meeting in two days. Bernice's stolen passwords had given Kim full access to all the board's business. The emails she was reading had her very worried.

That worry turned to full-fledged panic when Kim saw Lindsey approaching with a wave. Elliot waved back. "Do I know this person?" he asked.

Kim bolted from behind the table to intercept Lindsey.

"Hey," Elliot protested. "I have brunch plans."

Kim ignored him, intent on keeping Lindsey and her knowledge of Gloria's trove of Art Deco treasures as far away from Elliot and the rest of the guild as possible. She hustled Lindsey under a banyan tree out of view of the guild's booth. "Let's step into the shade."

"I just came by to bring you this," Lindsey said, holding out a gift bag and almost shouting to be heard over the music blaring from the string of restaurants across the street. Kimberly pulled out a glass ashtray. She recognized its classic Art Deco design.

"Gloria asked me to give it to you," Lindsey said. "She took me to look at her grandparents' collection yesterday. It's quite impressive. I wish I could think of some way to convince her to donate it to the Guild before I leave on my cruise."

"I do too," Kim said, turning the ashtray over and over.

"Have you tried calling her? Maybe you can convince her that her collection really belongs in Miami. It's part of the history of the place."

"I'll do that." Civic pride was one thing, but Kim had another idea that might prove to be more persuasive.

* * *

"$150,000 is a lot of money," Gloria said. Kimberly wished they could have met in person so she could read the other woman's body language, but Gloria was in Denver.

It *was* a lot of money. The Guild's entire bank balance. But compared to the costs associated with a fundraising gala or the time and effort involved in luring donors, giving Gloria a financial incentive to choose the Art Deco Guild as the recipient of her largesse was clearly the better option. It was a small price to pay to complete their Art Deco installation in one fell swoop. That's how Kimberly would explain it to the board when they found out that she used Bernice's password to send a crypto payment to Gloria. Besides, you can't put a price on your dreams.

"Of course," Kim said, "I will need to take at least a quick look at the collection before the funds complete the transfer. Just for due diligence."

"I'm the only one who can access the storage facility," Gloria said. "You need a padlock key. It's not one of those fancy places with smart locks and remote access. I'd have to travel back to Miami for that."

"I'm sure we can find a way to . . ."

"Listen, Kimberly, I'm ready to sign on the dotted line with the museum people here in Denver. And frankly, this whole discussion with you feels a little sketchy."

Kimberly racked her brain for a way to keep her board seat from slipping away. Lindsey had said the collection was impressive. Maybe other people had the same opinion.

"Did the Denver museum do some kind of appraisal before accepting the donation?" Kim said. "Maybe I could take a look at it."

A moment later, her phone pinged, and a scan of the appraiser's report appeared. It was even better than Kim had hoped. There was no way the guild could object to her methods when they saw the phenomenal pieces they would soon possess. They could even sell a few of them to recoup the whole outlay. The board would thank her; hell, they would give her an award. It would be her picture on the website, her hand holding the gavel at the meetings, maybe even her name on the completed installation.

"I'm in," said Kimberly. "Send me your banking information, and I'll confirm the transfer. You'll have the money within the hour."

Gloria sighed. "All right. Once it clears the bank, I'll overnight you the key and the storage facility information. We can handle the rest of the paperwork later."

* * *

Kimberly blinked, staring into the empty storage unit. Shock left her feeling colder than the air conditioning chilling the vacant space. She had arrived with key in hand and victory in mind, only to discover that she had been robbed. But not in the way she thought. The manager informed her that the unit had not been rented out for months. No one had stolen its contents. And no one was answering Gloria or Lindsey's phones, which had both been disconnected.

Gloria had stolen the Guild's money and Kim's hopes. And Lindsey had been in on the scam from the beginning, introducing them and urging Kimberly to pursue the donation. She had pegged Kim as desperate and unscrupulous from the moment she had seen her smiling at Bernice's injury and rooting through her bag. A perfect mark for a couple of perfect con artists. And with $150,000, they could cruise out of Miami and onto their next scam under whatever new names they chose.

All Kimberly had to show for the whole experience was the glass ashtray they gave her. A reproduction, obviously. Probably bought at the Wolfsonian gift shop. Good for nothing now but holding the ashes of Kim's torched Miami dreams. Buried in those ashes, though, were the embers of a white-hot anger. She knew it would propel her out of Florida and beyond this latest failure toward an even better plan, a flawless, foolproof scheme. She just needed to perfect its design.

MURDER IN MYAKKA PARK

Wendy Dingwall

Ah . . . spring in Sarasota, no more forty-degree winter weather. How beautiful!

I'm taking some time away from my mystery writing to be in nature. It's a crime to live in such a gorgeous city and be inside for days on end, sitting in front of a computer screen.

Today, I stayed away from the crowded beaches. I'm heading to the massive Myakka Park. It's over 37,000 acres and part of a conservation area that expands to 80,000 acres.

Besides my vocation as a writer, I've been studying Twenty-First Century Shamanism. Since I moved here, gifts from my childhood have resurfaced in a big way, leading me on a path as a healer. So, today's homework assignment is practicing a medicine walk. It's about being invisible to the native wildlife yet interacting with nature spirits, learning their ways of being and their purposes on Mother Earth. Indigenous Native Americans call this walking with one foot in the spirit world and one foot in the physical world. Today, I'm concentrating on the Winged Nation. Thousands of bird species winter here. Like many northerners, they love this idyllic habitat. Although most birds have returned north, I'm not worried. There are plenty of tropical species to experience year-round.

I've arrived early. Two other cars parked here. It's a good sign. I'll have peace and quiet. I'm to practice using—deer hearing, coyote smell, raccoon touch, owl eyes, and snake taste. Don't want an audience for that. Ha! As you may have noticed, I'm journaling my experience.

*　*　*

I've checked in at the ranger station and received directions to the Nature Trail. It's populated with birds and harmless wildlife—deer, squirrels, raccoons, turtles, bobcats, and so on. Growing up near the Everglades, I've seen plenty of alligators in my time. There are over a hundred that hang out here in an area called 'the deep hole.' I understand they are allowed to roam freely. Not up for that today.

Time to hit the trail, so I'll begin my fox walking to blend in and do my best to become invisible. Putting my journal away for now.

*　*　*

Hours have gone by, but it seemed like only minutes. First, I followed our lesson protocol by placing my hands, cupped, at the back of each ear. Standing, I faced one direction at a time, and listened. This magnified what I heard. Birds chirped, cawed, and trilled. Crickets reminded me of a buzz saw. A few squirrel screeches pierced through the other animal chatter. The faint sound of a nearby bush rustled. I hesitated. Maybe a critter foraging for food. I jumped at a loud snort. I held my breath a moment, then I saw it, a wild boar. It looked at me knowingly, turned, and walked away. It's like the Shamans say, never is nothing happening, and that includes the spirit world. It just happens, my power animal is a wild boar. I received a rush of energy, knowing it was here to help guide me.

As I walked looking for the perfect sit spot, I took short coyote sniffs, smelling the earth. Scents of dried tree leaves drifted in the air bringing dampness and faint fish smells from the nearby river. I reached down and touched the earth, felt the breeze, saying, "Hello, I'm here." I blurred my vision and focused wide-angled, looking around in all directions with owl eyes, saying again, "Hello, I am here." And last, I stuck my tongue out like a snake and tasted the air, mildly salty and reminiscent of dog breath. Up ahead, I saw the perfect sit spot by a shady oak tree. I continued my quiet nonobtrusive fox walk and imagined I was invisible, stepping through a veil. I sat, leaning my back against the tree, and breathed into that place of physicality, moving into spirit.

In a short while, I couldn't say exactly how long, I sensed the spirit of a female deer approach. I sent her love, felt her trusting energy. She stepped closer. I sensed she came for me. I asked if I could merge with her. I felt a whoosh, and we were one. She meandered through the forest, stopping to investigate pinecones, raccoon feces, purslane. She bit off the flowers and leaves of a spiderwort weed. *Hmm, not bad.* Her movements felt light and easy, yet she was hypersensitive, on alert. Her hearing and eyesight were a hundred percent better than mine. Several times she'd jump-sprint at the sound of tourists on the regular path. Once, I watched, filtered through the bushes as they tried to photograph her-us. She turned, leaped, and took us deeper into the woods.

She stepped slowly for my benefit. Deeper in, a rancid smell filled her nostrils. She didn't shy away from it but moved to investigate. I'd heard some animals have heightened smell, others have hearing, while still, others have vision, but the Deer Nation is the only four-legged animal that has all senses heightened. At one point, I assumed I'd merge with an owl or a sand crane, now I realized it wasn't meant to be. She sprinted closer to the overwhelming smell. A flock of black crows took flight, cawing their loud, raucous cries. They'd been picking at a human body, deep in the woods, in a place hard to find.

My heart raced, and in a split second, I was back in my sit spot by the tree. Remembering the stench and sight of the bloody body, the face, picked away by the crows—a wave of nausea ran through me. I pulled my arms from my backpack, dug out my bottle of water, and took a drink. I sat stuck to the spot, getting my bearings, not hearing nature sounds any longer.

I pulled out my journal. I wanted to record my soul journey while fresh in my mind and keep my facts straight. When I finished, I took a few deep breaths and headed back to the ranger station to report what I'd seen. My better judgment told me not to mention that it was through the eyes of a deer.

I rehearsed my story on the walk back. When I arrived at the Ranger Station, a young couple was receiving final directions to their reserved campsite. I waited for them to leave, then spoke to the ranger, a distinguished gentleman looking around sixtyish. He referred to himself as Ranger Dave.

"How can I help you?" His eyes widened in recognition. "Didn't I check you in this morning? You had that funny name."

"Yes, I'm Macha Jones. I asked you for directions to the nature trail."

"Right. How can I help?"

"I'll admit right up front, against your advice, I left the trail. I'm afraid I have bad news. I saw a deer and wanted to get a picture. I followed her for a short distance, then lost sight of her. I got turned around and ended up going deeper into the woods. Anyway, it took me a while to retrace my steps and find my way out." Nervous about my white lie, I took a quick breath. "To keep this short, I stumbled across a dead body. I think it's a man but couldn't tell for sure. The face had . . . been gnawed on." I grasped my arms, hugging my abdomen.

Ranger Dave stared at me for a long moment as if he thought I might be imagining this. "Stay right here." He went into his office and made a call. When he returned, he asked, "Will you be able to find the body again?"

"I think so. I tried my best to remember the many turns."

"Have a seat." He pointed to three straight-back chairs against a windowless wall. "Sheriff's deputies will be here in about twenty minutes."

I removed my backpack and sat. I wanted to say how gross it was to see and smell. But I didn't. I recalled the body was still pretty much intact. I decided it was a man based on the clothes and the bulk of the legs. I pushed away my image of the crows gnawing on the exposed parts of him. I took more deep breaths to calm myself. Then wondered, who would do such a thing? Maybe he had a heart attack. Something in my gut tugged at me. What had I seen that made me think he'd been murdered?

* * *

The deputies arrived a half hour later. I'd had several drinks of water, and the nervousness caused me to need a bathroom break. When I returned, I overheard Ranger Dave saying, "She seems a little spacey to me." I imagined his eyes rolling upward, but no matter, I saw what I saw.

Two fit-looking men in uniform moved their focus to me.

"Miss, I'm Captain Martinez. This is Deputy Hansen. We're with the County Sheriff's Department, and we'll be investigating."

Deputy Hansen pulled a mobile phone from his pocket. "We'll be recording your statement. Do you have any objections?"

"No."

The deputy held the phone out to catch my answers and asked, "What's your full name and birth date?"

"Macha Lee Jones, February 10, 1977."

"Can you tell us how you came to find the body?"

I repeated my story as told to Ranger Dave.

Next, we began walking back to the trail.

I hesitated several times, deciding where to turn, hoping I'd find my way back. It took about forty minutes to get to the site, and my energy waned. I hung back while they examined the scene.

They took care not to get too close to the body rather than obscure what might be evidence of foul play. Captain Martinez indicated that he had forensics on standby.

While they observed things as best they could, given the circumstances, I tried to remember what had bothered me about the scene when I'd been merged with the deer. I looked around, and my sight landed on a small shiny gold object. That was it. I moved closer and snapped a quick picture.

"Captain Martinez, I see something that might be important."

"Where?"

"Over here." My hand shook when I pointed to the small object poking out from under the ground cover.

After putting on plastic gloves, Deputy Hansen stooped down to pick it up. "It looks like an old Boy Scout badge. I doubt it has anything to do with this. It was probably dropped here by some bird that picked it up elsewhere."

Captain Martinez said, "Nevertheless, we'll keep it with forensics of the scene. Thank you, Miss Jones."

My gut disagreed with the Deputy's assessment. I felt it would end up being more helpful than he imagined. I have learned—always listen to my gut feelings.

Captain Martinez turned to Deputy Hansen, "Deputy, take Miss Jones back to the Ranger station. I want you to wait for forensics and the coroner so you can lead them back here." He turned to me. "Miss Jones, you may return home, but don't leave town. We may have more questions in the future."

* * *

Later that evening, I listened to the local news.

A popular newscaster reported, "The body discovered by an unknown woman at Myakka Park has been identified as that of Commissioner James Rayburn, affectionately known as Big Jimmy. He'd been reported missing by his wife, Sarah Rayburn, when after waiting many hours, he didn't return from an unscheduled meeting with a constituent. The cause of death has not yet been determined. The police are not revealing whether or not they suspect foul play."

I decided to search the Internet for information about Commissioner Rayburn. Being so up close and personal, I felt I needed to know more about him. His own website had glowing things to say about him and his accomplishments. Yet there were several negative articles and disgruntled citizens who felt he was abusing his power on the Planning and Development Commission. He'd make promises to vote for the good of the community or the ecology of the location. At the last minute, he'd change his vote, going along with developers, allowing questionable construction to move forward.

* * *

It's the next morning, as I write in my journal, I find myself wanting to go to Myakka Park. The experience with the deer still lingers in my mind. It had been an awesome experience, one I'd like to repeat, except for the ending. On the other hand, I'm curious and drawn to the scene where the body was found. Who had he met? How did he wind up in the park at that spot? I'm going to assume it's someone who knows the park area. Given there are more remote areas where they could have hidden the body, maybe it was meant to be found. All these things are swirling around in my mind. From experience, until I get some answers, I'm not going to be worth much to anyone, including myself.

* * *

I'd arrived early at the park again. A sheriff's squad car and forensics van were parked out front. Had they been there since yesterday? Or were they back to do more searching?

I checked in at the Ranger's Station. A middle-aged woman who called herself Ranger Donna greeted me. "Have you been here before? You don't look familiar to me. You're not a regular." She scowled.

What's with the militant attitude? "I was here yesterday. Where is Ranger Dave?"

"It's his day off. Where do you want to go? The nature trail is off limits today." She grinned.

"I figured as much since I was here yesterday."

"Are you the lady that found the body?"

"Yep. Where can I find the best bird viewings?"

Ranger Donna pulled out a map, circled an area, and handed it to me. "Drive up the road about a mile. The entrance will be on your right. Then you'll have about a 20-minute trail walk to the water. You'll see lots of birds." She handed me a brochure showing species of birds that use the area for wading and tree-side habitats.

When I left the station, it occurred to me I would need to drive away. She'd know that I walked to the nature trail if my car was still parked.

I drove up the road a short distance when I found a spot that allowed me to pull off, sheltering the car near some trees. I grabbed my backpack and hiked back toward the nature trail. I stopped a few hundred yards ahead when I noticed the sheriff's car and van pull out of the parking lot. They drove toward town. I continued my trek to the sit spot, looked around for my deer, but didn't see her.

It was eerily quiet. I stepped lightly, not wishing to startle any animals after the barrage of investigators in their territory. I felt comfortable with the woodsy area, little by little, the bushes rustled, the birdsong filled the air, crickets chirped, and other sounds and smells came alive. I stopped a few times on the way to wipe my sweaty brow and take a drink of water as the heat penetrated through the trees. I arrived where the body had been and encountered my friends, the deer, and wild boar. They looked up at me, then romped around the area, removing any sign of negative human energy.

Something startled the deer. She looked in my direction, then ran off. The boar stood his ground.

"What are you doing here?" Ranger Donna's croaky voice came from behind.

"Just looking around. There's no crime scene tape. I assume it's fine to be here." I turned and held my gaze steady, looking directly into her eyes.

She blinked. "I told you this part of the park is closed. Look, there." She pointed at the boar. "They can be dangerous. You might get hurt."

"I'll have you know that boar is my friend. He will not hurt me."

Ranger Donna broke out in a booming laugh. The boar took a step toward her. She took a step back. "You better leave. I can make this whole park off-limits to you, if I see fit to do so."

I stood stock still.

She shrugged her shoulders. "Okay, it's your funeral." She turned and left.

"Wait!" I had a thought. "Is there another way to approach this area other than from the entrance near the ranger station?"

"Why? What does it matter to you? I hope you're not planning to sneak in without letting us know you're here."

"No, I'm not like that." I glanced over at the boar. He seemed interested in listening to our conversation. I know pigs are smart. I wonder if that goes for wild boars.

"Well then, why do you want to know?" She tipped her hat back on her head, indicating she wanted to understand my question.

"I'm curious. How did someone get a body out here without being noticed?"

"I suggest you let the police worry about that. Don't forget, curiosity killed the cat." She laughed again and walked away.

She didn't answer my question. Maybe, I'll come back tomorrow and ask Ranger Dave.

* * *

Listening to the local news that evening, my suspicions were confirmed. Commissioner Rayburn had been murdered. Not evident at the park was the stab wound on his back. This gave me the chills. I often get them as validation that my intuition is right on. Then the Boy Scout badge flashed in my mind. Don't ask me how, but I knew it had something to do with the murder.

* * *

"Good morning, Ranger Dave." I gave him my friendliest smile. "I'm signing in. I want to go back to the nature trail. Like to see if I can get a photo of that deer I missed or any others that may be sprinting around."

"I hear you gave Ranger Donna a hard time yesterday. She has advised me to ban you from the area."

"It's just the opposite. She gave me a hard time. Has she got a bug up her butt or something?"

Ranger Dave laughed. "Don't take it personally. I've heard she gets a bit superior with all the hikers and campers. She only fills in for me on my days off. Don't worry. You're welcome here anytime."

Whew! He's not so bad after all.

I trekked back to my sit spot. I redid my Shamanic assignment, but no deer appeared to me. I journaled the sounds and smells, but all in all, I was disappointed with the lack of excitement. Aware of more hikers on the trail, I figured that might be why the larger animals were scarce.

I decided to work my way back toward the crime scene. I wondered if the Sheriff's Department had found the knife or whatever was used to stab the Commissioner. I took a good look around. Nothing. Next, I pulled out the park map. I saw that it was possible to work my way through the woods to another entry point five or so miles away. It could get iffy. I could get lost or encounter an alligator, a wilder boar, even a poisonous snake. Once I leave this area, all bets are off as far as my nature experience is concerned.

While going over the pros and cons of this idea, my better judgment kicked in. I limited my search to about twenty paces toward the other entry. After finding nothing suspicious, I decided to head back to the Ranger Station.

* * *

"Ranger Dave, mind if I ask you a few questions?"

"Sure, Miss. That's why I'm here." He got up from his chair and moved behind the counter. "What would you like to know? We may have a brochure that can answer your questions."

"I doubt that." I wiped my sweaty palms on my shorts. "I wonder if you know of a regular hiker or camper that is familiar with all these woods. Someone who would know the back ways into the park."

"Well, young lady, there are many hikers and a few campers that would have that knowledge. Please tell me you're not playing Nancy Drew and trying to solve the commissioner's murder? It could get *real* dangerous for you. Besides, Captain Martinez already asked me about that. I gave him the list."

He sounded genuinely concerned, but why did I feel threatened? "What do you mean, it could get dangerous for me?"

"Some of these hikers and campers are not the kind of characters that like people sticking their nose in where it doesn't belong."

I looked around his orderly wood cabin and realized that here was a man who knew what he was talking about. "I appreciate the warning." I thanked him and left.

* * *

Back home, on the Internet, I checked to find more news about the commissioner. The media spoke about groups that had picketed his office, angry that his change of heart allowed eco-friendly lands to be destroyed. Developers inadvertently killed or chased wildlife, including land bird species, into residential communities. But no specific disgruntled person was named.

I went to the County Sheriff's website and found no further information there. Next, to the Development and Planning Commission site, and there I found that a subsequent meeting was scheduled to discuss plans to sell thirty acres of Myakka Park preserve. A blurb about the previous meeting said park lovers and ecologists had voiced their concerns, but they had gotten out of control. Therefore the meeting was postponed. The main argument—once the commission consented to a thirty-acre takeover, developers would soon be petitioning for more of the protected lands. I noticed a link to a YouTube video of that meeting. I clicked on it.

The meeting started out cordial enough. Several speakers took to the floor to voice their opposition. I was surprised to see Ranger Dave walk up to the podium.

He gave a brief but powerful statement, mentioning that as someone who had grown up visiting the Park with his family and now watched over it daily, he knew best the importance to the area. Our park, he went on to say, is the second most biodiverse ecosystem in North America, and it's full of diverse plants. A domain where animals live free of urbanization while keeping the land organic and helpful to the integrity of earth itself. Thousands of bird species that migrate annually to the Park would have fewer options and would either die or invade rural communities since they need to rest and rejuvenate before moving further south, as they've done for eons. He explained the importance of adults and children learning about sustaining the land and wildlife habitats so future generations perpetuate the importance of the park. His talk ignited the crowd, and they began shouting down their opposition.

Prior to visiting Myakka Park, I'd checked out their website's staff descriptions and something about Ranger Dave flashed into my mind. I navigated there again and reread his bio. Sure enough, in the seventies, he'd made trips to the park as a Boy Scout. Furthermore, he's currently a volunteer high-ranking

Scoutmaster. I wondered if the badge found near the body might have been his. I felt my heart race. I retrieved my mobile phone and located the picture I'd taken of the badge. I went online to find out what it represented. Turns out it's not a badge. It's an award medal. The only one I found that resembled the gold-tone medal near the body was the Hornaday Award, given for excellence in conservation and protecting wildlife. Of course, it must be his.

Now what to do? . . . Call Captain Martinez. He did say if I think of anything.

I took a few minutes to get a cup of tea, and as it brewed, I gathered my thoughts. Seated at my kitchen table, I picked up the sheriff's card and dialed his number. He answered on the first ring.

"Captain Martinez, Macha Jones. I remembered something and wondered if you had pursued the boy-scout medal as evidence of the person who killed Commissioner Rayburn?"

"We've eliminated it as evidence. Ranger Dave told us he lost the medal part of his award, normally attached to a sturdy ribbon. He had no idea how it ended up out there."

"Are you aware that the Commissioner was targeted by conservationists for his record of voting with developers who destroyed crucial wetlands and conservation areas? Ranger Dave was one of those."

"Yes, we've been investigating that angle. What business is it of yours?"

"I'm the one who found the body. I want to know what happened. Are you aware the medal is for striving to save conservation and wildlife?"

"Yes. Is that all? I'm busy with a heavy workload of crimes here."

"What about Ranger Dave? Is he a suspect?"

"No. According to the time of death, Ranger Dave has a solid alibi. He was home, babysitting two grandkids."

"Do you mind if I ask? What was the time of death?"

"Approximately twenty-four hours prior. Around the same time in the afternoon, forensics transferred his body to the morgue."

"And Ranger Dave was not working?"

"Right."

"Was it that rude woman, Ranger Donna, who covered for him?"

"Look, Miss, just leave this alone. Thanks for trying to help. But we'll take it from here." Captain Martinez hung up the phone.

Guess that was one question too many. Now what? Back to the park tomorrow. There are several park rangers. Any one of them could have subbed for Ranger Dave, but I have a feeling it was Ranger Donna.

* * *

"Good morning, I'm Macha Jones. I'd like to visit the nature trail." Ranger Jeff handed me the daily code 653 to enter. "Where is Ranger Dave today?"

"It's his day off."

"I thought Ranger Donna subs for him."

Ranger Jeff's eyes narrowed to slits. His face was so plump that they almost disappeared. "Not always. Why do you care?"

"No reason, just curious. I thought she said she always subs for him."

"Well, she don't," he said. "Look, you want anything else? If not, I have work to do."

"Besides answer questions or chit-chat with park guests?" I looked around the visitor center, its brochure racks and pictures of wildlife, still neat as a pin. "Doesn't look like much needs doing to me." I turned and left.

Today, I decided to stroll through the whole nature trail and see where it would lead me. While I hiked, I caught a glimpse of a bobcat slinking away from the trail. I encountered a green turtle crossing the path. I love turtles, and seeing one is good luck. Bird song was in full force today. I couldn't help but laugh at the honking of a Sandhill crane. Not much activity, though. No deer sightings either. Twenty minutes in, I was startled when someone rushed from the tree cover behind me, poking me in the back with what felt like a gun.

"Turn in here," Ranger Donna said. I'd recognize that crusty smoke-riddled voice anywhere.

"What . . . why are you doing this?"

"Move." She pushed me hard.

I stumbled forward in the direction she'd pushed. Using a calm tone, "Again, why are you doing this?"

"I warned you about curiosity, didn't I? But you didn't listen."

"How do you know? I only met you that one time."

"You think I'm stupid?"

"No, of course not," I lied.

"First, Ranger Dave tells me you complained, then today Jeff said you asked about me. Now why would you do such a stupid thing?"

"You're right, but I was disturbed by what I saw. I needed to know what happened. Wouldn't you have felt the same?"

"I wouldn't have endangered myself finding out." She pushed me again. "Keep walking."

Into the woods we went until I lost hope that anyone would hear a gunshot. How far does the sound of a gunshot travel?

If I stall for time, will it even help? I prayed for a miracle. "Are you going to shoot me in the back? Or do you have the guts to face me?"

She whipped me around with her free hand, gun pointed close to my chest. I took a step back.

"Fine, take a few more steps backward. I don't want to get your blood spatter on me." She chuckled.

"Why did you kill him? Why frame Ranger Dave?"

She screamed at me, "I did it for the animals and that smart-ass Dave. But the snooty bastard laughed at me when I asked him out. I fixed him good. I put that damn medal he was so proud of near the body—payback for thinking he's so much better than me."

At that moment, the wild boar came running from the brush behind her. He gored her in the hip, causing her to fall forward, releasing a gunshot into the ground.

Instinctively, I screamed.

The boar backed up and charged her again, getting her in the thigh. She began screaming in pain, then passed out.

I took a calming breath and telepathically asked the boar to stop, thanked him for saving my life, and urged him to leave. He disappeared back in the direction he came.

I reached for the gun Ranger Donna had dropped.

I heard running footsteps. Ranger Dave and Ranger Jeff had found us.

"What is going on here?" Ranger Dave asked.

"She . . . tried to kill me. She killed the Commissioner and thought I suspected her. She had this gun in my back." I set it down on the ground. "She moved me away to avoid getting splattered with my blood. That's when the boar attacked her, saving my life. How . . . why did you come?"

"Jeff said Donna stormed after you in a blaze of fury."

Ranger Dave checked her pulse. "She's alive. Jeff, call an ambulance. I'll call the police."

THE FUNHOUSE

Tanya Goodwin

Ginny licked the whipped cream clean off the plastic fork and then stabbed it into the juicy strawberry shortcake.

Brian chuckled and tapped the corner of his mouth. "You have some strawberry stuff."

Heat spread across her cheeks despite the cool March Florida night.

Perhaps a first date at the Strawberry Time Festival wasn't such a good idea.

Brian pulled a napkin from one of his cargo pants pockets and dabbed the whipped cream from the corner of her mouth.

"Thanks."

He smiled. "Don't mention it. Happens to me all the time. Do I have any on me?"

Unfortunately, he did not.

She shook her head. "Nope."

"I have to say that this is, no doubt, the best strawberry shortcake I've ever had!"

"That's fair food for you. You've never been to this festival before…or uh…one sort of like it?"

Oh, that was stupid. Of course, he hadn't been to Strawberry Time. He'd just moved to Florida two months ago from New Jersey. They had to have fairs in New Jersey, but nothing like Strawberry Time. She came every year, first with her parents and then with girlfriends. But this was the first time she'd come here on a date.

"I've been to state fairs and end-of-summer local ones, but nothing can compare to this," Brian tilted his head and grinned, "including the company."

Scratch that. It wasn't such a good idea.

Ginny finished the rest of her shortcake, gazing at Brian's boyish face while he shoveled in the rest of his.

Crowds of festival goers jabbered in the background, but Brian captured Ginny's complete attention. The two of them bathed in the kaleidoscope of flashing lights. This year's festival was going to be the best one yet!

And she hadn't wanted to go.

"Go! Go!" her friends prodded.

No. She had to study for her pre-med midterms.

They slammed her books shut and handed Ginny her cell.

"Call him back! Your books can wait. You can study tomorrow. Don't pass this guy up. He's so into you. And he's gorgeous. And so polite."

Her friends had a point. Ginny was ahead in her studying anyway. And they were right about Brian, an amiable, newly hired bartender she talked with until closing time. The evening was so unlike her. She wasn't a bar person, but her friends ripped her from the security of her desk to a night of frivolity. Brian was so easy to talk with. And he didn't flinch when all she ordered the whole night was ginger ale. Ginny chuckled to herself. At least it was an *ale*.

He'd walked her to the exit door that night despite the fact she hadn't any alcohol in her blood, and then he entered his contact info into her cell, knowing darn well she could delete it if she wanted to, but she didn't.

And here they were on Saturday night, her choice.

Ginny and Brian tossed their empty strawberry shortcake plates into the heaping trash.

Brian took her hand. "Where to next? Show me around."

Could he feel the pulse shooting to her fingertips?

He squeezed her hand.

Maybe.

"The Ferris Wheel?" It was Ginny's favorite ride.

He scanned the height of the gigantic wheel with its spokes of neon lights.

"Awesome! Let's go."

She'd indeed chosen well.

* * *

Ginny pulled Brian's hand and hurried toward the Ferris wheel.

She craned her neck past the long line inching through the maze of ropes.

The Ferris wheel cars stopped and started while the ride handler loaded each one.

With the slow loading and unloading, they'd wait over an hour, she guessed, for a ten-minute jerky ride.

But what did she expect for a Saturday night?

"We can wait," Brian offered.

"I don't want to spend the night waiting in line. Let's try another ride, and maybe we can come back to this one later."

But given the crowds and the popularity of the gigantic Ferris wheel, where you could see the whole festival from the very top, Ginny tempered her enthusiasm that the lines would shorten.

Brian pointed. "Hey, look over there! No line at The Funhouse. Want to go?"

"Yeah!"

This time, Brian pulled Ginny toward the attraction.

They squeaked to a halt in front of the towering mustached carnie, who wore a black Metallica T-shirt and grass-stained jeans. His greasy wavy brown hair framed his weirdly popping blue eyes.

"That'll be three tickets a piece," he said.

Brian reached into his cargo pants pocket and handed six tickets into the carnie's waiting hand.

"Enter if you dare," he warned. "Can't vouch for the exit. Still want in?"

"Yeah, we want in." Brian looked at Ginny. "Right?"

"How can I say no! Who knows? Maybe once we go through this, we can try to get on the Ferris wheel."

Brian pumped his fist. "Let's do it!"

* * *

Brian stepped past the spinning tube, the Funhouse's first challenge, and entrance into the wacky attraction.

Ginny paused with her eyes intent on the rotating cylinder.

Brian held out his hand. "Come on! Don't think so hard about it. Just go. Or jump over it. I got you. I won't let you fall."

Don't be such a baby! Ginny drew a deep breath and hurried across with a step-step pounce.

"We're in!" Brian cheered.

She glanced back at the cylinder, and her eyes widened. It began spinning faster and faster. She couldn't back out now without falling and hurting herself. The last thing she needed was a busted ankle or a scraped knee, not to mention a bruised ego.

Suddenly, white strobing lights attacked Ginny's eyes, blinding her, and she squinted to ward them off.

Ginny groped for Brian's hand.

The strobe stopped as quick as it came, and she blinked the burning moisture from her eyes until she could focus ahead.

Brian was right in front of her. How could she have missed his hand?

"Damn! That blinded me too," he said.

"I was trying to grab your hand," she said.

He offered his hand.

"Grab it now while you can," he teased.

"I don't hear anyone behind us."

"Oh, they'll come along. Meanwhile, we have the place to ourselves."

Ginny's mouth went dry when she recalled the carnie's warning.

She pulled Brian to a halt, waiting for others to catch up with them, but their breaths only emphasized they remained the sole couple in this madcap menagerie.

Brian gave her a reassuring tug.

The strobes only made the maze dimmer, but Ginny could see the pathway forward.

She gripped Brian's hand, just in case.

They ventured farther while squeezed into increasingly narrowing walls until the two could no longer fit side by side.

Her hand slipped away from Brian's until her fingertips lost touch with his.

"You go first, and I'll follow," Ginny fought to suggest.

Follow, as in she'd be nipping at his heels.

Holographic stars and neon orange, green and blue swirls peppered the walls. She had to admit that the fluorescent kaleidoscope images were pretty neat.

She'd started to enjoy herself.

But that was the point of a funhouse, and the carnie's omen was all part of the fun.

Five steps later, a jet of air shot up her jeans and puffed under her blouse.

Ginny giggled and slammed into Brian's back.

"Oops! Sorry!"

"What happened?"

"Air blew up my jeans and under my shirt. Startled me! You must've missed wherever I stepped!"

"I should've been behind you," he joked.

"Ha ha!"

The walls widened again.

Not that she was claustrophobic, but the widened maze settled her heartbeat.

A heavy metal base beat banged over speakers that vibrated the walls.

So much for her heartbeat. Now, the boom assaulted her ears.

"That's really loud," Ginny yelled over the music.

"What?" he yelled back.

Ginny shook her head. "Never mind."

"Okay," he mouthed.

There was no way she'd do this funhouse again.

But the sooner they got out of here, the sooner they could stand in line for the Ferris wheel.

They approached a zig-zagging walkway that looked like a flattened escalator met Picasso.

"Cool," Brian exclaimed.

Ginny blinked. The wonky walkway made her dizzy.

"Here goes! Meet you on the other side," he called.

Brian bobbed and weaved across the moving sidewalk and leaped to the end while Ginny stared at the jiggling path. She waited until one step shifted to the right and jumped on that one, and then coordinated left, right, left, right until she reached Brian.

"Nice!" he cheered.

Ginny shrugged. "That wasn't too difficult. It's all about timing."

Brian grinned. "Yep, everything is always about timing."

From the outside, the Funhouse appeared no larger than a trailer, so Ginny figured they must be approaching the end.

She leaned on Brian, her shoulder abutting his.

"It's dark in here," she said.

Bam! They smacked into a wall.

Ginny reared back and shook her head.

"Ouch! What the heck!"

Brian hugged her. "I didn't see that coming. Are you okay?"

"Yeah. Just startled."

"We just need to back up a little and feel our way with our hands."

Brian let go of Ginny's hand.

Ginny raised her hands and patted her palms right and left against the walls, blinded, while she walked forward.

Lights flickered and then swelled to a lightbulb bright.

"Looks like we've entered a maze of mirrors. Brian? Where are you?"

"Over here," he called.

"Over here where?"

"Follow my voice."

Ginny began to walk toward Brian. She made a sharp right, right into a dead end of mirrors.

Dang!

She stepped back and stared at her distorted image, and laughed at her elongated forehead. She puckered her lips at her silly reflection. Then she turned to the left, anxious to view herself in that mirror. She was reduced to half her size with her legs squeezed to toddler size. Ginny whirled around to her right and landed at another funky image. This one made her look like a skinny giant.

"Brian, you've got to see this! I look hilarious every time I turn around."

Brian laughed. "I wish I could see. I'm encountering my own bizarre reflections. Let's find each other so we can see what we look like together."

"That would be fun. I got boxed in, but I'll make it out. How about you?"

"So far, I haven't smacked into anything. I seem to be making progress."

"I'm coming your way. Stay put."

"Okay."

Ginny made a 180 and exited. She maneuvered through right and left angles while stopping to chuckle at more distorted reflections. She couldn't wait to see how silly they'd look together.

Footsteps approached from behind her, louder and faster.

"Brian!"

A panel of mirrors rattled.

Must be a bunch of kids.

She hurried to catch up with Brian and caught herself at another dead end.

Ginny backed up but, this time, found no exit.

A deep laugh echoed through the maze.

Her heartbeat spiraled, and she began to run, only to smack into mirror after mirror.

Ginny looked behind her. No kids. No one behind or ahead of her.

Someone flashed by her.

"Brian!"

No answer.

She shot through the maze.

This wasn't funny anymore.

Ginny landed in yet another never-ending sequence of mirror after mirror.

She stopped to catch her breath and to think her way out of this bizarre, mirrored labyrinth.

"Brian?" Her voice squeaked.

A deep laugh roared right behind her.

Ginny raised her eyes and looked into the mirror.

Someone wearing a red-nosed clown mask and black cape popped up behind her.

A hot rush of adrenaline filled her chest.

She flung her arm back to hit the clown to escape, but it only crashed into a mirror. Crack! Glass shattered. Her hand grew warm and slick.

Again, the laugh.

Ginny raced through the maze of mirrors.

"Brian! Help!"

Silence.

Ginny grabbed her cell and dialed 911.

No service.

The clown jumped in front of her. The black caped demon raised a knife in his black-gloved hand.

"Help! Please help me!"

The clown laughed and disappeared in the jungle of mirrors.

Oh, my God!

Every breath hurt.

The carnie's voice vibrated in her head, "Can't vouch for the exit."

Brian didn't answer her calls. What if the wicked clown had gotten to Brian? She was all alone, trapped with this psychopath.

She had to find Brian. Drag him out. Save him. Save herself. Where the hell was the carnie?

Ginny slinked around each corner while rubbing her slick hand across the side of her jeans.

She crouched in a corner and clutched her cell. Her finger shook over the blood-smudged screen. 9 . . . 1 . . . 1.

"What is your emergency?"

"I'm trapped in a funhouse at the Strawberry Time Festival, and there's this clown chasing me, and my date—gasp—is hurt—gasp. He may be dead."

"You're at a Strawberry Time Festival funhouse?"

"Yes! I need help!"

"Miss?"

"Yes."

"Can you repeat that?"

"Funhouse. Strawberry Time Festival."

"Police are on the way."

"Hurry! He has a knife! He's going to kill me!"

The psychopathic clown barreled toward her, his black cape whooshing behind him.

Ginny sprang to her feet and ran.

"You're next!" he taunted.

Her sneakers crunched over broken glass. She'd backtracked! Now what? *Forward.*

She tripped over someone, and she tumbled, breaking her fall with her hands. Glass shards pushed farther into her sliced palm.

"Brian!"

Ginny leaped to her feet and rushed to Brian.

"Brian, wake up! Please wake up! We need to get out of here!"

"Huh?"

His shirt was ripped.

Ginny patted over his chest and neck. She didn't detect a life-threatening injury, and at least he was breathing."

Brian cradled his head. "Someone behind me knocked me on my head."

"Can you walk?"

"Mmm."

She held out her uninjured left hand, and Brian grabbed it.

Ginny pulled him to his feet.

He stumbled but regained his balance.

"The clown. He hurt you."

Brian nodded.

"Hurry. I'll help you."

Ginny slid her arm under Brian's armpit, supporting him. Sirens blared.

Ginny followed the blue and red strobes that flooded into the Funhouse.

And there it was, a black door, the exit to the Funhouse.

They'd reached the exit!

Ginny leaned against the door's silver bar while holding on to Brian, and they stumbled out of the Funhouse.

* * *

The policeman rushed up to them.

"We got you," he said.

He led Ginny and Brian toward the rescue vehicle's flashing lights.

"Can you describe who attacked you?" the officer asked.

"He was wearing a clown mask and a black robe. And he had a knife and black gloves," Ginny blurted, barely taking a breath. Her head spun, and this time Brian came to her aid.

"I'm okay now."

She drew a quick breath and pointed to Brian. "He was about Brian's height." She looked at Brian. "Wouldn't you say?"

"I couldn't tell because he snuck up on me, but yeah…maybe a little taller."

"Stay here, and they'll take care of you. We're going to go inside and check it out," one policeman ordered.

The carnie exited the Funhouse, breathless, his hair disheveled, and sprinted toward the police officers. "There's glass everywhere. You got to shut the Funhouse down."

"Sir, take it easy and wait over there with the others while we go inside."

"Be careful. He's still on the loose," the carnie warned.

The officers drew their guns. One entered the exit while the other one rounded toward the entrance.

Ginny pressed against Brian. "I can't believe this is happening."

He hugged her close. "It'll be okay. The police will find him."

She shook her head. "I don't know. I bet he took off."

"No. He's gotta be in there because we and this clown were the only ones in there."

Brian looked at the carnie. "Right?" he asked.

"Yeah. Spooky because no one else entered the Funhouse after you guys."

"How could that be? That would mean that the clown was already inside, or you let him in," she accused the carnie.

"No. No one got by me. I took over from Axel, who had ended his shift. He'd worked the festival since early morning. He's gone to his trailer."

"Trailer. Where's his trailer?" an officer asked.

The carnie pointed. "Over yonder behind the Tilt-A-Whirl, next to mine."

The officer tilted his head and spoke into his police radio on his shoulder. "The carnie who may have let our clown in is in his trailer."

"Roger that. All clear here so far."

"Lead me to Axel's trailer," the officer said to the carnie.

Brian grabbed Ginny's hand. "Let's go with them. It's not safe here to be alone."

She was so lucky to be with him instead of her girlfriends. Ginny's shoulders quivered. If she'd come with her friends, then they might have been…the psychopathic clown's victims. Brian, thankfully, clutched her hand harder.

She'd picked out the shards of glass from her palm, and the paramedics bandaged it.

Brian's bump on the head hadn't expanded, and both she and he declined any further treatment, so the paramedics rolled away in their rescue vehicle.

Ginny and Brian's breaths floated in puffs of gray on the chilly night while they strode close to the officer's back all the way to Axel's trailer.

"Stand back," the officer warned.

He rapped on the trailer's door.

The trailer door squeaked open and sleepy Axel swayed.

"Yeah, what do you want?"

Axel widened his eyes at the police officer.

"Hey, officer. I don't have anything in here."

"Please, step outside, sir."

"Okay."

Axel did as the officer asked.

The carnie cocked his head toward Ginny and Brian. "I think we can go now," he said.

Brian nodded. "Agreed."

Brian pulled Ginny away from the officer while he questioned Axel.

"Let's go to the Ferris wheel," Brian said.

They should've just waited in line. Then the whole macabre thing wouldn't have happened.

"I don't know. Maybe we should leave," Ginny said.

"We're not going to leave until we ride the Ferris wheel like we should've done in the beginning. Come on. It's safe. The Funhouse is clear on the other side of the fair, and that clown couldn't have gotten far."

Ginny hesitated. The clown could be following them.

"I still think we should leave," she insisted.

"Please. Just one more ride before we go. It's your favorite," he pleaded. "Look at all the people. Nothing's gonna happen. You know what they say. 'There's safety in numbers.'"

"Okay. But then we'll leave."

Brian took her hand. "Okay."

Brian was right. She needed to calm down. No one was going to attack them in a crowd. They'd probably already grabbed the guy. Besides, if the clown was still on the loose, they'd close the fair. And that hadn't happened.

"Let's go," Ginny said.

"Great."

They'd snaked through the Ferris wheel rope maze and were the next in line for the next car.

"That went pretty quick," Ginny said.

"Some things are just meant to be," Brian cheered.

"I guess so."

"I know so."

The Ferris wheel car swayed to a halt, and Ginny and Brian climbed in.

Brian secured the safety bar and wiggled it to make sure it locked.

The ride operator checked the safety bar and gave a thumbs up.

Off they went.

Brian rocked the car with his back against it.

"Whoa!"

"I thought you liked this ride?"

"I do, but don't rock it like that."

"Okay. Okay, I'm sorry. I'll quit. I just have some extra adrenaline going on."

Ginny's heartbeat pumped. "Me, too."

Brian scooted closer and wrapped his arm around Ginny.

"Let's just sit back and enjoy the ride."

"Amen."

The car rose and rose and then jerked to a stop at the highest point.

"What's going on? Are we stuck?"

"No, they're just loading more riders."

Ginny drew a deep breath.

She gazed at the whole Strawberry Time Festival. It gleamed as if gold glitter landed everywhere. She leaned against his shoulder. "Breathtaking, isn't it?"

"Yeah, it's cool."

Their car gently rocked at the summit.

"I'm not doing that."

"I know. It's the breeze. Doesn't that feel good?"

Ginny looked down and nudged Brian.

"Hey, it's that carnie from the Funhouse."

"Yeah, I guess so since they closed down the Funhouse."

"But he wasn't operating the Ferris wheel. He's just standing there with a black bag."

Ginny's stomach clenched.

"Why does he have that black bag?!"

"Probably his stuff from his trailer. The police are surely going through each trailer. Probably can't go back until it's all clear."

Brian waved to the carnie, and he waved back.

The car still hadn't moved.

"Something's wrong!"

"I'm sure we'll start up in a minute."

Ginny slid her arm around Brian's back. Her hand landed at his back pocket against something.

Must be his wallet. Good thing he still had it, given everything that had happened in the funhouse.

The cars began to move.

"See?"

His wallet peeked out, and with it, the tip of a black glove.

Ginny swallowed hard.

Her imagination was playing tricks.

She teased that tip, and yes, it clearly was part of a black glove.

She quickly stuffed it back into his pocket.

He didn't seem to notice.

Or maybe he did.

She reared away from him.

"I gotta go. I don't feel good."

Brian grinned. "The ride is still in motion. You can't jump out now."

The car swayed to a stop at the bottom.

Ginny rattled the bar.

"Let me out of here!"

"Okay. Okay," the carnie said and opened the bar.

"Where's the other operator?"

"Oh, he had to go."

The carnie and Brian winked at each other.

Ginny huddled in the corner of the car.

Brian held out his hand.

"Come on, Ginny. Ride's over. Time to go," he said in that deep voice.

"Help!" she screamed.

But that's the thing about crowds at the Strawberry Time Festival.

No one can hear you.

And if they do, they think you're just having fun.

HOW TO GET AWAY WITH MURDER IN FLORIDA

Margo Hammond

Thank you for inviting me to talk with you today on how to beat the rap, escape detection, and get away clean in the Sunshine State. For those of you who already are in the Witness Protection Program, congratulations. You're halfway there. For everyone else, I have compiled some tips on what to do if you are contemplating a career as a murder mystery writer and what not to do if you are tempted to commit an actual murder. My To Do List is inspired by those Florida experts in noir who found novel ways around murder.[1] On my Don't Even Think About Doing List are some of the most egregious mistakes made by Florida criminals (known in this state as Florida Man and Florida Woman) who got caught out of stupidity, bad planning, or just because they didn't watch enough Law & Order.[2]

Feel free to take notes.

---

[1] I'm looking at you John D. MacDonald, Elmore Leonard, Les Standiford, John Lindsay, Carl Hiaasen, James Hall, Randy Wayne White, Cheryl Hollon, Edna Buchanan, Tim Dorsey, Paul Levine, and John Grisham

[2] Gleaned from newspaper accounts of murders that took place in Florida from 1967-2022

THE DO'S AND DON'TS FOR GETTING AWAY WITH MURDER IN FLORIDA

Do move into a 52-foot houseboat in Fort Lauderdale and call it The Busted Flush. Tell people who ask you what you do for a living that you are a "salvage consultant." Keep a low profile. You may want to consider ditching that Rolls Royce that looks like a truck and is the color of your grade schoolteacher's hair. Stay clear of romantic involvements. If you must get entangled, be prepared to always end up alone.

Don't shoot a mobster from the Gambino Family in the back of the head on Halloween night as he makes his way through the Harbor Lounge bar to the Place for Steak Restaurant in a posh neighborhood of Miami frequented by celebrities and millionaires. Never target someone whose nickname is "Tommy the Enforcer."

Forget the houseboat. Buy your mother a four-unit motel in Pompano Beach. When you visit her, do spend your time reading crime shorts in the local daily newspaper (preferably the print editions, if there are any left). When someone asks you why you are drawn to Florida postcard land, mention retired car dealers in bright yellow shirts and paisley pants and tattooed *pachucos* who just got out of Cuban prisons. Look out for an attractive widow of a Mafia boss who is flirting with a bank robber turned dolphin trainer. Chat up an elderly gallery owner who remembers the 1935 Labor Day hurricane. Pal around with a redneck security guard who's been involved in a major drug bust.

Don't report your husband missing to authorities in December, telling them he went "duck hunting." Don't petition to have him declared legally dead after authorities find his empty boat in Lake Seminole and conclude that he must have been eaten by an alligator. Alligators don't eat in the winter. The water is too cold. Don't marry the guy who helped you take out a large life insurance policy on your husband shortly before he went "duck hunting" and was "eaten by an alligator."

Do move into a condo in North Palm Beach in time to catch a Nazi-Klan rally downtown. Hang out with a special agent at the Florida Department of Law Enforcement named James O. Born, the one who always wears a leather jacket. Ask him to tell you about the time the violent crimes task force rounded up escapees from the Everglades prison, including the country's most successful bank robber who was a dead ringer for George Clooney.

Don't date a girlfriend who posts all her activities on YouTube and Instagram. Don't take a trip out West in a van with her and then fight with her in full view of eyewitnesses. Don't leave evidence of those clashes on a police body cam and on 9-1-1 emergency dispatch call recordings. When your girlfriend goes missing, don't drive the van back to your parent's house in Florida and claim you have no idea where she is. Beware of what will be uncovered when flood waters at Myakkahatchee Creek Environmental Park recede.

Do make friends with a Palm Beach County judge named Marvin Mounts, who can supply you with transcripts of amusing hearings and trials. Ask him to regale you with the escapades of a horny fellow judge nicknamed "Maximum," a former model with an active sex life who keeps a toy electric chair and a diaper-wearing pet chimp named Toto in her chambers.

Don't date a guy with a criminal past. Don't hatch a plan in a Denny's restaurant to bump off your mother, no matter how controlling she is. Don't use a syringe to inject her with bleach to try to kill her. Don't stuff her corpse in a garbage can in the woods near Tampa. Don't flee to Texas in a high-speed chase.

Do get a job as a Miami building contractor. Call yourself "Galahad with a nail gun." When someone asks you why you like to live in Miami, tell them it reminds you of the bar in Star Wars. Mingle with terrorists, Chinese gangsters, shady developers, and mobsters.

Don't send out hitmen to execute your drug competition. When they fail, don't send them out again during a

St. Petersburg Martin Luther King Jr. Day parade, telling them to make the hit more public to "send a message on the street." Don't call yourself "General." Don't underestimate science and the efficiency of digital ballistics technology.

Do hang out with a guy who works as a blood splatter technician for Miami-Dade Police Department by day and kills fellow serial killers by night. When someone asks you why you married a Hemingway, tell them it was an arranged marriage. When someone asks you why you like living in Florida, mention its distinctive smell: a mixture of vegetation and fruit, seaweed, and something else.

Don't chase a kid with a stapler in your history class at Hialeah Junior High School. Don't moonlight as an accounting instructor at Miami-Dade Community College. Don't fire off shots from your house and break a window with a pellet gun. Don't pick grapefruit from a neighbor's tree wearing only your underwear. Don't collect aluminum cans. Don't use a bicycle as your getaway vehicle.

Do move to Palm Beach, the home of Presidents and First Ladies, to be near a private club called Casa Something. At the private club, rub shoulders with older, wealthy women who are divorced or widowed or divorced and widowed. If someone asks you what you do for a living, say that you are a "wildlife wrangler extraordinaire" who knows a lot about Burmese pythons. If someone asks you what it's like to live in Palm Beach, tell them it's like the Hamptons with extra sunblock and that all your friends are plastic surgeons.

Don't use the GPS system in your rental car to find the Bonita Springs address of the woman you've been hired to kill; providing a digital map for police to trace your entire trip via data from cell phone towers and security camera footage. Don't enter the address of a local Walmart into that same GPS and then let the store's video camera capture you buying wipes, trash bags, black towels, black shoes, and a lock-picking kit. Don't leave a bloody hammer behind.

Do read up about the mermaids at Weeki Wachee. Know that Cassadaga is called the "Psychic Capital of the

World." Check out the Rainbow Family, aging hippies who camp together every winter in Ocala National Forest, usually peacefully, except for that one time when one of them was murdered by someone in a passing truck. Get to know drug smugglers, backwoods, thugs, alligator poachers, and drug dealers.

Don't brandish a weapon and fatally fire your gun at FBI agents when they come to your apartment complex near Fort Lauderdale to serve a warrant related to a child pornography case. Don't be that guy your neighbors later describe as "awkward, antisocial, and living alone with little furniture."

Do move to Key West, where you can eke out a living tying bonefish flies. Team up with a private eye to right wrongs, avenge the death of your parents, friends, and lovers, and thwart animal smugglers, cruise ship hijackers, rogue medical experimenters, and other villains.

Don't tell your fiancée that you hate that loud "rap crap" playing from a truck as she goes into the gas station in Jacksonville, where you have stopped to buy wine and chips. Don't shoot at that truck and later say that you feared for your life because the teenager in that truck wielded a "gun or a stick" when you never mentioned the gun or the shooting to your fiancée when you both went back to your hotel room, ate a pizza, and never called the police. Don't think that just because George Zimmerman got away with evoking Florida's "stand-your-ground" law that it works every time.

Forget Key West. Even Hemingway said it was too crowded, and that was in the Thirties. Instead, move to Sanibel Island (after it recovers from Ian). When someone asks you what you do for a living, tell them you are a tropical bum who prefers wilderness and empty beaches to fancy resorts. Or tell them you are a marine biologist. Do hint at a mysterious past in undercover work. Wear cool t-shirts and hats and travel with military-worthy gear. Hire kids that may or may not remind you of the trio from the Harry Potter series to help you out, teaching them to catch and tag bay sharks as part of a research project.

Don't take psychotropic drugs that drive you to violence and then crash your SUV with blood on your hands and ammunition in the car near your home in a gated community in the upscale equestrian community of Wellington.

Do move to St. Petersburg. When someone asks you what you do for a living, tell them you used to design and build military flight simulators. Tell them you inherited Webb's Glass Shop on Central Avenue and you are giving flame-working classes. When someone asks why you like living in St. Petersburg, do mention the $5 Martinis at Three Birds and the green bench with the melted clock in the Avant-Garden at the Dalí Museum. Leave out the part about the body propped up on the bench covered with a newspaper.

Don't feed arsenic to your husband, collect on his life insurance policy, then feed arsenic to your boyfriend, collect on three different life insurance policies on his life, and then also try to poison your son. Don't take your son, paralyzed from arsenic, out on a lake, capsize the canoe, and when his leg braces weigh him down and drown him, collect on his military life insurance. Don't then give another boyfriend a "vitamin C" capsule when he comes down with a cold, and when that doesn't kill him, plant a bomb in his car. Don't leave the wire and tape in your bedroom that match the remains of the bomb.

Speaking of newspapers, do try to land a job at one of the few that remain, preferably on the night metro desk, where you can listen to the cop scanner and hear about police corruption, killer hurricanes, crimes of passion, and serial killers.

Don't incinerate your wife in a 50-gallon barrel behind your house west of Fort Meyers, leaving a jawbone with an intact tooth in the burn pile. Don't leave her wedding band and engagement ring in your safe with 13 vials of steroids and more than a dozen unregistered silencers. Don't leave traces of blood in your truck where it can be found when the police apply Luminol. Don't tell the police that the blood came from loading groceries.

Dump the newspaper job—no one reads newspapers anymore anyway. Instead, befriend a serial killer, this time one who only kills people who deserve it, like people destroying Florida's environment or rental investors ripping off the little guy. When someone asks what's wrong with your friend, tell them that he is attention-deficit, anal-retentive, obsessive-compulsive, paranoid-schizophrenic, and that he may be the only human being ever suffering from a self-inflicted case of shaken-baby syndrome. When someone asks you what's it like to live in Florida, do mention glistening condos, royal palm trees, headless bodies in oil drums, long lines for the early bird special, space shuttle launches, mermaids, orange juice with more pulp, and waterfront Mediterranean stucco sprayed with automatic weapon fire.

Don't announce your intent to murder the boy who had sex with your ex-girlfriend in a text to that girlfriend. Don't lie to another girl and tell her your girlfriend was raped, so she'll help you lure the boy out of his apartment complex in Miramar. Don't get caught on the surveillance tape at that apartment complex on the day of the murder. Don't come armed with a sword.

Do quit your corporate lawyer's job when your firm asks you to defend asbestos manufacturers. Tell them for you that's a bridge too far. Instead, pal around with a former Penn State linebacker who is now a colorful lawyer in South Florida. Follow this jock-turned-attorney as he struggles with the gaps between the justice system and justice and copes with health problems brought on by his years playing a killer sport.

Don't ask Siri where to hide your roommate around the time of her disappearance. Don't use your iPhone flashlight nine times at that same time, leaving behind digital circumstantial evidence when her body is found in a shallow grave in a forest near your college in Gainesville.

Do build an oceanfront house on Amelia Island, but when people ask you where you spend your winters, call it "Camino Island." Go undercover at the bookstore on Centre Street. When someone asks why you like it there, brag that it's a good place to loaf around. Mention the oak tree in the middle of Ash Street and Christner's Prime Steak & Lobster on Lee Road.

Do drop in at the Sea Turtle Inn and Pete's Bar in Neptune Beach. Then take a side trip to a Panhandle casino. When someone asks what you do for a living, tell them you are an investigator with the Florida Board on Judicial Conduct.

Don't think you won't be caught because most people believe serial killers are males with a female companion in their life whom they resent. Don't think Johns won't be missed. Don't pawn an object that you stole from your victim and then leave your thumbprint on a receipt.

Don't think you won't be caught because most people believe serial killers are white. Don't think prostitutes won't be missed. Don't smoke, but if you must, don't leave a cigarette butt available for police to pick up, test for DNA, run through a genetic database, and track you down through your relatives.

Follow these do's or don'ts, and you'll be sure to get away with murder here. But meanwhile, never forget the Florida Rule: This state is out to kill you. Think hurricanes, sinkholes, riptides, heat exhaustion, sharks, alligators, panthers, black bears, killer bees, flesh-eating bacteria, fire ants, rabid bats, wild boars, jellyfish, venomous snakes, wrong-way crashes, pedestrian and bicyclist fatalities, accidental shootings, and homo sapiens using strangulation, swords, knives, fists, and—most commonly—handguns.

You can outwit The Rule, though. Fake your own death. Leave a suicide note, a long goodbye in blue ink on yellow-lined notepaper. Sign it with a pseudonym. John Deal, Thorn, Dexter, Britt Montero, Angie Armstrong, Doc Ford, Serge A. Storms, Samantha Webb, Jake Lassiter, and Travis McGee have been taken, but I hear Dallas McGee is still available (now that the Kennedy assassination is a distant memory).

Good luck. It's murder out there. Don't say you haven't been warned.

BURIED SECRETS OF SPANISH POINT

Stephanie Palmarosa

The footsteps were getting louder, and there were definitely more of them now. The sliver of moon behind the clouds on that hot Florida summer night wasn't helping visibility, but if she couldn't see well, then they couldn't either. Her hiding place behind the dank clump of palmetto bushes made her nearly invisible, but that wouldn't last. She was going to have to choose which path to take and choose it soon, except she couldn't remember which way was the right path.

Straight ahead lay a fork with one way leading to the parking lot and a busy Tamiami Trail where she was certain she could find help, and the other way led to the Native American burial grounds. Why couldn't she think?

She'd been here so often she should know the place like the back of her hand, but fear kept her rooted in place. If they caught her, they wouldn't let her live to tell the truth about what she'd discovered.

Ginny felt panic setting in. Her breathing was getting harder and more erratic. *Wouldn't it be ironic if I died of a heart attack? That would certainly make it more convenient for them.* The sounds of snapping branches brought her back to herself.

Now or never. Time to pick a path and stake her life on it.

Taking a deep breath, she bolted down the right fork, all the while praying she'd chosen correctly.

The searcher's footsteps turned into slaps on the ground when they'd heard her take off. The noise seemed to be coming from all directions. Toward her.

Up ahead, a light was shining in the distance. She felt elated that she'd chosen the right path.

The joy spurred Ginny on and helped her increase her speed. Suddenly, the path took a sharp right turn which didn't make any sense since she was sure it was a straight shot to the parking lot. Too late, she realized that she'd taken the wrong path. The light she'd seen was a small floodlight on the outside of one of the demonstration pavilions. She was headed straight for the burial grounds and a dead end.

Oh, God. Ginny thought as she darted her head left and right, looking frantically for another path, but just as she turned to look left again, her foot met only air, and she was falling.

She hit the ground hard on both knees. The pain of impact shot straight into her skull. Her momentum pitched her forward and onto her face. Pushing herself up, she spit out the dirt from her mouth. Dazed by the pain, she didn't realize that the night had gone quiet. There were no more sounds of pursuing footsteps. Ginny realized her peril when she finally heard the sound of people breathing heavily above her. Her last thought as she raised her eyes was, *Why did I ever open that book?*

* * *

"Kayleigh, stop playing in the dirt, me girl!" Kayleigh's mam had said that to her at least once a day for her entire childhood. The memory always brought a wistful smile to her lips.

There was nothing better in all the world than a good rummage around in the dirt.

"You never know what you'll find," Kayleigh said in her still noticeable Irish accent.

"What was that?" asked one of the interns standing nearby, imparting a look that clearly suggested he was concerned about her mental stability.

"Not a thing, Jack. I was just thinking about dirt. And I do a fair bit of talking to meself since I know I always give good advice." Kayleigh smiled at her own joke.

Jack looked at the trowel in his hand, then down at the hole at his feet and back up at her. "I suppose that's a good thing."

"Aye, Jack that it is. How's your test pit coming along? Found anything yet?"

"No, Professor. I thought I found some bones earlier but turns out it was scleractinian coral." The disappointment on his face and sadness in his voice made Kayleigh want to laugh or walk over and give the young man a hug, neither of which was appropriate. "Every archaeologist wants to make a great find, but most of archaeology is discovering the places where the archeology isn't. You just need to keep digging."

Jack nodded at her remark and knelt back down. By the time she'd turned to head over to the command center tent, she heard his trowel scraping the ground again.

There was no better sound than a trowel scraping off the topsoil bit by bit, except for maybe the sound of it hitting something solid. That's when the real fun began. It was like slowly peeling back layers of wrapping on a long-awaited Christmas present. The anticipation of finding the gift you'd so longed to receive was just as thrilling as the gift itself.

They'd already dug ten test pits just to try and gauge the boundary of the historic indigenous burial grounds. Spanish Point was one of the best old Florida nature preserves and Native American burial grounds, and they were taking excellent care to preserve the site and use it as a teaching tool for future generations. So far, they weren't having any luck at all. The site manager believed they hadn't dug down far enough to find the archeology, but Kayleigh suspected his map was just plain wrong, and they were digging in the wrong place.

She'd told Professor Adkins that on several occasions during the past week, and she was about to tell him again. "Let's see if he'll listen to reason this time," she mumbled. She'd just reached the tent opening when she heard raised voices inside. No surprise there. Nick Adkins might look like a mild-mannered old professor with his wild salt and pepper hair and unkempt beard, but he had a hot temper that almost matched her Irish one. Kayleigh didn't mind a good fit of temper if it was for a good cause, but she found his was rarely that. Shaking her head, she walked straight into the lion's den, saying, "Oh, will ya stop all your bluster, Nick. One of these days, people'll start thinking you're a stubborn old goat."

The woman taking the brunt of his ire was standing with her hands on her slight hips, her long brown hair pulled into a ponytail that went halfway down her back with a look on her face that said she knew Nick was full of hot air. She turned to smile at Kayleigh.

"He is a mean old goat," Katherine said.

"Wait just a darn minute. She said I was stubborn, not mean," Nick stated indignantly while pointing his finger at Kayleigh.

Kayleigh walked over to the tables they used for examining finds. "He's correct there, Katherine. But it doesn't mean they both don't apply."

Nick huffed and plopped his bulk into his director's chair.

"I was just trying to tell Nick," Katherine began while shooting an annoyed look over at him, "that we need to move the dig parameters because we're wasting resources digging in this quadrant."

"Chance is a fine thing," Kayleigh replied. "That's exactly why I was heading in here meself. Nick, you old goat, you either have a bad map or a bad compass, but either way, it's time to move this dig."

Nick shook his head, "Kayleigh, you may be a digging prodigy, but I've got thirty years more experience, and I've dug other Native American sites. I still think this's a good map."

"Then why hasn't it produced one single bit of bone, pot, or any spoils?" Katherine questioned. "There should have been some amount of pot shards at the very least if people lived here at some point."

Kayleigh added, "And, before you start with your same argument, Nick, we've dug deep enough in some of the pits to hit the natural soil. I'm planning on closing those pits in the next hour."

Nick's face showed that he was starting to believe them, and the look exchanged between Katherine and Kayleigh implied that they knew they'd finally won.

"Perhaps you're right, and we should move the dig. Where do you suggest?" he asked Kayleigh.

She replied, "I say we move the grid to the west and start there."

* * *

Six months ago, Professor Adkins knocked on Kayleigh's University of Florida office door, telling her there was a great shakeup in her adopted hometown. The Florida Bureau of Real Estate Services commissioned him to lead a dig at Spanish Point.

Apparently, someone studying the Calusa Native American Tribe, who were some of the earliest inhabitants of the Sarasota area, found a set of lost maps in an archive from when the land was originally owned by the tribe. The old maps on file at the Governor's office didn't line up with the rediscovered maps found in the archive. Knowing who had the correct map was imperative since the burial grounds were sacred. If the sacred sites were actually located somewhere that tourists had been hiking for decades, that would be an incredible disrespect to the Native American people, a possible environmental hazard, and an extremely embarrassing Florida political bombshell to boot. They had to get to the bottom of it.

The group of diggers, interns, and volunteers gathered under one of the pavilions after the lunch break. Nick got everyone's attention by saying, "It seems like we need a new place to dig, eh?" There was a chorus of chuckles at his attempt at humor. "We don't yet have the results of the geophysics and radar for the new location, but we expect them later this afternoon. In the meantime, I'm going to turn the dig over to Kayleigh McKenna, our renowned archeologist, who most of you know as the professor you're trying to get credits out of by being here in the middle of the sweltering Florida summer heat." That remark got considerably more chuckles, especially from Kayleigh herself.

"Remind me not to ask Professor Adkins to be my opening speaker when I win my Gold Medal for Distinguished Archaeological Achievement," Kayleigh responded. "I've drawn up a bit of a crude map of grids for us to do more test pits this afternoon. This time we're going farther west and will be over a 3-acre plot. We'll keep the test pits to a meter square, and as before, if you find anything, give me or Professor Adkins a shout. Don't try and lift any of the archeology until we've seen it and it's been properly recorded."

There were head nods of understanding as Kayleigh looked around to make sure everyone understood the instructions. When she was satisfied that they understood, she continued, "Okay, come up in pairs, and I'll assign you a lettered square, and you can be off." After everyone was assigned a spot, Kayleigh grabbed her tool bag and headed to her dig spot, which was the farthest away from the group and in what she believed would be the worst spot to dig. She didn't like to assign the hardest work to her students just because she could, which was what made her such a popular professor.

She arrived at her grid spot before her dig partner, Kim Sue, arrived. *It ought to be a good experience working with Kim Sue. She's a good student and passionate about archaeology.* As Kayleigh put her tools down, she noticed that much of the ground had been disturbed. "This mess had better not've been made by feral pigs. I don't mind wild animals as a rule, but I'll not mess with wild pigs. They're vicious." She took a moment to listen and make sure she didn't hear any characteristic shuffling in the dense woods around her.

After Kayleigh was satisfied they were working in a safe area, she measured out her one-meter square and put her shovel into the topsoil, not waiting for Kim Sue's arrival. Kayleigh smiled as she always did on first breaking ground. "Wonder what we'll find for ourselves today," she said as she knelt down to use her hand trowel. She'd removed the topsoil and started into the subsoil when it dawned on her that she'd chosen this location because the ground should've been hard-packed and difficult to work through, but she wasn't having any problems at all. She'd gotten only another inch or so before hitting something. She scraped at it as if she would if she were uncovering a stone or bones, but this surface wasn't the right texture for either of those things. She stuck her trowel straight down into the dirt and pulled harder. Out popped what looked like a large earthworm. She put on her gloves in case it was poisonous and picked up the worm to examine it. To her horror, it wasn't a worm. It looked like a finger. She dropped it and jumped up. "There's no way that's what I bloody well think it is. Get a grip, girl."

She took a breath and knelt back down, taking her trowel to the spot where what she still hoped was a worm came out of the ground. After a few more scrapes, sure enough, the rest of the hand was visible. "Holy sweet Mary," she said as she sat back on her haunches. Just then, a scream pierced the air from directly behind her. Apparently, Kim Sue had finally arrived.

* * *

Two hours later, after being questioned by two different detectives in the command tent, Kayleigh learned that the hand she'd uncovered was still attached to the entire dead body of a young woman in the political science department named Ginny Johnson. One of the summer volunteers named Cherity was a close friend of Ginny's, and she had recognized the description of the body they'd been given.

After Kayleigh's questioning had finally ended, she grabbed a cup of tea and found a quiet corner in the craft services tent to gather her thoughts. *Why would Ginny be here at Spanish Point? She wasn't an archeology student and wasn't one of the summer volunteers either.* Kayleigh looked around at the shocked faces, some of them the same age as poor Ginny, and it broke her heart that a young life had been cut short. Not far from the tent, she could see Cherity sitting cross-legged on the ground, slowly rocking herself, so she went over to her.

"Cherity, I'm so very sorry about Ginny. Is there anything I can do to help you?"

Cherity wiped her eyes with the back of her hand, which just made things worse since her hands were grimy from the dig, but Kayleigh didn't think mentioning that would be helpful.

"Ginny was the sweetest girl and such a good friend. I just don't know why anyone would do something like this to her."

Kayleigh sat down next to her and put her arm around her. "I don't know either. It's a terrible thing to happen to anyone, but especially to a young woman just starting out in life."

Cherity nodded. "She was so happy that she'd gotten an internship at the Governor's office for the summer. She had to work really hard to get that internship. She was so proud of herself."

"That's quite an accomplishment. I'm sure her parents were very proud of her for that," Kayleigh said.

"They were," Cherity began. "They wanted her to be the first Native American Governor. She was only a quarter Cherokee, but her family's very proud of their heritage."

"Aye, they should be," Kayleigh replied.

A young man standing nearby cleared his throat. "Excuse me, Professor, but Professor Adkins is looking for you."

"Thank you, Thomas. Cherity, as hard as this feels right now, they will find who did this and bring them to justice. Just keep your faith and your memories of Ginny close. I'll be around if you need me."

Kayleigh made her way over to the command center, where Nick and Katherine were waiting.

"Let's call it a day and see what happens tomorrow," Nick said. "The police will let us keep digging as long as we don't go anywhere near the crime scene. They'll get to the bottom of this."

"Good on ya, Nick. Does anyone know why Ginny was here anyway? Does her family live in the area?" Kayleigh asked.

Katherine answered. "I heard her folks live somewhere near Homestead, so it's strange that she'd be here. She wasn't part of the dig."

* * *

It was almost sunset. Kayleigh was sitting by her parents' pool with a lovely glass of Chardonnay in her hand and going over the day's events in her mind. *Why was Ginny at Spanish Point and not in Tallahassee, where she was supposed to be?* Since no one said they'd seen Ginny at the dig site during the day, then she must have been there late at night after everyone had left for the day. *Ginny must have had a reason to be at the dig site in the middle of the night, but what was it?* She'd give one of the detectives a call tomorrow to see if they had any more information. At least she'd like to get the address of Ginny's parents so she could send them flowers and a note of condolence.

* * *

"Looks like another hot one today," Kayleigh said as she stepped out of her air-conditioned car. "And it won't be getting any better." Seeing one of the detectives getting out of his car as well, she strode over. "Good morning, Detective Henderson." Kayleigh thought that for a man in his mid-forties, he looked very tired and like he'd seen too much bad in the world.

He nodded. "Good morning, ma'am. You're one of the professors in charge of the dig, correct?"

"Yes, I'm Professor McKenna." She held out her hand, and he shook it. "I'm sorry to be so blunt, detective, but you look as if you could use either a long vacation or, at the very least, a long nap."

He smiled. "Both would be good. And it doesn't surprise me in the least that a redheaded Irish woman is blunt."

"Any news on why Ginny was here and not in Tallahassee?"

He stopped. "You seem well informed."

"I spoke to Ginny's friend, Cherity, who told me of Ginny's internship."

"Hmm. I'm not sure why she was here and not either in Tallahassee or at her folks' home."

Kayleigh responded, "In Homestead, you mean?"

"You are well informed," he said unhappily.

She shrugged. "I like to ask questions. Did Ginny have anything on her when you found her? I mean, a girl never travels without a purse or a bag or something. Perhaps that might tell us why she was in town?"

"Us? There is no "us." There is a professor and a detective, and the detective isn't going to give any information to the professor."

"Will you at least tell me how the poor girl died? Everyone's going to ask me that, and if I tell them something, maybe they'll leave me alone – and then I'll leave you alone."

"Promise?" he asked, looking more hopeful than she'd seen him so far, which she found a bit insulting.

She sighed. "I promise."

He looked straight into her eyes to gauge whether or not she was telling him the truth before responding. "She was shot. One bullet. Straight through the heart. And before you ask, she didn't suffer. She died instantly." Then he turned and headed down the path that led to the crime scene.

Kayleigh thought knowing how Ginny was killed would help her, but instead, it just made her feel more hurt and confused. *Who would shoot a young woman like that? And why?*

She wasn't wrong that everyone asked her questions. Although everyone was relieved the police didn't shut down the dig completely, they were full of the whys and hows of it all.

After Kayleigh explained the little information she'd gotten from the detective, the crowd grew quiet. By the time Nick called everyone to order, a distinct pall hung over the crowd.

He cleared his throat, "Okay, everyone. We all want to know what happened to poor Ginny, but in the meantime, let's do our best to help the people we can help. Remember why we're here. If we can find the burial sites for the souls that were laid to rest here centuries ago, then we'll be able to help generations of Native American descendants, like Ginny, to honor the memory of their ancestors. So far, we haven't found anything. But the absence of evidence is not the evidence of absence."

Nick's speech did the trick. People nodded about the important work that was being done there. "Let's get to it." He turned toward Kayleigh. "First off, we need to find you a new place to dig."

"Too right about that. I don't see Kim Sue here, so I'll go at it alone today. She can join me later if she shows up."

They headed for the command tent and the map of the test pits when they heard the first shout. "No way, they found another body," Kayleigh said to Nick as they rushed toward the shouting. Turned out they had.

The intern who found the ancient grave site was so happy she looked about to faint. As Katherine and Nick worked on clearing the test pit, there was a second shout from the next acre over. Another set of ancient bones had been found. They spent the day uncovering a total of six ancient grave sites. They extended the pits into trenches to be able to measure the correlation between the graves. *Finally! We're getting somewhere.*

It was almost the end of the day before Cherity arrived at the site. Seeing her, Kayleigh went over to her. She could see that Cherity's eyes were red, and her face was drawn. "How are ya holding up?"

"I couldn't sleep last night. I didn't fall asleep until dawn. I'm sorry that I didn't make it in today to help."

"It's perfectly all right, my girl. We didn't expect you at all."

"I need to stay busy, to keep my mind off what happened. I keep seeing Ginny in my head, walking around the campus with her trusty pink backpack and her huge smile. She was always so friendly and happy. I'm really going to miss her."

Cherity started crying, so Kayleigh put her arm around her. "I'm sorry that you're hurting, Cherity. This is a terrible thing to have happened, but I need to ask you another question if you're up for it."

"Sure, Professor. What do you want to know?"

"Can you tell me more about Ginny's backpack?"

"It's pink, like I said, and it has a drawing of a dream catcher on it. Ginny's had that backpack since high school. It was one of her favorite things in the world."

That confirmed Kayleigh's suspicion that every woman carried some sort of bag, and it sure seemed like the detectives hadn't found it. Cherity turned to go, but before she got far, Kayleigh asked, "One more thing. Have you spoken to the detectives yet?"

"No. Do you think I should?"

"They may want to interview you since you knew Ginny."

Kayleigh couldn't decide if she should go tell the detective about this information or if it would just upset him that she was nosing around in his investigation. Besides, if they did interview Cherity, they would find out about Ginny's pink backpack.

* * *

Later that evening, while sitting by the pool again, Kayleigh couldn't get Ginny's backpack off her mind. *There's just no way that girl was here without her backpack. And if she did have it, then why wasn't it with her body? Could she have left it somewhere?*

Kayleigh knew she wasn't going to sleep with this thought plaguing her, so she drove back to Spanish Point to do some investigating of her own. The sun hadn't yet set when she arrived, but the ancient site was deserted. Pulling out her flashlight, she started her search at the front entrance and worked her way down each path. After an hour of searching and not finding anything at all, Kayleigh was starting to feel a bit foolish.

There were two more sections left that she hadn't explored, the Butterfly Garden and the on-site classroom. "Well, I've come this far, might as well not give up now."

It was just behind the Butterfly Garden, as Kayleigh shone her flashlight through the thick bougainvillea bushes, that she caught a glimpse of something pink. Kayleigh's heartbeat kicked up a notch. She went over and knelt on the ground just outside the bush to get a closer look. "Nice place to hide it, Ginny." Kayleigh was impressed. Bougainvillea bushes were full of nasty thorns, and you wouldn't stick your arm in one unless you had to. She took a deep breath knowing the sting of the thorns was a necessary pain, and she reached in and pulled out Ginny's backpack.

Kayleigh sat back and stared at the dreamcatcher, which was lovingly drawn by a young woman full of promise. *Should I look inside or take it to the cops?* Knowing how annoyed Detective Henderson was when she spoke to him previously, she figured if she turned in the backpack without opening it, she might never know the contents of it.

Opening the front pocket, she found headphones, a phone charger, gum, lip gloss, and other detritus. Opening the top zipper, she pulled out an old leather-bound book. Flipping through the vellum pages, she realized what she held between her hands. "It's a Plat Book recording of Florida land purchases and owners."

Halfway through the volume was a business card used as a bookmark, so she flipped to that page. It was hard to decipher what land it described since the handwritten notes recorded things like "ten feet from the beginning" and used degree markings, but what caught her interest was the listing of who owned the land. "The Calusa people, including but not limited to any and all of the descendants of the Calusa people, in perpetuity."

"Holy cow." Things were starting to add up, but Kayleigh didn't like where it was going. When she and Professor Adkins had been given the grant for permission to research the Spanish Point site, they'd discovered that Spanish Point was privately held by an LLC. Disturbingly, the LLC had recently purchased the site from the State of Florida with the governor's help using eminent domain.

Spanish Point land was worth millions and made a healthy annual revenue as well. The Plat Book she held clearly showed that Spanish Point was owned by the Calusa descendants. "This won't sit well with the general public if the government stole Native American lands. Again."

Is this what got Ginny killed? Did the person who owns the LLC find out that Ginny had this journal? Kayleigh's mind was racing through the implications of this information becoming public just as she heard approaching voices and saw flashlight beams. Ducking as close to the bougainvillea bush as she dared, Kayleigh knelt while holding her breath and waiting to see if the people would pass her by.

"She must've left the backpack here somewhere. We've searched her apartment and her car. We know the parents don't have it. Spread out and look. It's pink."

Recognizing the commanding voice, Kayleigh gasped. *Katherine.*

Kayleigh quickly shoved the backpack up her shirt so the pink wouldn't be seen and ducked under the prickly bush. Thorns were nothing compared with bullets.

From her hiding place, Kayleigh could see the flashlight beams coming closer and could feel her pulse throb in her ears. She realized the one thing she couldn't cover up was her red hair. *I can't stay here. I'm a sitting duck.*

Since she couldn't use her flashlight, she'd just have to take a gamble. Kayleigh crawled back out from under the bush, grimacing from the punctures she received in her rush to move, and she ducked behind the Butterfly Garden.

"I'll look over here, and you take over there," said a large man dressed all in black.

Kayleigh knew she needed to move again. She walked as quickly as possible to a large Banyan tree nearby, trying to keep her footfalls silent. When Kayleigh got there, she looked back toward her last hiding spot just in time to see her pursuer standing where she stood only moments before.

Kayleigh squeezed herself into a large opening in the Banyan tree and waited for what seemed an eternity, praying the entire time that she wouldn't be found.

Kayleigh waited hours before emerging from the safety of the Banyan tree. After she emerged, she headed straight to the police station. By the time she'd finished her tale, they'd gathered the entire SWAT team together. As paramedics tended to her wounds, the gathered force headed out to find Katherine and the rest of Ginny's killers.

* * *

It was a lovely fall morning on the day of the dedication of the new Calusa Native American Cultural Park. Ginny's parents had pride of place in the front row. The new Florida Governor gave a short speech and handed the beautiful dedication plaque that would hang at the entrance of the park to Ginny's parents. Kayleigh sighed. It turned out the former Governor was a silent partner in the LLC. He had awarded Katherine a large grant in exchange for her help in silencing Ginny. *It's bittersweet that Ginny can't be here to see what her tenacity brought about, but now her legacy would live on forever.*

MADDER

Cynthia Harrison

Reba felt lost in space. Was this place too small or too vast? A noise interrupted her thoughts. Was that Rick talking to himself? Bargaining with himself? Reba hated when he went off to that other place. Plotting with himself. About what this time? She realized she was in the trunk of his car when he sprang the lock and ripped the duct tape off her mouth. She tried to scream, her voice a low rusty squawk.

Rick laughed. "Not so bulletproof now."

She attempted to fake smile, but her mouth wobbled, wouldn't work. Rick had not been invited to the party. They'd broken up. How did he get her away from her sister? Her father, a cop, had taken pains to keep the party private. Nobody bullied her or Doll . . . until today. But she'd watched her dad all her life. She could be strong. She would save herself.

She had to pee. And puke. She told him, but he didn't listen. Rick liked her here, lying helpless and bound. He planned to take his time letting her go.

Fifteen minutes later, Rick returned. "Damn!" He leaned over and gagged when the urine fumes, and then the vomit hit his nostrils.

She didn't care.

He slammed the trunk and left her like that. She breathed through her mouth. Waiting. He'd be back. He wasn't that smart, but he'd never kill a cop's daughter. Sarasota was still a small town. Everyone knew Rick's family had a trailer park on the edge of town. Everyone knew they'd dated. Well, Doll knew. She and her twin shared everything.

He came back with a blanket and plucked her from her own puke and piss. The sun was coming up. *Rosy-fingered dawn*, she remembered from an AP English class. The trailer park. She'd been here before. His trailer. She'd been here too. He held her like she was a dangerous animal, which is how she felt. She curled her fear and anger tight inside. He cut her wrists free and dumped her in his crusty tub. He threw the blanket and her clothes on the floor and called to someone to burn them.

"Clean yourself up." He walked away with that strut she used to adore. How had she ever?

She felt weak but managed to turn the faucet and hold a sliver of soap. She didn't want to know what kind of gross was on the floor of the tub, but it couldn't be worse than the vomit chunks in her hair. She worked on her hair first with cold water that never warmed. She scrubbed every inch of her sore body. She saw bruises but didn't know where she'd gotten them. It was like a section of her memory had been knifed and lifted out. She'd been with the others, ready to board the party boat back to Sarasota from St. Pete. That was all. Rick had found her somehow. He had taken her. He was not *her* Rick. He was another person, a guy she'd seen glimpses of once or twice before she broke things off.

This other Rick had three moods: happy, mad, and madder. The key was not to make him madder. Madder Rick had done this. Kidnapped her. She reached up to grab the almost empty bottle of generic shampoo on a plastic shelf covered with pink mold. She lathered until her hair squeaked. She rinsed her mouth out with tinny-tasting water ten times. She realized she'd been crouched on her feet this entire time so as not to touch the tub floor.

"Y'all alright?" Here was an in-between Rick. He held out an old T-shirt for her to wear and a small hand towel for her to dry herself. She could work with this Rick.

"Yeah. Can't remember what happened last night. How'd I get in your trunk?" She had to play this right. "It wasn't funny. I could have choked to death on my vomit."

"But you didn't."

She took his hand as he helped her out of the tub. He gave her the small thin towel and the T-shirt. When she asked for toothpaste, he squeezed an ancient tube, getting the last little bit onto a used toothbrush. She quickly dried off, but not in time to throw the T-shirt on. He handed the loaded toothbrush to her like it was gold. He bowed. She played along and curtsied on weak legs. She turned to the sink and started to pull the T-shirt on.

"Not yet," Rick said.

* * *

"What did you give me?" she asked. She was careful not to act scared. Not to mention the word rape. Not to do one thing to make him mad. She pretended things were as always. Like they'd never broken up.

"Never mind, just some pills," he said, trending toward happy. He liked messing with her head *and* body. He always had, the creep. She pulled his T-shirt over her head and finger-combed her hair.

She seemed to be coming out of the effect of whatever he'd given her. Why couldn't she remember? She hadn't been drunk, just buzzed. She'd been able to fake sober for her parents.

"Here," Rick said. "Take this. For the pain."

She took it because she was desperate to stop the stabbing aches everywhere. If she was going to run away, she needed a pill. Once she swallowed it, she wondered if he'd lied. If it had been the pill that had stolen her memory. So was she really going to run away? In a T-shirt and no underpants?

Rick's phone rang, and he left the room as his sister Penny came in. She held out a turquoise tube top and a pink skirt so short Reba asked for underpants.

"You won't need 'em," Penny handed Reba another pill. "For the pain."

Reba took the pill and the glass of water after she put the skirt on. She refused the tube top. The skirt was about an inch longer than the T-shirt. She sipped the water and tucked the pain pill or whatever it was into the waistband of the skirt while Penny decorated the lamp with a red scarf. Reba could run on one pain pill, but she'd never taken two. Her mind worked fiercely while Penny opened a roller suitcase and pulled out a blow dryer. "I could use a coffee."

"Yeah. I could use a change of location." Penny took hold of the suitcase handle. "Come on out to the kitchen."

Rick was nowhere in sight. Penny placed make-up and hair products on the kitchen table. She sat Reba down on a chair. She pointed to the countertop littered with empty beer bottles, Nacho Cheese Doritos spilling out of the bag, and a package of Oreos, ripped open. "The coffee's there."

Reba got up on shaky legs and made her way to the countertop. She stole a cookie and some blue pills from a prescription bottle with no label. Her mom used the blue pills, so she knew what they looked like and what the effects were. Her mom fell asleep after she took them. To cover her slipping the pills into her waist, she rummaged for mugs in the dishwasher. "You want a cup?" she asked Penny, still setting up her pop-up beauty shop.

"Yeah, alright," Penny said.

Reba found two cups in the dishwasher, and while she had her back to Penny, she put the pills into Penny's cup. She spotted a sugar bowl and nabbed a spoon to crush the pills, then added sugar to both cups before pouring coffee and stirring.

"Oh, I put sugar in yours!"

"Yeah, good," Penny said. "Sit, so I can finish your hair."

After the barrel curls were complete, Reba took a comb and teased a high crown. Just as Penny reached for her coffee, Reba grabbed a can of hair spray. She made exaggerated movements while spraying her hair and getting it all over the area. "Watch my coffee," Penny said, sipping. "Yep, tastes like spray." She finished it anyway.

"Want more sugar?" Reba asked, gulping the caffeine down for energy.

"Nah. Let's do your eyes." Penny picked up a mascara.

Reba wondered where her dad was. Instead, she asked, "Where's Rick?" She noticed Penny had done a decent job on her eyes. She grabbed a lipstick and did her own mouth.

Penny globbed a powdery blush onto a brush and flicked it over Reba's cheeks.

"He'll be back. With company." She handed Reba the tube top and picked up her phone, which was playing the opening riff of "Enter Sandman." Reba took off the T-shirt, not caring about her hair or make-up. She knew what company meant. Or she thought she knew. Boys who wanted to bang her. For money. Penny was nice enough, but she had a bad reputation. Reba did not want that kind of life.

Penny talked on the phone, setting up a date, when she went into the bathroom.

Reba, with no shoes and no underwear, grabbed the T-shirt and opened the door to the outside. Rick was just pulling up, his car roiling with drunk guys. Her mind raced. Barely morning, but how many hours had her dad been searching? Maybe eight, she added in her head. She knew he would not stop until he found her. Meanwhile, she had to keep herself from harm.

"Hey babe, looking good," Rick said, revving the engine.

Rick's grandma came out of her trailer. She saw Reba and the boys and said, "Get that whore off my property."

Rick laughed, but he went over to his grandma to hug her and have a private conversation. The guys stayed in the car. Afraid of an old lady.

Reba ran behind Rick's trailer and out the back dirt path to the road. As she ran, she tied the T-shirt around her skirt, giving her a bit more modesty. Dad, she thought, now would be a good time. But he didn't come. The road was empty. She heard Rick's car start up, and she ran for the mess of mangroves on the other side of a ditch. She crouched in their scratchy depths as Rick and his friends roared past.

She felt dizzy with relief. Still, she wasn't able to run. She was barefoot in brackish water with worms and swamp crabs. She grabbed a tree branch just to hold herself up and felt a snake slither over her knuckles. Something nipped at her toes. Mosquitos swarmed and bit. She might not want to move, but she had to. Road or water?

She let go of the branch and squished through the mud to the road. She lay down for just one minute on the gravel. She felt like she might black out again. *Peaches*, she thought, hovering in the twilight, awake but incapacitated. She heard a car. Rick. She tried to make herself small, but she could barely move her limbs. More cars zoomed by and screeched a turn. Into the trailer park.

"Oh, sweetheart." Her dad held her in his arms. "You saved yourself."

"Where is he?" Dad asked, still holding her tight.

"Rick's not there," she said. "Ask Penny…" She began to cry.

"Bastard slipped you a mickey."

"Hospital. And Mom." She sniffled, working to control herself.

"You got it." He eased her into his work SUV. She'd tell her mom about the rape. She didn't mind confessing to her dad that Rick had kidnapped her. What could mad Rick do now? He'd be going to jail for a very long time. Her smile at the thought was wide and not a bit wobbly.

NO WAY OUT

Anne Carter

"Are you positive we can't get arrested?" I bite my lower lip. "What if someone is sunbathing in the altogether on their private beachfront? I don't want to spend my birthday in a Florida jail."

Birdie laughs and shakes her head. "It's off-season. No one's home in these showy Shell Key estates. This narrow stretch of hot sand during the summer is isolated. Walking along the water's edge, we're not breaking any laws." Changing the subject, Birdie points to the property coming into view. "Jenny, look at the back of this house. It's got more columns than Caesars Palace in Las Vegas." She twirls around, kicking sand in my direction.

"How do I let you talk me into these escapades?" I chuckle at the memory of our first meeting.

* * *

Diana Hawk, also known as Birdie, has been my best friend since our first day of kindergarten.

"I can't do this, Mommy." I gripped my mother's hand.

"Please, don't leave me." I whimpered, wiping my tears on my sleeve.

"Yes, you can." I heard a child say. Looking up, I saw another five-year-old with freckles and two missing teeth.

"I'm Birdie." She grinned from ear to ear. "They have good lunches here."

She took my hand, and I followed, never looking back. For the next fourteen years, that pattern of friendship continued until I rushed into marriage at nineteen. Birdie detested my husband.

She didn't care for the second one, either. That's what this trip was all about. Reconnecting. Plus, I was hitting the big 4-0 tomorrow.

* * *

Passing Caesar's Palace, I notice a window washer on an upper balcony. He waves, and I return the gesture. I bend down and scoop up several translucent shells as Birdie takes off running. How can she run so fast in this oppressive Florida heat? I wipe the dripping perspiration from my brow.

"Stop! Let's go back," I yell. "I've had enough sun and fun for one day."

Birdie sprints down the powdery white sand beach, not responding. I watch as she waylays a small dog before he can enter the frothy surf. I jog over. The pup is busy licking Birdie's face. I stop mid-stride, realizing the dog is covered in blood. A pungent metallic odor invades my nostrils, and I feel myself gag. Birdie continues to examine the squirming animal, undaunted by the gory discovery.

"Is he injured?"

"It's not his blood. But someone around here is hurt. That's a lot of blood."

Birdie raises her hands. They're stained a bright crimson red. I shudder at the sight, feeling nauseated, and swallow hard. My eyes dart up and down the beach, searching for a possible victim as I attempt to gain my composure.

Birdie reads the dog's collar tag. "His name is Precious. He lives at 220 Beach Road."

We walk toward the residence. It's as ornate as the others. A long, weather-stained wooden promenade winds itself upward toward the back of the house.

I feel my pulse quicken. "Look, a window is broken." I point to a pile of shattered glass lying on the deck. "And the patio door is open." Precious jumps from Birdie's arms and runs into the house. I grab hold of Birdie as she starts after the canine.

"We can't go inside uninvited. That's trespassing and the dog's home."

My stomach muscles clench, and a tightness creeps into the back of my neck. "Please, let's just leave. The owners might blame us for the damage."

"With all that blood, someone's injured. They might need our help." Pulling free from my grasp, she enters the house. Precious is sitting in front of a polished wooden staircase. He bolts up the stairs as we enter. Birdie follows behind. About to protest, I freeze when I hear voices coming from the front of the house.

"Stop! Come down," I hiss, dismayed at my friend's behavior. Birdie dismisses me with a wave of her hand and disappears out of sight. I take two steps at a time and make it to the top gasping for air. "Birdie, please. We don't belong up here, and someone is home." I gulp down loud breaths.

"That little bugger ran in there." She points to a door that's ajar and enters the room, disregarding my plea.

The master bedroom is furnished with elegant cherry wood pieces. Silk curtains hang on the windows, and swags of the same fabric drape over a king-size four-poster bed. Sunlight streams through the parted panels, allowing a hanging chandelier to glisten like diamonds catching the brilliance of the sun's rays.

Birdie stops short. I plow into her and let out a startled gasp. The dresser drawers are open and empty. Their contents fill the floor. Toiletries and framed photos are smashed and strewn about. But that's not what caught Birdie's attention.

Clutching my arm, she points toward a lavender settee, partially shielding two bare feet with ruby red toenail polish sticking out. Birdie covers my mouth, stifling my scream, as Precious runs from behind the settee leaving a trail of bloody paw prints as red as the victim's toenails.

"Turn around, Jenny. Let's get out of here. Whoever did this might still be downstairs. They didn't hear us come inside, or they'd have followed us upstairs. We've got to be quiet, or we'll wind up dead like the woman behind the settee."

I take a step backward, not wanting to believe what I'm seeing. "I can't do this."

"You can and you will, Jennifer Morgan. You're the toughest woman I know."

We hear two men talking, followed by footsteps up the staircase. "Oh my God, we're trapped." My knees buckle.

Birdie grabs me around the waist and pushes me into the bedroom closet.

"Get some photos of the stool pigeon." A man with a gruff voice says. "Mr. Stanley wants proof. He's not paying us a dime unless he's positive she's dead."

"You take the pictures, Larry. I ain't no photographer. I'll check her closet to see if there's anything else we can add to the score."

The closet door opens, and I pray that the collection of Cinderella ball gowns will offer enough camouflage to keep us from being detected.

"Damn, Cuz, there's two full-length mink coats in here." A hairy arm reaches in and grabs a garment bag. I taste my Breakfast Burrito.

"One of these beauties is going home with me. Gloria will jump my bones when I show up with one of these." He slams the door, and we fall into each other's arms, exhaling the breath we've been holding.

"You're not taking anything home, Marty. You can buy your wife a different fur coat with your payout. This needs to look like a robbery gone bad. Nothing can trace back to the heist. Take those furs down to the van. I'll get the photos."

We hear a loud, exasperated gasp.

"Geez, Marty, what were you thinking? There's blood all over the place. We're supposed to put her body on the bed. No way I'm touching this stiff broad."

"Leave her where she is, then. No skin off my nose."

"Now what," I whisper as we hear the men exit the bedroom. My hands begin to quiver like that cherry Jell-O my daughter Tracey loved as a child. Birdie takes out her phone.

"Oh, no! No bars." She pushes my arm with her finger. "See if you've got service."

Cold sweat trickles down my back. "I left my phone in the car."

Birdie attempts to stand up. "I'm going to check the windows."

"Don't go." I pull her back down. "Let's stay here. We're on the second floor, and I'm afraid of heights."

"We're hiding from killers, and you're afraid of heights?" She stands. "We can't sit here like trapped animals. We don't know when they'll leave, and every minute we wait gives them another opportunity to find us." Pulling free from my grasp, Birdie opens the closet door.

I rest my head against the back wall, wrap my arms around myself, and recall the time we were ten and climbed up into a hayloft. The ladder toppled over, trapping us eight feet off the ground. Birdie swung down on a hanging pulley and landed safely in a pile of hay. It took me five minutes to find the courage to follow. I dropped to the hard floor and broke my arm.

I sigh. This was supposed to be a relaxing vacation in paradise. For certain, it wasn't living up to my expectations. I flinch as I hear sounds from outside the closet. Birdie slips back in, carrying Precious.

"Look who I found." She hugs Precious to her chest. "That's the good news. The bad news is that every window on this level has child-proof locks Houdini couldn't open."

She pauses at the sound of heavy footsteps on the stairs, alerting us to the hit men returning. Birdie puts her hand around the dog's muzzle and speaks softly to the antsy animal. Once again, we huddle in silence, praying for a miracle.

"You're a moron. There's a safe in one of these rooms that we're supposed to empty." The man with the gruff voice says. "You didn't write down which one, and there's eight bedrooms. I'm not calling Mr. Stanley. We'll need to search for it."

The throbbing in my head escalates as they walk closer to where we're hiding.

"Might as well start with this one. Mrs. Stanley won't mind." His ghoulish laughter turns my stomach.

I stare wide-eyed at Birdie as the closet door opens. Precious dashes out, and both men shriek.

"What the Hell. I should have killed the little mongrel. How'd it get back into the house?"

"It's his kid's pet pooch. We can't harm a hair on the mutt's head."

"Catch him. We'll lock him in the cage in the kitchen."

We both cringe as we hear them stomp down the staircase in pursuit of Precious.

I look down at my hand, and blood is dripping through my fingers. I realize I've bitten into my palm to keep myself from screaming.

"Sweet Lord." Birdie rips off a piece of her T-shirt and bandages my hand to stop the bleeding. "We need to move to a new location before they return. Don't worry, Jenny. That dog is much faster than those two hoodlums."

Once out in the hallway, we hear the men thrashing around downstairs. Precious is leading the pair on a merry romp throughout the house.

"We're going to find a way out of here. Trust me." Birdie rubs my shoulder, offering support.

We stop and open a door that has an angel playing a harp painted on the outside. An enchanting child's bedroom presents itself. A little girl's room decorated in pink and white with ruffled gingham curtains at the windows.

A rainbow-hued teddy-bear mobile hangs over a crib. I'm sure it cost more than my car. Two bookcases contain a multitude of children's books. I notice one of Birdie's among the titles. We open the wardrobe, and it's filled with enough clothing to outfit a daycare center. Birdie pushes me in and leaves before I can react. "Where are you going now?" I ask empty air.

I grab a pink stuffed unicorn that's sitting on the closet floor and clutch it to my chest.

My daughter loved unicorns when she was little. She'll be off to college next month, and I won't be there to share the experience. Tears cascade down my cheeks, and I wipe them away with the stuffed toy. The door swings open. Startled, I bite down on my tongue.

"Look what I found." Birdie grins like the Cheshire cat from Alice in Wonderland.

She holds up a charging cord, unplugs a porcelain ballerina lamp, and plugs in her phone.

"Damn, still not getting a signal," Birdie says, sounding defeated. Voices in the hallway send her dashing back to the closet.

"I don't know where that little beast went." Marty could be heard fumbling around the girl's room.

"Forget the stupid dog." Larry's tone is sharp. "We need to find the safe before the private security company does their routine five o'clock house check."

"We've got two hours. It's only three o'clock, and I'm hungry." Marty whines like a bratty two-year-old. "How 'bout it, cousin? Did you get a gander at the stuff in their refrigerator? I've never tasted caviar or truffles. There's a full bar too. Let's take a lunch break."

Appalled, we listen to the depraved duo head back downstairs. They're off to delight in a scrumptious repast while the lifeless body of their victim lies congealing in her own blood. Crawling out of the closet, Birdie tries every electrical outlet in the room.

"The power must be turned off in the house."

"It can't be. Not if the fridge is cooling food. That

charger must be broken." I stare into my dear friend's woeful eyes. For the first time today, I see genuine fear.

Birdie begins to sob, and I wrap my arms around her trembling body. In the thirty-five years I've known Birdie, I've never heard her cry.

"Please don't cry. We have to stay strong for each other." We flinch in trepidation as we hear scratching at the closet door. "Precious, you're safe." I scoop up the frenzied animal and sit him on my lap.

I glance at the new Mickey Mouse watch my daughter gifted me before I left home. It was three-thirty. "Larry mentioned that a security check takes place at five. We need to survive another hour and a half. And if the rodent can make it to ninety-four, I can survive hitting forty."

I grab Birdie's hand and pull her up. "We're not giving up without a fight," I felt a surge of self-reliance. "Let's see if we can find something to use as a weapon."

We creep down the hallway, scrutinizing the many bedrooms. Birdie opens the last door on the landing, and I let out a contented sigh.

"Mr. Stanley is a sports fan." I point to the memorabilia hanging on the wall. Birdie grabs a signed baseball bat, and I grip a monogrammed hockey stick. We've agreed when the men return, they'll probably split up to save time. They'll work their way toward the middle of the corridor. "The child's room is our O.K. Corral," I decide.

We tiptoe back down the hall and drop to our knees when we hear sudden shouts.

"You idiots. You screwed up big time. Good thing Mr. Stanley has us on his payroll."

We peer between the sculptured iron railing and see two men in black jackets with Security USA logos printed on the back. One has a gun, with a silencer attached, pointed at the two agitated hitmen.

"What the Hell! We did everything just like Mr. Stanley instructed." Marty sneers. "His wife is dead. I cut her throat myself. We tossed the place and loaded up all the valuables in the van."

The taller guard pushes Marty up against the wall and puts the gun to his temple. "You let two women in the house. There's video of them walking into the residence, but none of them leaving." He grunts in disgust. "It's a damn good thing we decided to ride over early and check our camera feeds."

Larry and Marty stare at each other in obvious shock. "You're crazy, man! You don't know what you're talking about," Larry shouts. "We never saw no dames, and we've been over this house from top to bottom. Put the gun down, and we'll help you search the place again."

The lanky guard turns his head, Larry lunges at him, attempting to grab his weapon.

We hear a muffled pop accompanied by a flash of light and watch in horror as Larry is executed.

"Please don't kill me. I got a family," Marty begs, hands clasped in prayer.

His body hits the floor with a dull echoing thud.

"Mr. Stanley isn't going to be happy about this," the taller guard says.

"Collateral damage," The other guard says. "Those two women are still in this house. Dumb and Dumber were too busy stuffing their faces to do a thorough search. Time to finish the job."

* * *

Overwhelmed, we crawl back to the child's room on our hands and knees like two cowering animals. For the next ten minutes, pandemonium ensues—doors slam, objects crash to the floor, and then even more worrying ... silence.

Surprising the two security guards is our only way out. I've positioned myself behind the bedroom door, hockey stick ready. Every nerve in my body is on heightened alert. Birdie, bat in hand, is hiding alongside the high boy dresser to my right. Her renewed look of confidence lightens my expanding feeling of pending doom.

I take a long deep breath and lean the hockey stick against the wall. I form a heart with my fingers and raise my hands over my head. Birdie smiles and returns the gesture. We're ready for the fight of our lives.

The door swings open, hitting me, and I suppress a groan. I push back against the wall, mustering all my strength, ready to strike.

"It's his kid's room," one of the guards says. "You know how Mr. Stanley feels about his daughter. If we toss her room, he'll kill us."

"Maybe those women snuck out while you were changing the security tape," the other voice says. "We're running out of time. I'm all for rolling those goons up in carpets and going back to the office. We can call in the robbery and Mrs. Stanley's murder from there."

The door slams with a loud reverberating bang, and we hear them retreat down the staircase. I put my hand to my chest, shocked to feel my heart still beating. We step out from behind our hiding spots and stand in suspended animation, not believing our good fortune. The shrill screeching of brakes announces their departure.

We sprint down the staircase and begin our descent down the wooden beach planking. We're halfway to the sand below when an ominous figure blocks our escape. "We're screwed," I say out loud, frozen to the spot.

"Going somewhere, ladies?" The taller security guard laughs, waving his gun at us as a mocking smile twists his lips. "You outsmarted yourselves. The kid's room has a Nanny-Cam."

My spine stiffens in outrage as I lash out at the sneering predator. "You knew we were in the room all along! Why the charade?"

A bubble of laughter escapes his throat. "Get blood all over darling little Lisa's room? I don't have a death wish, sweetheart. It was much easier to wait for you to leave. Sorry ladies, it just isn't your day."

Birdie steps toward him, a flash of temper lighting her eyes. "We have families, and we'll be missed."

He seizes Birdie by the hair, nostrils flaring. "You dumb broad. Do you really think I'd let you go? Turn around and get down on your knees. Let's make this easy on all of us. You'll never know what hit you."

We do as instructed, knowing there's no way out. Birdie grabs my hand.

"I love you, Jenny." Her voice trembles in fear as she casts her eyes downward.

"I love you too," I say as tears stream down my face. Closing my eyes, I began a silent prayer.

A deafening crack resembling a boom of thunder ensues. An uncontrollable shudder spreads throughout my body, and I wonder why I'm not feeling any pain. My eyes dart open.

I see three uniformed police officers, guns drawn, standing at the top of the beach walkway. Birdie squeezes my hand tighter as she vomits into the sand.

I turn my head and watch as the menacing security guard, blood oozing from his shoulder, is handcuffed by two men in navy blue nylon jackets that identify them as Drug Enforcement Agents. One walks over and helps Birdie to her feet, and hands her a handkerchief from his back pocket.

She looks at him, startled. "Raul, what in the world! What are you doing here?"

The agent smiles, asks that we return to the house, and escorts us inside. Birdie can't take her eyes off him. We're led through the front hallway and pass a blood-stained ceramic floor.

My insides twist as I recall what we've witnessed.

A Sarasota Police Lieutenant awaits us in a lavish parlor room. We take a seat, and the DEA agent leaves the room. Birdie watches his exit in shocked silence.

"Agent Green will be back shortly." The officer introduces himself as Lieutenant Kennedy. He hands us each a bottle of water. "Is there anything else I can get for you?"

We shake our heads without answering, still in disbelief of our circumstances.

"I know it's been a harrowing day," he continues. "We will need a detailed report of what you saw and heard today concerning the death of Mrs. Gwen Stanley. Her husband will be detained at JFK when his plane lands later tonight."

Agent Green returns to the room carrying a tape recorder. Birdie repeats her unanswered question. "Raul, what are you doing here? I don't understand."

He takes a seat, turns on the recorder, and answers Birdie. "I have a confession to make. My real name is Ronald Green, not Raul Garcia, your neighborhood window washer."

I realize the agent is the worker I waved to earlier in the day. We both lean forward in anticipation of his explanation.

Agent Green clears his throat. "I've been involved in a surveillance operation monitoring Owen Stanley for the past three months. His real name is Orlando Ricardo. He's the head of the largest drug cartel on the Eastern Seaboard. His wife, Gwendolyn, has been feeding us information about his organization. She was due to go into Witness Protection at the end of the month. Somehow, he found out and arranged for her murder while he was out of the country. A perfect scheme until you two ladies got involved."

I let out a gasp, shocked at the agent's commentary. Birdie's cheeks flush with a radiant pink glow.

"All this time, I thought you were just the best window washer in Florida." She twirled her hair between her fingers, a sly grin lighting up her face. "This is my best friend, Jenny Morgan."

"Nice to meet you, Jenny. Birdie and I have had some interesting chats these past few months during her daily power walk on the beach. I hated deceiving her, but it was necessary."

Birdie giggles.

I've never heard my sweet friend giggle in her life. "How did you know we were in trouble?"

Agent Green moves his chair closer to Birdie and watches as she crosses her shapely sun-tanned legs. He pulls out a small notebook, flips to some recorded data, and continues.

"I saw you out walking earlier. Though Birdie rarely alters it, she has a routine of dropping her delicious homemade oatmeal cookies at Mrs. Billings' residence. Her estate is at the end of Shell Key. They have afternoon tea together and share their love of good books. When I didn't see you two return, I grew concerned."

The agent pauses, watching Birdie react to his detailed information concerning her whereabouts. She looks at me, stunned, as he flips the page in his notebook.

"I waited an hour, and when you still didn't return, I checked with Mrs. Billings' housekeeper. It happens that Mrs. Billings is out of the country for the next month. When your car hadn't moved, I knew something was wrong."

We take long sips from our bottled water, remaining silent as Agent Green continues his narrative.

"I alerted the Sarasota Police, and they sent out a SWAT team. Surveillance was set up around the perimeter, and sharpshooters assigned to roof positions. We watched when the security guards carried two rolled-up rugs out to a van. I must say, I was concerned they may have contained your bodies. But one drove off and the other high-tailed it around toward the back of the house. We followed, assuming the worst had yet to occur. You, ladies, were certainly resourceful to have stayed out of sight the entire time you were trapped inside."

Agent Green gives Birdie a wink as we begin our detailed testimonial. Two hours later, he drives us home. I watch Birdie flirt with the eye-pleasing agent as if nothing has occurred today other than winning a first date. Once back at Birdie's cottage, we double-lock both doors. Agent Green checks every window before departing. A patrol car remains in the driveway overnight.

Rather than discuss our nightmare experience, we take long hot showers. After several glasses of wine, we sleep for the next ten hours.

Agent Green arrives in the morning with coffee and doughnuts. He no longer looks like the unshaven window washer from yesterday. Dressed in a tailored suit, freshly groomed, he reminds me of the actor Matthew McConaughey.

We sit around Birdie's hand-painted kitchen table as Agent Green explains the procedures we will encounter today.

"I'll escort you to the station so you can officially identify the two security guards," he says, sipping his Starbucks Café Latte. "Every precaution is in place so your identities will be preserved." He watches closely when Birdie licks jelly from her doughnut off her fingers.

"I promise I'll be with you today and every day during the trial." He stops speaking as we shake our heads 'no' in unison. "I know the entire scenario is crazy scary." He reaches over, patting our hands. "I do ask that you reconsider assisting my agency." His serious tone reflects the importance of his request. "Your depositions will put away a very dangerous man who's responsible for the deaths of countless thousands, not just his courageous wife."

* * *

Birdie and I ride in silence to the Sarasota Police Station. Hidden behind a two-way mirror, we relive our terrifying ordeal. We sign numerous legal documents and are asked again to be part of the investigation and murder trial. Although reluctant, we both agree to be witnesses for the ongoing prosecution.

The next four weeks are spent inside a Florida courthouse. Our identities are concealed, and our voices altered. Three months later, we watch from a secluded room as the jury finds Orlando Ricardo guilty of all charges. The drug lord is sentenced to life in prison without the possibility of parole. His daughter Lisa is sent to live with her grandparents in England, and Precious is by her side. Both security guards escape a life sentence by turning state's evidence concerning the drug cartel. The mansion on Shell Key has a For Sale sign out front.

* * *

A month later, Birdie's engagement to Agent Ronald Green arrived in the mail. I flew to Sarasota and spent a week with the happy couple before deciding to permanently relocate to Florida in three months. I'm buying Birdie's colorful cottage.

She's been busy moving in with her new fiancé and recently writing and illustrating a new children's book entitled "Precious Saves the Day."

My last night in town, we had dinner at a quaint café overlooking Sarasota Bay. Birdie, eyes gleaming with a happy inner light, asked me to be her Matron of Honor. I answered by dancing on the eatery's tabletop.

However, after examining her stunning hand-drawn wedding invitations, I did have one request for a bulletproof vest. Mrs. Ruth Billings is hosting the gala event. No issue there, but the nuptials are being held at her beachfront estate on Florida's beautiful Shell Key.

DO YOU BELIEVE IN MONSTERS?

Barbara Ryan

In the eighth grade, a substitute teacher, whom I'll never forget, taught my class for three days. Miss Purdy dressed like an old-fashioned prude, wearing a white blouse, dark skirt, and wide boxy shoes. Pulled back into a tight bun, her mousy brown hair rode on top of her head. Her lips, always tightly pressed together, indicated she had no empathy or imagination like our regular teacher, Mrs. Chapman.

Miss Purdy showed us a different movie about the Loch Ness Monster every day. I asked her if there really was a monster, and she said, "Yes, of course, Alec. These are documentaries." When I looked skeptical, she said, "That means it's documented." It was then I knew monsters existed.

The school library had DVDs of the films Miss Purdy had shown, and the public library had even more books and DVDs. I read the books, watched the videos repeatedly, and vowed to someday see the Loch Ness Monster for myself. In high school, I read *Twenty Thousand Leagues Under the Sea* in preparation for my quest to see the Monster.

The Loch Ness Monster would not frighten me since I lived in Florida, a place of grotesque snakes like the 215-pound Burmese python found last year in the Everglades, rattlesnakes, exotic birds, and Bufo toads with poisonous toxins. We had lovebugs that swarmed my dad's car and blocked the entrance to our house. Lots of weird stuff happens here, not to mention the swamps and marshes with screeching insects that fill the grates on airboats.

At school, kids made fun of me—called me Gump after Forest Gump—because I believed the Loch Ness Monster was real. I don't know if they bullied me, but I think they did. A group of boys sometimes stole my lunch and threw the carrots and celery around the lunchroom, trying to hit people on the head, especially mine. If we played dodgeball in gym class, I was always the last picked for a team but the first to have the ball thrown with high velocity to the back of my legs as I tried to escape.

* * *

After high school, I joined the Marines to become a man. While stationed in Okinawa, we went to Iwo Jima to see the site of the great battle. I brought some black sand home in a bottle. We traveled to South Korea, visited the demilitarized zone (DMZ), and learned that we were in Okinawa to deter North Korean leader Kim Jong-Un from attacking Japan and other Asian countries. We flew to the Philippines to help people recover from a hurricane and did six weeks of training in the Great Victoria Desert of Australia. I learned to do deep dive snorkeling and free diving with no snorkel or fins in the Pacific Ocean. I loved the underwater world with colorful creatures cohabitating among bright orange and yellow coral.

Okinawa houses every branch of the U.S. Military. The island is overrun with American service members, who are rowdy when drunk. I was seeing the world, but even though I now wore a uniform and had made it through three months of basic training— twice as long as the Army—I still had bullies making fun of me.

I am a small person, five feet seven inches, and skinny. Strenuous sessions at the gym lifting weights and working with a trainer increased my strength, but I wanted to be even stronger. So, I started taking steroids and testosterone. I vowed to survive the toxic masculinity by beefing up my body. My muscles developed along with my confidence. Now I was getting into fights every weekend—still getting beat up but winning some, too.

Karate and other martial arts originated in Okinawa. Learning Karate made sense because Okinawans were small but mighty in self-defense and taking people down. I studied in a dojo and developed knee and elbow jabs, knife-like hand and palm strikes, kicking, and throwing skills. Throwing a much bigger person to the ground was a thrill.

I would have been okay if I had stayed with martial arts training and stopped the steroids. But I didn't, and the steroids and testosterone turned me mean. I almost killed a sailor in a bar fight and landed in the brig. I agreed to detox and underwent psychiatric treatment for six months to stay in the Marines. When I returned to military life, no one bothered me. They thought I was dangerous, perhaps crazy.

I stopped drinking while in rehab and no longer wanted to visit bars. Instead, I spent my time reading and exploring sea life. Scuba diving allowed me to go deeper and encounter even more exotic creatures. I hired a fisherman to take me far out in the ocean to see what roamed those isolated waters. Armed with an underwater camera, I videotaped many species and had a few close calls with sharks but encountered no monsters. After seven years and all I'd been through, it surprised me to recognize my old obsession—the Loch Ness Monster—still existed. So, I saved my money, and for R&R, my last year in the Marines, I went to Scotland instead of Hawaii or home to Florida. Here was my chance to finally see the creature.

My visit to Loch Ness was a pleasant interlude to my military service. I planned to see the Monster, and all the locals assured me it did exist.

"Aye, lad, I've seen Nessie m'self," a crusty fisherman told me.

An older shopkeeper in town insisted she'd laid eyes on the Monster. "Most don't see her 'cause she hides in the deep. Nessie looks scary, for sure, but she's a warmhearted soul."

By this time, I knew Loch meant lake, and Ness was the name of the river flowing from the Loch's northern end in the Scottish Highlands. The Monster, affectionately called Nessie by the town folk, had been seen by many people and photographed by a few. Nessie looks like a prehistoric, long-necked dinosaur with two humps on its back. The creature is believed to be a survivor of the extinct plesiosaurs and lives in the Loch because of its depth, 780 ft., which allowed the Monster to escape the Ice Age drama that killed off land-based species.

Day after day, I sailed on the lake looking for Nessie. But no luck.

* * *

After my four years in the Marine Corps, the lure of seeing Nessie—or any sea creature that might be trolling the depths—drove me to learn more. Maybe I could become an officer with the Coast Guard or captain of a fishing boat taking people out to catch the *big one*. Or go to school and study oceans and marine life.

I enrolled at the University of Florida in Gainesville to study oceanography and marine biology, getting a B.S. in Marine Sciences. After graduation, I sought a job accommodating my academic, coastal, and monster-seeking interests. I was thrilled to get a job at Mote Aquarium in Sarasota on the Gulf Coast. There, I gave short lectures to tourists and school children on *Monsters of the Deep:* giant eels, stingrays, sharks, octopus, floating jellyfish, and everyone's fascination— manatees and alligators.

I always included manatees in my lectures because they are prehistoric, like the Loch Ness Monster. After mentioning my interest in Nessie, I explained that manatees are easier to spot as they are massive, over 1,000 pounds, and up to 10 feet long, but are gentle in nature, unlike alligators. They breathe air and go to the surface every 3-5 minutes, although they can stay underwater for up to 20 minutes. Manatees are deeply loved and have been named Florida's state marine animal. People throughout South Florida cried when they learned Snooty, the oldest-known manatee, age 69, died because an access panel loosened. Snooty swam into a controlled space at the Manatee Aquarium and couldn't escape the air-less area. His death made front-page news, and his memorial drew thousands of visitors from across Florida.

Usually, I closed my lectures by wondering how long other sea creatures could stay underwater and how many we had never seen or known. Sometimes I saw people roll their eyes, but maybe red tide—nasty algae bloom in Gulf waters—made their allergies flare up.

After I'd been on the job for over a year, the program director requested I see him in his office. I imagined it was to praise me for how audiences enjoyed my lectures and perhaps reveal a raise in my salary. I could use more money since I was planning another sea trip.

"Alec," Mr. Hanson said. He hesitated, his double chin quivering. "There have been several reports from parents and teachers that you've been telling students that our manatees are related to dinosaurs."

"Yes, sir. That information is from scientific journals."

"There has been some speculation, but it's an unproven assumption. We prefer to tell students that the elephant is a close relative to manatees, something we know is accurate, and they can more easily relate to."

Fat and old, what would he know about young people and what they liked? I felt compelled to inform him. "But children know about dinosaurs; they collect little rubber ones and go to Dinosaur World in Plant City. They love them."

"Yes." He sighed. "Children do love dinosaurs. The problem is that you draw a further connection between manatees and dinosaurs to the Loch Ness Monster, which is a myth."

"Mr. Hanson, I've visited Scotland. I've been on a boat on Loch Ness and talked to townspeople who have seen the creature and have pictures to prove it." I started to sweat, and my leg began shaking, a nervous habit I exhibited when I felt stressed.

"Scientists have never proven the legitimacy of the Loch Ness Monster, regardless of what local villagers believe or shopkeepers who welcome tourist dollars may say. I am asking you to stop talking about a mythical creature as if it were real. We are a scientific organization here."

I couldn't help responding when he brought in science, especially since I considered him a bureaucrat more than a real scientist like me. "Sir, NASA is studying UFOs and have stated that understanding the unknown is the very definition of science."

He stared at me without speaking. His eyes looked hard and cold.

I decided to introduce more examples. "You may not be aware, but at Three Castle Head in West Cork, Ireland, on windy days coming off the Atlantic, there is a froth on the water described as the White Lady. She is said to walk the lake, but it's best not to look at her because if you do, you won't see another day. This was told to me by more than one person."

"Alec, how can you be so naïve? You graduated from U.F. with a B.S. in Marine Sciences. You know the difference between myth and science, or are they not teaching reality these days?"

"There's much left to prove, sir. We need to keep open minds."

A deadly silence followed though I wasn't sure why. Perhaps I astonished him with how much I knew about science and monsters. I continued. "We have sea monsters in the U.S. like the Lake Washington Sea Monster in Seattle discovered by the Wonkatilla Tribe. They named it Willatuck."

Just as I thought, Mr. Hansen was unaware of this little-known monster. His mouth turned down in an ugly way as if in pain. He started to speak but stopped. Again silence. I decided to ask questions that might allow him to show what he knew. "Are you familiar with the Northeastern monster called 'Champ' or 'Champy' in Lake Champlain between New York and Vermont?"

Silence is even deadlier when you ask a question that doesn't get an answer.

The scowl on his face was intimidating. I decided to change tactics. "Mr. Hanson, are you religious? Do you believe in God and hell and Heaven? The Bible talks about ghosts, dragons, demons, and monsters. Science can't prove that these are real. And yet, a priest rowed to the middle of Loch Ness and did an exorcism."

Mr. Hanson turned red. "Alec! You either forget about the Loch Ness Monster or lose your job. Do you understand me?"

So much for opening his mind. "Yes, sir," I said. What else could I say? I didn't want to be fired.

* * *

That night, I thought about Miss Purdy. I liked her and enjoyed our correspondence because she believed in the Loch Ness Monster. Boy, was I wrong about her. My mom thought Miss Purdy had brainwashed me and didn't know I'd secretly kept emailing and texting her. My father said seeing those films over three days was a form of indoctrination on a young mind. They might be right, but so what? I was fascinated with the Loch Ness Monster and committed to proving that creatures like that existed.

In Sarasota, I heard fisherpeople say they'd seen a sea monster in the Gulf of Mexico. The sighting happened after a hurricane caused gigantic waves. Some even called it Nessie II, the southern cousin of the Loch Ness Monster. Why would sailors lie? It was time for me to put my money where my passion was and prove that sea monsters did exist.

After counting my savings, I put an ad in the *Sarasota Herald-Tribune* and *Tampa Bay Times* seeking a boat and crew to take me on an expedition to discover monsters of the deep in the Gulf Coast waters. Only one sea captain answered my ad, a crusty old salt from Tarpon Springs named Nicholas Constantine Papadopoulos, nicknamed Captain Nik, and a first mate named Demetrius. Their boat looked a little iffy, but after some negotiation and a lot of money, Captain Nik agreed to take me far out in the Gulf to explore the deep.

I couldn't sleep the night before, and that morning I practically skipped as I gathered my backpack and hummed a light-hearted tune. Thoughts of my findings published in journal articles worldwide filled my head. We met at Sarasota Bay's Marina Jack boat dock and took off at 5:00 a.m., heading directly west. After six hours, we were in bottomless water with no land in sight. That's when I became nauseous and dizzy, including throwing up. Demetrious asked if I had seasick pills, but I had forgotten to bring them.

Upon seeing that I vomited on his boat, Captain Nik shouted, "Why didn't you put your damn head over the side?" Demetrius said he had something that would do the trick, winked at the captain, and gave me some pills. He told me to go down below and lie on a bunk with my eyes closed. Soon I fell asleep.

Later, I woke up. Don't know how long I slept and didn't remember where I was. When I tried to stand up, I felt lightheaded and dizzy. But then I noticed the boat rocking and rolling. Disoriented and bewildered, I ran up the steps but saw no one. I shouted for the captain and went up more steps to the bridge. Empty: no Captain Nik or First Mate Demetrius. Running down to the cabin and head, I found them vacant too. Where were they?

Back to the bridge, and out of breath, I saw a lifeboat with Captain Nik and Demetrious rowing away from the ship. I hollered. They looked up but turned away after the first glance.

Why did they leave while I slept? Had we hit something? Were we sinking? But no, the captain must go down with the ship. Was Captain Nik unaware of what happened when the Italian cruise ship, *Costa Concordia*, struck an underwater rock and capsized? As Captain Francesco Schettino rowed away, 32 passengers still aboard drowned. He is serving 16 years in prison for manslaughter and abandoning passengers at the time of the sinking.

A sucking sound drew me to the ship's port side. Green tentacles with small suction cups on the underside clung to the hull. I ran to the starboard side. More tentacles. "It's a monster," I shouted. I raced below for my camera. In my excitement, I tripped on the steps, nearly losing the camera. Looking over the bow, I began snapping away, but I couldn't get a good angle. I ran down the steps and snapped more photos, leaning over the side. Moving to the other side, I reached so low I nearly fell in. I was getting great still shots and video. It wasn't Nessie, but it was a monster, and now I had proof. I tried to make contact, calling out, "Hello, monster of the deep. Don't be afraid. I'm your friend."

The monster didn't seem to understand what I was saying as it flung a tentacle at me, grazing my head and nearly knocking me overboard. I thought that might have been an accident, but another tentacle came at me from the other side, hitting my hand, the one holding the camera. Oh, no, the camera flew off into the water. "No! No! No!" Another flinging tentacle hit my shoulder, forcefully knocking the wind out of me. Pulling myself up, I looked over the bow and saw that the monster had captured the boat with tentacles grasping each side. It crept up, making loud gasping sounds. Suddenly I felt my skin crawl as I realized the monster was coming for me.

I looked but found no other lifeboat. I'd have to fight the creature myself with anything I could find. What resources were onboard? I saw a hatchet, a rifle, and a handgun on the bridge encased in glass. I broke the glass, gathered the weapons, and checked for the monster. It made steady progress toward the deck. I began shaking.

Only after all my efforts to communicate with the creature failed, and with great sadness, I raised the rifle and aimed for where the head might be, firing repeatedly. The Monster stopped for a moment and then began a rapid ascent. The rifle empty, I pulled out the handgun and continued shooting to no avail. One tentacle crept over the rail. I raised the hatchet as high as I could and swung hysterically. The end of the tentacle flew off and flopped on the deck. Yellow pus and blue blood oozed out of the open wound. My panicked heart thumped with regret and fear.

A second tentacle slid over the rail while a third tentacle slithered up the other side. I swayed back and forth with a continuous chopping motion. Again and again, the monster and I danced this violent tango – grip and chop, grip and chop. "How many tentacles do you have?" Shouting and crying with snot dripping down my chin, I continued chopping. With no escape, I could only keep fighting.

And hope for a miracle.

The wind picked up, increasing in strength every minute into gale force. The ship rocked violently, nearly throwing me overboard. I ran to the bridge and saw that the monster's short tentacle grip had become loose from the force of the wind, and it fell back into the water. It now looked like a colossal squid, which I knew could grow to over 40 feet long.

My legs collapsed and I sank onto the deck. Battered in body, broke and penniless, the vindication and verification of my lifelong quest felt hollow. Some creatures, some avenues of research, may be best left alone. I knew I wouldn't speak of monsters again.

With great effort, I crawled up to the bridge and could see that this now short-tentacled monster would never again be able to wrap around a boat—unless it was a small craft.

I grabbed a pair of binoculars. My breath caught. The tentacled brute was closing in on the pathetic little lifeboat that rose and pitched with each wave.

The monster enveloped the lifeboat. And then, the beast dove deep to explore its catch of the day.

A SARASOTA LEGACY TAIL

Tracy Ann

He slouches down quickly as she glances in his direction. "Damnit!" he whispers as his right knee hits the steering column. "When will I get a car that fits my body *and* my garage?"

Her face flashes a brief sign of recognition, followed by a sweet smile. She waves past him at the couple parked a few spots to his right. The three of them intersect at the edge of the sidewalk just outside their destination. Nokomis, Florida, a few miles south of Sarasota, is one of those places where tiki bars are plentiful, even in strip malls. School has started, not many tourists hang in this part of town, and not many snowbirds have returned, *ergo* the crowd tonight is likely too thin for him to sit inside and get a closer look.

His younger self would have blown his cover by pushing too hard. His experienced self has learned patience. He has identified the target, her car, and two of her acquaintances. Enough success for today. This assignment poses a few unique challenges, not the least of which is his patron's insistence he make a minimum of five observations before concluding his work. He laments that this job could easily be done with less scrutiny. Fortunately, his experienced self has also learned that his reputation for impeccable attention to detail and total compliance to specific requests commands a larger payday than most of his competitors.

She enters the restaurant with her friends, unaware that his first observation has been completed.

He retreats to Wawa for a sub sandwich and a black coffee.

* * *

KD slept soundly until the sun from the open slider blinds brought the morning light and warmth into her bedroom. She smiled and thought about how waking up without an alarm on a Saturday morning was one of life's simple pleasures. Although she did not consider herself overly high-energy or Type A, it took a morning like today to remind her that it was okay to have a lazy start once in a while, despite her predilection for a productive lifestyle.

She executed an awkward scoot up the headboard to reposition herself into her people-watching perch. Just several dozen giant steps beyond her bedroom slider was The Legacy Trail. From the comfort of her bed, KD peered past the patio furniture, the fire pit, a few arboricolas, several unkempt crotons, and two pygmy palms to surreptitiously study today's trail users. Notable partakers on this morning included a small boy blowing bubbles while he walked with his grandpa, a group of cyclists with Big Ten jerseys, and a spritely young woman with five leashes connected to five very obedient dogs of varying breeds and sizes. Her favorite observation was a middle-aged couple with two dogs. The first dog was a plodding, slightly oversized black lab whose gait was matched by the man. The second dog was a surprisingly mild-mannered English setter that fit the woman to a tee. When KD spotted the Big Ten cyclists, which she had first observed riding south on their return trip north, she realized it was time to begin the productive part of her day. On a morning like today, she measured time by how many trail users she witnessed going both directions past her nicely camouflaged windows.

While she showered and dressed for the day, an unsettling awareness crept over her. It was a small matter that almost slipped past her, yet once realized, it rolled through KD's thoughts incessantly, like a sticky marketing jingle that replays in the brain for hours. She recalled an individual man from her people-watching session. He was dressed the part of a local, with lightweight khaki pants, a short-sleeve poplin shirt, and a Tampa Bay Lightning ball cap. He blended in with the scene so well KD was surprised she remembered him. She first saw him walk leisurely north. He had stopped on the far side of the trail and was looking across toward her house, smiling at the boy with the bubbles who was on the edge of her backyard. The singular curiosity that troubled her was that she saw him walk northbound a second time. On his second pass, he again slowed down across from her house and looked in its direction. This time, however, the boy and his bubbles were long gone. KD tried in vain to recall a view of him walking south either time. It was possible she missed him while she grabbed a cup of coffee or checked the emails on her phone. Several unanswered questions loitered in her mind. First, why would he double up his route when most people only pass once in each direction? Second, was he simply looking in the direction of her house or actually looking *at* her house? And, the most important question, can someone walking on the trail actually see into her bedroom? KD made a mental note to walk out to the trail and evaluate the potential visibility when she left the blinds open. It was a simple task that would hopefully quash her growing sense of paranoia.

Running errands proved to be a perfect cure for her morning suspicions. KD had lived alone for over eight years. During those rare times when her overactive mind created false doubts or anxiety-filled narratives, KD simply smiled in remembrance of all the times her late mother and her countless aunts had warned her about the dangers of not getting married. Most importantly, being single suited her.

In addition to her customary errands, she shopped for the perfect birthday present for her 9-year-old nephew. She regretted that although her brother and his family lived within a reasonable driving distance, she did not see them as often as she wished. If not for Aunt Dell's funeral in June, it would have been a year since her last visit. She spied a display of superhero watches and decided her hunt was over. Now if she only remembered if Blake preferred Spider-Man or Batman.

KD walked back to her car, happy with her find and feeling smug for having executed the perfect solution. She had simply purchased both watches and planned to call her brother Justin for advice on which one to send. Unlocking her car door, she threw the plastic bag on the passenger seat, drove down Clark Road, and decided to treat herself to a decent lunch. Turning south on Beneva Road, she headed for restaurant row in Gulf Gate. In her rearview mirror, KD noticed a dark mid-size sedan had pulled onto Clark Road just behind her and had also turned onto Beneva Road. When she turned onto Gulf Gate Drive and cruised past the library, the sedan executed the same turn. Eventually, when she turned onto Superior Avenue, the sedan continued straight on Gulf Gate Drive. Her confident, analytical side gently chided her suspicious side.

She enjoyed two slices of New Jersey pizza and a Diet Coke at her favorite cheap lunch hangout. As KD approached her car, the sight of a dark mid-size sedan parked in front of the Moose Lodge on the opposite side of Superior gave her pause. She feebly attempted to convince herself that there was an abundance of dark mid-size sedans driving around the Sarasota area. She was instantly frustrated with her dismal ability to identify car models. As a matter of caution, she looped around the street and drove past the sedan, using her cell phone to snap a photo of the license plate. It seemed a silly gesture, yet she felt better.

* * *

Despite his quick success in initiating surveillance of the local target, he knows this job is a strict two-for-one. The second target may be more challenging. It is highly unusual for him to take on a job with two targets, especially when they are located three hundred miles apart. He reminds himself that the contract is especially generous, and the patron has never reneged on terms or defaulted on payment. "At least the two are related," he

210

says aloud while making travel plans. "At least they live in adjacent states," he adds, trying to quell his unexplainable uneasiness with crossing state lines.

After packing his overnight bag, he walks the half mile to his friend Susan's house. She has generously offered to lend him her SUV for the trip. While dropping off some of his famous homemade pepper jelly last week, he had prepared a great story with just the right amount of detail to convince Susan to lend him the car. To his surprise, he had just started his bid when she insisted he take her car rather than bother with a rental. *Maybe he should bottle that pepper jelly!*

* * *

In the midst of a busy week, KD noticed the plastic bag with two superhero watches sitting on her kitchen counter as she rushed off to work. Midday, she called her brother to get the all-important verdict on the best gift. Justin's office phone broadcasts his out-of-town travel status. He traveled quite a bit these days, usually just for a day or two, but enough to disrupt the routine at his house. Rather than pester him with questions about pre-teen superhero preferences during a business trip, KD called her sister-in-law, Lynne.

* * *

Lynne decisively chose Spider-Man as Blake's favorite. They chatted a bit about upcoming holiday plans, but Lynne seemed uncharacteristically disconnected. At first, KD assumed she was just off her game due to Justin's travel, but Lynne was a champ and rarely unsettled. Their conversation drifted to an awkward silence, and KD finally blurted: "Okay, what's up?"

Lynne sighed, said nothing for a brief moment, then disclosed, "You are going to think I'm nuts, but I swear I'm being watched."

* * *

That night KD gave in to her temptation and Googled, *"How do I know if someone is following me?"* She laughed at herself after dissecting an article outlining Green Beret methods for the prevention of international kidnapping. After all, her potential pursuer was in a dark sedan. Lynne's mystery man drove a white SUV. KD went to bed reassured by the conclusion Lynne and she had agreed upon after comparing stories. Their lives were much too boring to pique anyone's interest.

* * *

KD woke up ten minutes before her alarm and quickly threw on semi-clean shorts and a T-shirt. Grabbing a mug of coffee, she lumbered through her backyard onto the smooth pavement of The Legacy Trail.

Although she had not seen her unwelcome shadow all week, she had promised herself she would spend at least some effort beefing up her personal security this weekend. Besides, she was certain there was someone who would approve of her choice to take a first-in-the-morning walk as a healthy alternative to people-watching from her bed.

KD walked south on the trail for ten minutes before turning back towards home for her inspection. She had deliberately left her bedroom blinds open and put a bright royal blue sweatshirt on her bedspread. As she passed the cozy ranch she had been renting for the last three years, KD gazed, then peered, then stared towards her bedroom slider. Despite her best efforts, she was unable to see the sweatshirt on the bed. Satisfied that she could continue her occasional people-watching adventures incognito, KD continued her walk for a bit more before returning home with a smile. Her urgency to ramp up a security plan had been extinguished. She would no longer need to alarm all her windows or buy a guard dog.

* * *

The last few weeks at work were a blur. They had gotten approval for the hospital's yearly budget, and less than a week later, KD was tapped to be the lead coordinator for all upcoming grant submissions. *No rest for the weary.* On Friday, at lunchtime, KD grabbed a sandwich and an iced tea from the snack bar just outside the hospital courtyard. Sitting in the courtyard, she ate lunch and enjoyed her free thoughts. The breeze was pleasant, and the outside temperature no longer oppressive. She felt rejuvenated and had started the walk back to her office for an afternoon of meetings and spreadsheets. She passed a group of comfy chairs in the hallway near registration and did a double-take. Her calm instantly evaporated. Was *that* man really at the hospital? Her hospital? She initially fought the urge to walk past him again, then relented and returned, feigning a need to interact with the volunteer standing near registration. Her potential nemesis was quietly reading in the hallway and was not wearing the telltale Tampa Bay Lightning ball cap. His height was difficult to discern while seated. He did not look at her or at anyone else, for that matter. He just sat and read. Her brain, professional and work-absorbed, dismissed the identification. Hundreds of people come to the hospital every day. Dozens sit in those chairs. Her gut, the great equalizer, screamed danger and convinced her it was time to act.

Feeling a bit sheepish, KD took a detour on the way back to her office and made her way to the hospital security area. Fortunately, she intercepted her favorite security officer in the hallway, which allowed her to talk to him without the audience of the entire security team. KD hurriedly described the events of the last couple of weeks. She talked so fast that she was out of breath by the time she reached the end of her story. Her eyes started to water, a mixture of fear, frustration, and vulnerability. Clarence listened patiently. KD no longer felt alone or embarrassed. They walked together back to the registration area. The man was gone. The chair was now occupied by two small girls sitting together like puppies while their mother watched from the registration desk. Clarence was scheduled to work all day Saturday, so he promised to stop by her house on Sunday afternoon to help her create a personal security plan. Striding back to her office, KD felt both vindicated and relieved. She had spoken up and gained a capable ally.

* * *

Back home, he pulls out his laptop and opens the document he started a few weeks ago. "Paperwork! Who'd a thunk I would be spending such a beautiful afternoon doing paperwork?" He resigns himself to the fact that this report is not going to write itself and updates his surveillance notes. He documents the date, the time, and the location of all the observations for both subjects. For each observation, he describes the activities he witnessed, lists all observed interactions with others, and with a flair he believes will please his client, even documents the subject's clothing. He adds a summary of his conclusions regarding each subject. With his task complete, he emails the report to his client, suggesting Monday morning to finalize his contract on the local subject.

"She almost caught me twice. Either she's good, or I'm losing my touch." He chuckles. "Although, she never did see me at the nail salon. It cost me sixty bucks for that pedicure. Good use of my expense budget, for sure!"

His computer chirps as an email response arrives from his client. Monday morning is a go.

* * *

Clarence arrived at KD's house on Sunday afternoon as promised. Walking around her house, he checked her doors, her windows, and all the other imagined sources of entry. He asked her about old boyfriends, new boyfriends, and anyone else who may have hoped to achieve that status. KD was thankful for his help, yet in the light of day, it all seemed like a bit of overkill. After all, she may have seen the same man a few times over the last few weeks, but he never approached her. She was not even certain it was the same man. Clarence wrote down the license plate from her Gulf Gate encounter and made her promise to file a precautionary police report first thing Monday morning. KD suggested she file the report on her lunch break rather than arrive late to work. He insisted that she file the report before 9 a.m. on Monday, then convinced her to accept his offer to drive her to the police station himself. KD shook her head while conceding that he was the expert in this area. She wondered if his offer to drive was based on chivalry or to keep her from changing her mind.

* * *

Arriving in KD's neighborhood with time to spare on Monday morning, Clarence was feeling relaxed and confident. As he turned down her normally empty street, he noticed a dark mid-size sedan that had been driving slightly ahead of him pull over and park two houses past KD's house. Pulling over, he parked just short of her house to watch the sedan's occupant as he exited his car and stood near the trunk. The man was wearing a Tampa Bay Lightning ball cap, and he had both his hands in his pants pockets. Clarence texted KD with instructions to hide in her spare bedroom closet, turn her phone to silent, and wait for further communication. Touching his waist reflexively, he felt vindicated in his decision to bring his old service revolver.

The man from the sedan stood calmly by the trunk, apparently waiting or maybe surveilling. As Clarence formulated his next move, a blue minivan arrived and parked behind the sedan. The driver, a young blonde woman, exited the minivan. She was quickly joined by the man from the sedan. As they approached KD's front walk, Clarence's heart sank when the front door opened. Apparently, KD did not get his text, and she was not hiding in the closet. Clarence exited his vehicle in a full sprint as the blonde woman reached into her oversized Coach bag.

* * *

KD walked into the legal office with a bit of trepidation. The waiting area was well-appointed, but devoid of any feature that felt welcoming or comfortable. To be fair, she was still a bit shaken after the events of the last few weeks, and not even a proper office with a receptionist dressed in a nicely tailored wool suit was able to shake her unease. She distracted herself a bit by wondering how many women in offices downtown were still locked into a wool suit dress code while living in tropical Sarasota.

She was efficiently ushered into an immense conference room. A sizable man, also in a wool suit, entered, and a young woman followed close behind. KD felt small and anxious. Sensing her discomfort, both the man and the woman smiled. KD recognized the woman as the person who had been at her house the previous Monday. Following a flurry of papers and hasty signatures, KD had finally started to relax when the door opened a second time.

It was him. The man she had first seen on The Legacy Trail several weeks ago sauntered in, wearing the same Tampa Bay Lightning ball cap. KD immediately stiffened. The man countered with a big grin that softened his face. The lawyer quickly introduced him as Michael Holmes.

"My friends call me Mickey." Reaching out his hand, he gently took hers. "And I hope that despite the recent chaos I may have inadvertently brought into your life, you will call me Mickey too."

He explained that her deceased aunt had included a morals clause in her will which prevented any inheritance from being disbursed to a beneficiary until a professional assessment confirmed the individual's moral suitability. KD laughed as she let her head drop a bit, and she relaxed her shoulders. Smiling, she remembered Aunt Dell's frequent guidance regarding clean living.

KD left the office with a receipt for the inheritance funds electronically deposited into her personal bank account. She hurried back to the hospital and finished her day with the same focus and efficiency her coworkers had expected from her. That night, she stopped at Publix and grabbed a pre-made salad and a split of mid-priced Champagne.

Back at home, KD began to take stock of recent events. She enjoyed her celebratory dinner while her thoughts turned to Justin and Lynne. She trusted they also received a financial windfall from Aunt Dell and wondered how they would spend it. The non-disclosure agreement she signed prevented her from asking outright, but she assumed she would be able to infer an answer in the coming months. Before going to bed, she set her alarm for the next day of work and immersed herself in two Internet searches: one for a local realtor and the second for wine country vacations.

* * *

Mickey smiles as he opens his mailbox. Inside, he finds a vibrant postcard with a beautiful rolling hillside vineyard in the background. Overlaid in the foreground are two bottles of wine with a bold Napa Valley winery label. He reads the short note on the backside and laughs with delight: "I guess she *does* forgive me!"

He begins walking back to his house and stops midstep: "And how does she know I am an avid postcard fan? Apparently, I'm not the only detective in this town."

MADDIE TATE BUILT A TABBY WALL

Martha Reed

February 17, 1848
7 miles north of St. Augustine, Florida

Baba's corded arms struggled to keep the weighty iron poker jammed into the charcoal embers until its twisted metal tip glowed cherry red. The wrinkled, white-haired old woman looked grimly determined.

Huddled on her pallet in a corner of their tabby cabin, Pearl twisted her hands, looking ready to cry. "Papa? Sure this needs done?"

"Don't want the same thing happening to me that happened to your momma." Fifteen years old, Pearl was Maddie's only remaining child, his only hold on hope, the last slim thread that bound him to the cherished memory of her mother, Emmaline, and as precious and rare as his dead wife had been. Thinking of Emmaline, Maddie felt a piercing loss so fierce he couldn't breathe. Emmaline had picked up cracked heels working barefoot in the cane fields and suffered a lingering, stinking gangrene death that took six hellish weeks to put her in her grave.

"You had no business chopping cane by yourself," Baba muttered, hunched over, turning from the firelight. "Shoulda lef' that to them First Gang young'uns."

"I had my reasons." Gritting his teeth, Maddie tensed. Pearl was on the cusp of becoming a woman. No matter the pain or the cost, she needed him alive to keep her safe. "Hit me."

The smoking iron seared his pus-filled suppurating forearm wound. Maddie screamed like a swamp panther before everything turned black.

* * *

Raising the hand-painted, imported porcelain cup, plantation owner Leland Tate sipped his sweetened milky coffee, aware of and fully enjoying the sunlight dappling the coquina stone terrace and the oh-so-pleasant breeze blowing inland off the Tolomato River.

"Dearest, are you sure you need to go?" Two vertical lines creased the skin between Felicity's nearly invisible blonde eyebrows. "Birmingham, England seems so very far away. Wouldn't a letter suffice?"

"Can't be remedied." Setting the cup down, Leland picked up an estate-grown orange, stripping its thin, curling peel with his thumbnail. "Plantation business, my dear. My partners insist on seeing me in person."

Twisting her hands, Felicity looked concerned. "It seems like an unnecessary risk when we've only just finished juicing the cane." The breeze ruffled her Belgian lace cap. "Everyone is saying how dangerous these new steamships can be. What if you meet with a hurricane? Or the … what do they call it? The boiler explodes like the one in Louisiana did?"

"Sour. No juice." Leland discarded the pale half-eaten section, listening to his wife with half an ear. Once she got started, Felicity tended to ramble. "While I appreciate your concern for my safety, my dear, it's the wrong season for hurricanes. Steamships offer a modern and faster trip." Dusting his fingers, he smoothed his waistcoat. "I can be in Manchester in eighteen days. A sailing clipper could take six weeks, with luck. Some of them have been known to take fourteen weeks and run out of fresh water and provisions." He reached for her plump hand. "You wouldn't wish that on me, would you, my dear?"

"Of course not." She simpered. "I just object to the idea of you being away for so long. Why don't I go with you? We could visit London, do some shopping. I'd love a new dress."

"I'm afraid this trip is all business. I'll come back as soon as I can. Buy the fastest return ticket I can find, and bring you a special gift," Leland promised. Releasing her hand, he gestured. "Pearl? Fetch our guest."

"Guest? What guest?" Resettling her cuffs, Felicity smoothed her day dress, gazing at the house. "I didn't know we had a guest."

"You'll see," Leland teased. "He arrived late last night. I didn't want to disturb you since you had retired to your room." He paused. "My dear, we need to discuss one more thing before I leave. I've tried to protect you from the upsetting news, but the harvest numbers confirmed it. The sugar cane yield is dropping. It may be time to sell the plantation. That's why I need to speak with my partners in person. This land may be played out."

"You told me we earned $22,000 with the harvest this year." Felicity looked affronted. "Your accounting must be wrong." Pulling a lawn handkerchief from her sleeve, she dabbed her sweaty upper lip. "Leland, this plantation is 20,000 cleared acres. It was my daddy's pride and joy. That much land *can't* be played out. Besides," her tone turned peevish, "it was *my* dowry." She resettled her skirt. "I wasn't entirely pleased when you renamed it the Tate Plantation."

"Tate is your legally married last name now, dearest." He flicked an ant off his sleeve. "Besides, times change. We need to change with it. They're finding gold in California. I'm considering whether we should relocate, move our slaves to California to work the new gold fields."

"California?" Felicity's voice rose as she repeatedly blinked. "That's the other side of the world."

"The other side of our American continent." He smirked. "On the Pacific Ocean."

She looked unsettled. "I assume, Leland, you're speaking of taking the men to California. What about the women and children?"

"Sell 'em." He shrugged. "Wouldn't pay to ship them. They'd be a drain on our resources, nothing but a carried burden."

She curled her shoulders around her folded hands. "I don't much like that idea either."

"As I've said, it's not entirely my decision. My Manchester partners will have an opinion on where our finances stand." Striking a sulfur match against the stone paving, he lit a cigar. "I did hire you help while I'm away."

"No, thank you." Felicity stiffened. "I'm capable of managing plantation affairs. I managed for two years after my daddy died before I married you."

"Your daddy never owned eighty slaves." Leland puffed sententiously. "You think you could oversee the distillery, the sugar house, the loading dock, the cotton, and the mule trade? You really believe you could manage all of that, my dear?"

"I've never been asked to try." Felicity boldly raised her chin. "And exactly where did you find this new and helpful person?"

"My partners suggested him. Their letter of recommendation stated he's of good character, a sober and industrious individual. He's produced a very good testimonial from his previous employer in Barbados."

"I can see you've been considering this overseer suggestion for some time." Her voice trembled.

"Dearest wife." Setting it in a pink Queen conch shell, Leland left the cigar stub to burn. "You're adorable, but you must leave running the plantation business to me. Oh, good. Here he is." He stood as Pearl returned to the terrace, looking flustered. She scurried out of the way. "Madame, let me introduce Mr. Rox Abercrombie, our new overseer. Rox, this is my wife, Mrs. Tate."

The new man bowed low over her extended hand. "Honored to meet you, ma'am."

Felicity looked appalled. "Where are your people from, Abercrombie?"

"England, ma'am."

"I think not, with that carrot-red hair," she stated, her tone scathing. "You certainly don't look English."

"By way of Belfast, ma'am. I'm Ulster Scot."

"So, you're *Irish*." She rose. "That's an entirely different matter. Come, Pearl. I'll leave you two *gentlemen* to it."

Leland remained silent as his wife left the terrace. Rox narrowed his eyes.

"I believe, sir, I've offended your wife."

"Take a seat, Abercrombie," Leland genially stated. "Mrs. Tate needs time to wrap her head around any new idea. It's why I hesitate to suggest them. She'll be fine. She knows her place." He proffered his monogrammed silver cigar case. "You know our deal. I may be away for six months, perhaps a full year."

"Anticipating the pleasures of London, sir?" Rox smirked.

"That's my business." Leland's pale lips thinned. "I expect you to increase the plantation stock while I'm away. I'll need that extra revenue when I decamp for California." Steepling his fingers, he studied the rippling river. "You'll see a sizeable bonus if you can double the population."

"Only double, sir?" Rox chortled, tipping back his head and gripping the cigar between his eyeteeth. "No worry on that score, sir. You'll find plenty of fresh babes in arms on your return, *whenever* you decide that may be."

* * *

"Someone's comin,' boss." Squinting into the sun, Augustus Tate pointed his machete. Gus, as he was called, was Emmaline's brother and Maddie's best friend. "Two someones, looks like."

Maddie removed his battered palm frond hat, careful not to disturb the neat calico bandage Baba had tied over the clean scab on his forearm. The two men rode up on their standardbred horses, stirring up a cloud of bitter dust. Wiping his sweating brow with his short shirt sleeve, Maddie hacked a cough.

Leland pointed his riding crop. "The big one's Maddie. The skinny high yellow is Gus. Maddie's in charge of all three crews. Him you can trust."

Despite the livestock tone, Maddie warmed at the praise. He had busted his hump for nine years to become the coveted field crew boss, biting his tongue bloody to mindlessly follow orders, restrain his opinion, or to express any suggestions or ideas of his own. His increasing rise in plantation authority had given him enough back door influence to secure Pearl a position in the Kitchen House with Baba instead of working as a cane field hand on the deadly First Gang crew.

First Gang crew members started out young, wiry, and tough, but Maddie had seen their eventual and guaranteed destruction with his own eyes. After ten years, chopping cane broke their bodies. Everyone ended up with crippled backs and missing fingers or whole limbs. Maddie did what he could do, shifting them to Second Gang, where they spent their final years weeding the cane rows with the Grass Gang children. Between the crushing lifetime workload, the many sicknesses and infections, the stinging insects, and the poisonous snakes, after thirty years, every field hand was dead.

Maddie had joined his own Grass Gang crew 22 years ago when he was ten. He had known even then what needed to be done to protect his family and himself. He felt very proud of Pearl. She had heeded his advice and worked up to ladies' maid in the Big House on her own.

"Get the crews back to working, Gus," he directed.

"Hold up." The red-headed stranger slid off his horse, tossing Gus his reins. "They need to learn who I am."

"Agreed." Leland rested his forearms across his horse's withers. He raised his voice. "Mr. Rox Abercrombie is the new overseer. I've granted him full and complete authority."

Dread thumped Maddie's stomach like a falling coconut. Plantation changes upset everything. They were never good.

Rox toed a basket of rotting manure with his boot. "I see we use the cane-holing method."

"I inherited the fields that way. Mrs. Tate's papa believed in it. We get the manure from the mules and the outhouses."

Crouching, Rox knelt on the bank of the six-by-six-foot field squares. His head snapped up. "You said production yield's been falling?"

"Yesss. The land's playing out. Why?"

"There's more than one way to damage cane, sir." Dusting his hands, Rox slowly stood. "Someone's been hacking at the roots."

Maddie suddenly felt light-headed.

"That might be your problem, sir. Damage the roots, and the cane won't regrow. Maybe the plantation's not playing out. Maybe someone's been sabotaging your field."

Maddie unglued his tongue from the roof of his mouth. "It was borers, Mr. Leland. Borers got into the roots. Crew needed to cut them out before they rotted the whole field."

Leland slowly blinked. "Abercrombie? That true?"

"I'll need to survey more rows, sir." Watching Maddie carefully, he slid his boot into the iron stirrup and swung back onto the saddle. "I'll make a report."

"You do that."

Gripping his left wrist with his right hand, Maddie controlled his trembling as they rode away. Only Gus knew that he had been hacking the cane as revenge for Emmaline's death. Gus had caught Maddie in the field late one night, chopping the exposed roots with a sharpened hoe and sobbing his bone-rattling grief under the moon. It had been Maddie's only relief, leaving him hollow and spent until the next wave of sorrow unseated his mind. He had never given a moment's notion on how his secret anguish might play out.

Bile torched Maddie's throat. Now the plantation might get sold because of the reduced cane yield and played-out land rumor. What little remained of his family would get auctioned off and scattered. What would happen to Baba? Who would buy a toothless worn-out old woman? What about Pearl? How could he protect them?

His fear needled him deeper. Could he still trust Gus? What if Gus ratted him out to the new overseer? Would Gus do that to win Maddie's field crew boss job? Maddie's guts twisted as the trembling started again. Gus had two half-grown kids of his own to protect, a sturdy boy and a slim, sickly girl. Both were already working on the First Gang crew.

* * *

Felicity picked the half-eaten scone into crumbs. The pastry had tasted like chalk.

"Try eatin' some, missus," Pearl gently suggested. "You're gettin' thin."

"It seems pointless." Staring at the river, she toyed with her teacup. "With no one to talk with and nothing to do but wait for a letter."

"That new overseer would gladly join you."

Felicity inspected her sterling silver fork. "I'd rather starve."

"Maybe, missus," Pearl offered, "what you need is something special to do. Something interesting to do outside. It's cool enough mornings. Fresh air would build up your appetite." Gesturing at the terrace, she made a bold suggestion. "Why don't you plant a nice garden like the one the Jassey Plantation has before the weather turns hot?"

"I do adore jasmine," Felicity admitted, perking up. "It's like angel's breath. I could call on Melanie Jassey and ask for her advice." She set the teacup down decisively. "I'd love to see the look on Leland's face when he returns and sees that I've improved the plantation in his absence."

"My daddy could help you build it."

"Remind me again. Who's your daddy?"

"Maddie Tate, Missus. The field crew boss," Pearl proudly stated.

Felicity drummed her fingernails on the tablecloth. "Send for this Maddie Tate."

* * *

Maddie stood in the shade of the live oak tree, studying the Big House. The stately clapboard building sat high on an artificial rise, perched on coquina blocks to avoid fevers and flooding and to catch any cooling breeze. Cedar shutters framed double-hung windows filled with plate glass so brightly polished they winked the sunlight into Maddie's eyes, leaving black blots in his vision.

He fingered the smooth quartz pebble in his hand, hating those windows with his whole being. Although he had memorized the number of panes, Maddie counted them again. Eight panes in each window, twelve front-facing windows meant one hundred panes of imported English plate glass, with spares, at what a terrible cost. Mr. Leland had Maddie and Gus replace the older wavy glass when he had married Miss Felicity to modernize the look of the place. Maddie wished he had a fat white pebble to bust every single one of those glass panes. Mr. Leland had sold Dante, Maddie's only son, off a Fort Augustine auction block to cover the renovation expense.

Maddie hadn't known about the auction until he'd come in from the cane fields to find Emmaline crouched in one corner of their cabin cradling her broken arm and missing her front teeth, her blackened eyes swollen into slits.

"They come for Dante," was all his wife would say.

Maddie's thumbnail nicked the pebble. If only he had known, he might have done something.

Mrs. Tate stepped onto the porch, closely attended by Pearl, who shot him a quick, shy smile. Loosening his grip, Maddie dropped the pebble into the dirt, waiting for the missus to speak first.

"I want a new garden, an arbor of tropical beauty." Raising her chin, she flicked her hand in the air. "Like the one the Governor has on his St. Augustine estate. I'll fill it with rare ornamentals. It will be the talk of the county."

"I can build you whatever you want, missus," Maddie started slowly. "What's arbor?"

"A garden, with seats. Where I can take tea and admire the flowers."

"Flowering plants?" Maddie doubtfully frowned. "You'll need a wall then to shade them from the sun and keep out the wind."

"There goes that idea." Felicity looked dejected. "I don't have the pin money to purchase bricks or coquina blocks for a wall." She savagely twisted her wedding band. "Leland gave the bankers control of my money."

"Don't need bricks or coquina, missus. I can build you a tabby wall outta oyster shells. Same as I used to build the cabins." Maddie gestured with his chin. "Oyster shells are free."

"I love this idea." For the first time since Leland Tate left, Missus looked animated. "Use the children to collect the shells and help build the wall. It won't take any time at all."

"Grass Gang kids can collect the shells," Maddie quickly backpedaled, "but building the wall's my doing. Gotta be extra careful working with tabby. Breathe shell dust, and it'll turn to glass in your lungs." He tapped his broad chest. "Fresh slake will eat the skin off your hands down to raw bone. Need to be careful enough just collecting the shells."

"I don't believe you." Felicity pouted. "There's no such thing as a dangerous oyster unless you eat them in a month without an 'r' in it. I do know that much."

"Them shells can kill you," Maddie insisted, thumbing his fresh pink scar. "Cut you like a razor. Poison your blood."

"Do be careful then." She tapped her lips. "How long will building my new arbor take?"

Maddie scanned the cloudless sky. "Depends some on the weather. Need to tamp tabby in layers. I can use the forms I made for the cabins. Each layer needs one sunny day to firm up before I add more on top."

"Pearl, fetch my gloves and order my carriage." Felicity looked satisfied. "I need to start collecting plants from my friends."

* * *

Wearily resting his arms on the shovel, Maddie studied the new arbor enclosure. Mixing tabby had been a crushing load of hard work, but the waist-high walls were up, trim and square with the new plants bedded in. It was a job well done.

Filling his sore lungs, Maddie eased his breath, feeling at one with the world as he stretched the tension from his shoulders. The cicadas were singing in the trees, and the bullfrogs were thumping from the creek. Sometimes working with his hands was all a man could do to leave his mark on the world, but at the end of his days, he could be judged by the quality of the things he had built and by what he had left behind. Maddie had this wall to show for his time, and Pearl. It was enough.

"Caught you admiring yourself." Baba handed Pearl her rush basket.

Resting the shovel on his collarbone, Maddie followed them toward the cabins. His nose smelled hot food, and his stomach gurgled. "What's for supper? I'm half-starved."

"Fried catfish, collards with rice, and cornbread. Watched you working from the Kitchen House today. Knew you'd be extra hungry like you got a worm."

"Hold still. Gimme that basket." He playfully wrestled with Pearl. "I know you got what I need."

"Get offa me!" She screamed. Shoving him hard, she thrust the basket at Baba. "Don't touch me."

Maddie felt stung and confused. "I was just playing. Pearl? What's got into you?"

Hitching up her skirt, his beloved daughter burst into tears, racing barefoot past the Sugar House for the cabins.

"Baba?" Maddie's heart snapped in half. "What did I do?"

"It's not you," the old woman muttered darkly. "That new man's been gettin' after her."

"New man? Who? The overseer?" Maddie's eyes filmed over red. Breathing hard, he turned for the Big House. Pain seared his brain clear as Baba grabbed his freshly scarred arm.

"What you gonna do?" She hissed. "You think any of this is new just because it happened to your girl? She's a grown woman now, and he knows it. Maddie, listen to me. Listen! You try to stop him, and he'll beat you dead. With you dead and gone, it'll be worse on me and Pearl. We'll have nothing left."

Dropping the shovel to the ground, Maddie gripped his pounding head with both hands, his heartbeat hammering his ears. He wanted to scream his lungs empty to release his pent-up rage. *I'll make them pay for this.* His failure to protect Pearl choked his windpipe until only one gasping thought remained: *But how?*

Smelling cigar smoke, he looked up.

Rox Abercrombie leaned against the open Sugar House door.

"Saw Pearl run past just now." He leered. "Nice legs. When you catch up to her, send her back."

Stoutly stepping forward, Baba blocked Maddie's path. "Find somebody else. Pearl's sick."

"Liar." His smoke ring shimmied in the still air. "Seemed fine enough to me this morning. Twice." He flicked his fingers like he was shaking off water drops. "Hurry along now. I'm waiting."

* * *

Crossing the terrace, Maddie followed the tabby wall into the new arbor. Pert mockingbirds flicked their tails, darting between the citrus trees, striped Spanish dagger, and King Sago palms. Even the new ornamentals had settled in well enough to bloom. Leggy castor bean, oleander, and flame lily vine framed the view. *The missus has a good eye for plants, even if most of them is poisonous.* It was a restful spot.

Gonna tell her my idea even if it costs me. Maddie firmed his resolve. *Got to make this work.*

"There you are." Felicity returned her teacup to the saucer with a click. Pearl refused to look up. "I've been considering the leftover shells the children gathered and how they might best be used."

"Missus, I've been thinking on them, too." Maddie hurriedly risked an interruption. "We could use them to lay a shell path around the cabins. Make them prettier," he pointed, "since you can see them from this arbor."

A shell path will crunch. We can post a watch. Women in the cabins will hear Rox coming. Might give them — and Pearl — warning time to hide. It's not much, but it's something.

"Those cabins are a hideous eyesore," Felicity admitted. "But I have another use for those shells, and I like my idea better."

Maddie's heart sank to his knees. *Nothing I come up with is good enough.*

"I want you to extend the garden wall." She sipped her tea. "And build it higher."

"Add more tabby?" Maddie stuttered.

"Exactly. How tall is the wall now? Four feet? Raise it to six. And extend it so that it screens the cabins from the arbor. That should improve the view."

Maddie's heart soared like a seagull in the wind. *A stout six-foot tabby wall between the Big House and the cabins would keep Rox out. I'd like to see him climb over that.*

"Missus." Tears of gratitude watered Maddie's eyes. "I'll start mixing fresh tabby first thing tomorrow morning."

"One more thing." Felicity tapped her prominent front teeth. "We'll need a gate. Abercrombie wants access to inspect the cabins. Build a gate in the extended wall, a large arched gate decorated with shells made to look like flowers. Let's keep to the theme."

"Yes, missus." Maddie wanted to scream.

* * *

"Pearl, I have done my best." Maddie sat slumped before the cabin's small flickering fire, his hands between his knees, the flames highlighting the bags under his eyes. "I'm out of ideas. Don't matter what I do to protect you. They outfox me every time."

"You got that nice wall done." Baba rested a gentle hand on his shoulder. "That's something."

"Don't do no good keeping Rox out with that big arched gate I built into it."

"Seems to me what we need to do . . . is to start using his own fears against him. What's this Rox afraid of?"

"He ain't afraid of nothing." Maddie spat onto a hot brick. His thickened spittle sizzled.

"He thinks a bird in the house means death is coming," Pearl spoke from her pallet. "He's afraid of banshees."

Maddie turned. "What's a banshee?"

"A devil woman who steals your soul. He called me a banshee once, teasing me."

"What's this banshee look like?" Maddie rose, his bulk outlined by the fire. "Pearl? What she do?"

"She combs her long hair waiting for a man to come walking by. Then she confuses his mind and steals his soul. Rox said never pick up a comb if you find one laying on the ground, 'cuz it's a banshee setting a trap."

Reaching into the twiggy tinder basket, Baba handed Maddie a cedar shake.

He grasped it slowly. "What you giving me this for?"

"Sharpen your knife." She stared through the open doorway. "Start whittling combs."

* * *

Puffing on the cigar, Rox paused. His belly was full, the French wine more than ample, and the moon shone across the river like a beacon. Five months on the job, and he had a lot to be thankful for. The new cane shoots looked lush and promising, with no signs of pests or drought. Leland Tate had written to say he was extending his overseas stay for another six months. Mrs. Tate seemed satisfied enough puttering around her new little garden, and he had his choice of more cock trap than an Istanbul sultan.

Somewhere ahead in the slave cabins, a woman was singing, her low sweet tone carried on the wind. Dropping the cigar, Rox crushed it underfoot, gleefully picking up his pace. As he stepped into the arched gate, he heard a brittle snap.

Looking down, he froze as gooseflesh pimpled his forearms. His right boot had cracked an ornate wooden comb in half. Trembling and treading carefully, Rox raised both arms to shoulder height as he cautiously backed away from the gate.

"Told you," Pearl whispered, clutching Maddie's sleeve.

"Do I really need to do this now?" Rox drunkenly wondered aloud. "Yes, I believe I do."

Taking three giant strides to the right, he leaped up, hooking both arms over the top of the tabby wall. His boots scrabbled for purchase as the brittle exposed shells splintered. His thin linen shirt ripped.

"Goddamn it!" Rox howled before falling off and landing on his back. "That hurts," he whimpered.

* * *

Relaxing in the balmy December sunshine, Leland toyed with his crystal glass, admiring the pleasant new garden. Taking another sip, he grimaced. The acidic lemonade aggravated the open sore on his lip.

"Finding the lemonade disagreeable, dearest?" Felicity pointed to an etched decanter. "Try the cordial. I made it myself."

"You take such good care of me." He sighed, gesturing with his free hand. "Truthfully, my dear, I've missed your smile and this sunshine. Manchester was dreary. It rained every other day. You'd have hated it."

"Your business partners were satisfied with the plantation receipts?"

"They were. According to Rox's last letter, sugar yields have returned to normal."

"No more plans, then, for relocating to California?"

"No." Leland scowled. "They chose someone else. A younger man, unencumbered. Besides," he muttered, "those prospecting fools have poured into the gold fields. The profitable leases are already taken."

"Well, that's that. You haven't said anything about my new arbor. Don't you love the way the pink oleander sets off the spotted water hemlock? So delicate, just like Queen Anne's lace. My lady friends particularly recommended these ornamentals, and they were right."

"It's paradise. Did Abercrombie give you the idea for this garden?" He glanced at the Big House. "Where is he, by the way?"

"He did not." Felicity tucked her chin. "Didn't you get my letter? He's been dead these six months."

"No, I did not get your letter." Leland sipped the cordial. "Malaria? Yellow fever?"

"Blood poisoning. It was wretched and disgusting. He developed these horrible black streaks up and down his limbs to his . . . groin. Dr. Dimmons did his best, everything he could do. He amputated Abercrombie's arms and legs, but the infection was too deeply seated."

"Poor man." Leland drained his glass.

"I had his remains sealed in a cask of rum and shipped to your Manchester partners. I hope that was the right thing to do. It was the only address you left with me, dearest. The only address I had."

"I bet they got a surprise when they opened that cask." Chuckling, Leland refilled his glass. "Six months dead? Who's been running the plantation?"

"Who do you suppose?" Felicity straightened her sleeves. "I've proved quite capable and proficient while you were away." She tapped the decanter with her fingernail until it rang. "I've even perfected Melanie Jassey's cordial recipe. The essence is distilled from herbs grown in this very arbor, mixed with enough cane juice to remove the bitterness. Melanie said it would cure what ailed me." She winsomely smiled. "Enjoy another glass full, dearest. After your long voyage, I believe it will do you . . . good."

THE PURSE DETECTIVES

Monica Faeth Myers

Before you blame me for the fire on the causeway bridge, hear me out.

I don't know if you've been to the annual St. Mary's rummage sale. Somebody once tried to bill it as the largest collection of abandoned, poorly aged, culturally irrelevant, and just wrong-at-purchase stuff that somehow missed a dumpster, but the school principal, Sister Ursula, vetoed that. Now we just print the dates.

I'm the volunteer who sorts through the donations, arranges them by junk style—household, clothing—and on sale day keeps the crowd from stripping down to their underwear in the school cafeteria to try on a three-dollar skirt. For my services, I, and other volunteers, get to shop before the crowds. My particular draw is purses. Cheryl's is too, but I'll get to her later. I have dozens of them now, some designer-level ones like the Brahmin I got for thirty dollars, others like a leather bucket from Dooney and Burke I got for two. I have them stored in boxes in our condo storage area and in suitcases stuffed under the bed. Yes, I have thought about what I am getting from buying purses I am unlikely to ever need or wear, but who thinks about that when buying accessories, particularly on the cheap?

Growing up in St. Pete, I think my mother used the same raggedy handbag for at least ten years, and it was lower-rack K-Mart to start. Her mantra was that spending money on a decent purse was a waste because nobody she knew had ever noticed a handbag. Wrong, Mom! Now I'm carrying a Longchamp shoulder bag I got for five dollars, and it came with the dust bag.

At noon, one hour before closing, anybody can stuff a grocery sack of whatever's left for $5. The crowds are standing by, waiting for the bell that Principal Sister Ursula swings like a logger after counting down on her watch. Mothers throw their kids in the ring with a "Run faster than the old people! Go! Go!" Afterward, the leftovers are carted away or dumped. Even though I've looked at this junk for days, I'll still buy a brown bag. You never know. I could have missed something. That's how I found the roll of film.

And that's when I called Cheryl.

"Do you remember somebody donating a brown leather Fossil shoulder bag with a kind of ratty strap? "I said.

"That sounds like ninety percent of them at the sale."

"This one had a roll of film."

"Okay, that's the other ten percent."

"I developed it."

"If you bought the purse, that's your option. Can you recognize anybody in them?"

"Like celebrities? No. Most of the film was unusable. The three pictures that could be printed looked like an old house or cabin by the water and an old station wagon, the kind that smells of dog blankets.

"Well," she said. "I suspect you're calling me not to discuss landscape photography but to figure out where this place is and who shot the film."

"I thought you liked landscape photography. But since you brought it up," I said. "What's the use of having a friend who's a former naval intelligence officer if we're just going to make condescending remarks about people who can't take pictures on their phone? That's only good for ten minutes."

"And you want to condescend for much longer."

"If we can make it work. Meet me at Bellair Coffee. I'll bring the entire mystery kit—purse, pictures, and negatives. You can do your spook stuff. I'll buy the coffee."

The afternoon was slow, and we managed to get two chairs next to a handmade wood table.

Cheryl inspected the film and the Fossil bag.

"Somebody got their money's worth out of this." She inspected the purse, turning it inside out. There was a tear at the bottom of the lining and a business card for one "Leonard Deiderman, Your Friend When You Need a Friend," that had become trapped under the rip. The purse was full of lint and metal foil pieces from gum wrappers.

"What can you tell me about it?" I said.

"Like, can I look at this picture and recognize it enough that I can train a satellite on the spot, that kind of thing?'

"Wouldn't that be fun? I saw that in movies."

"It's not how it works." She pulled out her cell and looked to be sorting through the app store before uploading an image of the cabin at the water.

"This app will match the photographic image with other images on the web. Then we'll know if this is even in the area."

Cheryl worked quietly for a few minutes while I drank coffee. Then I got up and bought two chocolate croissants because you can make wrong decisions when you're hungry, even though I wasn't the one making decisions. Cheryl flipped to a magnifying app on her phone and inspected the picture closely.

"This looks to be it," she said. "Thomas Grainger Park in Largo. Probably taken in 2019."

"You got the date from a search on the web?" I said.

"No. I looked at the tag on the car. It says 2019."

"So, the film has been sitting around for a while," I said. Frankly, I was pleased with myself for both finding and developing it. It wasn't as interesting as that Mont Blanc pen I discovered in a rummage purse once. But it was a good reason to get together for coffee.

"Look at this, Loretta. It's a newspaper article the search found. The picture accompanying the article is almost exactly of the same spot and car." She passed her phone to me.

The headline read, "Body of Murdered Largo Woman Found in Grainger Lake." According to the police report, Stella Nordler was found in the lake approximately 36 hours after being reported missing by her husband, Stan Nordler. After reporting her gone, Stan drove through the neighborhood looking for his wife the night before she was located. He hadn't thought to look at Grainger Park because it was not someplace the two of them had visited. The paper reported Mr. Nordler as "inconsolable."

"Who would do this?" he said. "My wife was a saint. Everybody knew that. I hope they find that person or persons and throw the book at them. The world is at a loss now that she's gone."

"Who took the pictures, then?" I said.

"I suspect it was the saintly Stella. If I had to guess, the two of them went to the park, and he killed her, then somehow, he managed to throw her body into deep water. He took her purse and belongings to make it look like it was an attack by a stranger. He dumped the contents, which most likely included her wallet, the camera, etc. But he didn't think to look in the side pocket for the film she shot."

"You have a very bleak view of humanity if you think it was the grieving husband."

"He knew she took pictures, so he took the camera. He may have avoided her taking any pictures of him as a failsafe. Probably never looked at it again. A missing purse suggests a stranger, maybe with a robbery motive. But would a stranger donate a purse to a charity rummage sale to get the itemized receipt for ten dollars? Look for the creepy murdering husband."

"Somebody donated used socks to the sale and asked for a receipt. They had holes. "

"But why did he keep it this long?" She ran her fingers over the inside seams.

I had been searching my own phone for information.

"Apparently, the police investigated, but nobody was ever charged. There was a big funeral service," I said. "And no doubt there was one of those memorials at the park that has flowers, teddy bears, and signs written on poster boards 'You're our angel now in heaven, Stella.'"

Cheryl sat for a second, her coffee cup on her lap. "Do you know what would be fun?"

Her eyes shone in anticipation. "We should go visit Mr. Nordler and ask if he donated the purse. See if he wants a donor receipt."

"Wouldn't that be dangerous?"

"He might itemize. He might be grateful we came by. Besides, we won't be in a park."

"Are you thinking what I think you're thinking?" I once saw Cheryl wrestle a fake fur chubby jacket from a woman trying to stuff it inside her palazzo pants. I knew Cheryl to be a woman of action.

"We'll only show him the photos to demonstrate an even deeper level of rummage sale support if we think it's appropriate."

"Okay, but we should tell our families where we'll be just to be safe." But it turned out we didn't tell them. What could we say?

Stella Nordler, in life, lived in an anonymous white cinder block home in Pinellas Park. There was a white van in the gravel driveway that said, "Acme Siding." There was also a newer model silver Ford Mustang convertible, and a Toyota SUV.

"Let's ring the bell," Cheryl said.

I paused. "I'd be happier if we had a couple of *Watchtowers* or something to hide behind." I started to think this was a bad idea.

"It's two o'clock on a Saturday afternoon. Nothing is going to happen."

"You have the Navy training. I was just an analyst. My watch doesn't even think I'm athletic."

Cheryl rang the bell. A paunchy middle-aged man in a faded polo shirt that looked rummage-ready answered the door.

"Are you Mr. Nordler?" Cheryl asked. I looked at her because she sounded so chirpy.

"Yeah?" His forehead accordioned in suspicion.

"We're from the St. Mary's Rummage sale. I'm Cheryl Craig, and this is Loretta Franklin. You donated this and didn't get your tax receipt. They're so *valuable. It's* a big reason why people contribute. Plus, we like to check in on our contributors."

"I didn't donate that. I don't know what you're talking about."

Behind Nordler, a very buxom woman in her twenties rose from a sofa littered with unfolded laundry. The room smelled of old take-out. She had long dark hair in a messy scrunchie and a T-shirt tied in a knot and tucked up under her bra. I could be wrong, but she didn't look like his daughter.

A purse sat on a chipped mirrored side table under a lamp.

"Is that your Yves Saint Laurent Sunset bag? I hate to be nosy, but did you get it retail or from Poshmark? I think Poshmark is such a savings."

"Are you kidding? This is current season." She grabbed it from the table and stuffed it under a pillow as if my staring at it would reduce its value.

"I know. And it looks to be python," I said.

"That's why I got it."

"I am so jealous. Cheryl and I just admire beautiful handbags, and yours is a treasure. I can see why you'd want to get rid of the Fossil. It's not your style at all. What flair you have! What *panache!*"

It was Cheryl's turn to look at me.

"I don't know what panache is," Python Girl said.

"It means feather," Cheryl said.

"I don't have any feathers."

"Are you an influencer?" I said. "I know the important fashion companies often supply influencers with their best products. Maybe that's how you got it."

"Stan got it for me. But I have a TikTok. You can follow me. It's @toohothot. I have two-hundred-seventeen followers."

"Is that your name? Toohothot? Thank you, Ms. Hot, but I've never TikTok'd before."

She looked at me as if she was reading a big L on my forehead.

"*No.* My *name* is Taylor Kransky. My *TikTok* name is Toohothot because everybody knows I am. Aren't I, baby?" She glanced at Nordler, who slowly turned his head in her direction.

"Do you want the receipt for the purse you donated?"

"Give it to Stan. I just wanted to get rid of it."

"Of course. I've so enjoyed seeing your purse. Thank you," I said.

Cheryl gave me a side-eye.

Then she reached inside her Radley of London zip-top tote in tan to pull out the pictures for Stan Nordler. She only gave him one.

"We found a roll of film in the purse and developed it for you. It's how we found you were the donor. I'm sure you'll want these. Happy memories, I hope."

"What's this all about?" His forehead wrinkled in confusion.

"As a reminder," Cheryl said. "St. Mary's Fall Festival and Dance is October 15th. Tickets are thirty-five dollars a couple, and there's a silent auction. Goodbye!"

With that, Cheryl turned swiftly to leave. "Time to go."

I scurried behind her down the drive as Nordler watched. "That was a thirty-eight-hundred-dollar purse."

"She didn't pay for it. Or this car either, I bet."

"Seeing that lovely Sunset bag in that squalor makes me sad. It's probably reeking of frozen pizza and chili fries right now."

"We're doing this for Stella," Cheryl said. "Who probably never owned a purse she didn't get at Macy's with a coupon."

"What next?" I said.

"Why don't we visit the Acme Siding Company? You know, the school association is getting ready for their Fall Festival dinner dance and auction. They're looking for donations. People may tell us about how poor Stan is recovering from the death of his wife. Because it takes time to grieve."

"And you are looking for siding?"

"It could be the star of the silent auction. Who doesn't want siding?" Cheryl laughed. "Stan's probably hanging a lot of siding to pay for Ms. Kransky's appetites. Long days slapping it up on houses and trailers."

"She-sheds and dog houses," I added. "No wonder he had that vacant stare. Probably difficult to stand from the exhaustion. Okay, but save that for Monday. Why don't we check out a few things about Ms. Toohothot right now? She wants to be noticed, after all."

"We'd have to get a TikTok account. Otherwise, we don't know anything about her unless we go to the police."

"We can learn pretty much everything we want from a tenant check on Whitepages.com. It will tell us about any criminal background, aliases, eviction reports, and even her credit score."

I was on my phone this time, keying in data.

"Well, for $29.95, we find that Ms. Taylor Kransky has a selection of former criminal charges, including one for passing bad checks and a second for speeding. She lists her occupation as entrepreneur, and she has two former aliases. What a colorful young woman! Because she seems so settled in with our Mr. Nordler."

"She could have found Jesus," Cheryl said. "She could have been baking pies when we rang the doorbell."

"She could have. Or, she could have helped dispose of the body. She looked like she has a lot of upper body strength."

"Probably from lifting heavy things," Cheryl said.

"That would do it."

Late Monday morning, Cheryl and I introduced ourselves to the receptionist at Acme Siding in her second-floor office. There was a nameplate, Sumata Monanth, which in my experience, lends status and authority without financial compensation. A lovely Michael Kors satchel was nestled next to the printer behind her desk.

"We're here from St. Mary's School Fall Festival and Dance, soliciting contributions to the silent auction," Cheryl said.

I stared in admiration. She can just say any variety of things with a gravitas that comes from a military background, and people believe her. I mean, there was a Fall Festival, but I think that's all either of us knew, and that came from reading the church bulletin. I don't even know if there is a silent auction. Wouldn't Sister Ursula be surprised if a couple of pallets of vinyl siding were suddenly dumped on the playground on Monday?

"I'm Cheryl, and this is Loretta. Did you have a chance to go to our rummage sale?"

"When was it?" Sumata asked.

"A week ago, Saturday. At least one of your co-workers went. Do you know Stan Nordler or Taylor Kransky?"

"I know that pair. I'm surprised she was there. She never lets him buy anything but designer for her."

"She has a TikTok name of TooHotHot. I think that shows confidence," I said. "I haven't had a chance to check it out yet, though."

"That would be Taylor. She has a lot of confidence. Mostly she thinks it's in her T-shirt."

"There's so much pressure on women today," I said. "It's toxic. I bet you feel it here in your job. You're in such a responsible position. You probably know everything about the people in the company."

"Stuff they wish I didn't." She slapped the point of her free office pen into her desktop.

"We learned that poor Mr. Nordler lost his wife. That must have been a nightmare for him," Cheryl said.

"Not that big of a nightmare, as it turned out," Sumata said. "You saw Taylor."

"Some men just can't live alone. I guess that's why they got together," I said.

"They were *together* for almost a year while his wife was alive. They'd get *together* in the company truck during lunch hour. We could see it bouncing on the tires from this window." She walked over and showed Cheryl and me the exact spot where she and unnamed others probably offered guesses on the amount of torque observed in Nordler's van as lunch progressed.

"Your windows are so clean," I said. "You can see to the WaWa."

"Did the police ever come and ask about Nordler and Ms. Kransky?" Cheryl asked.

"They did. But everybody felt so bad for Stan nobody wanted to rat him out for Taylor," Samata said. "A week later, he was back at work. She didn't take any time off at all. Not even for the funeral."

"And then they were back working together again?" Cheryl said.

"Heck, no. Taylor quit. Stan takes on extra jobs to buy her the stuff she wants. I don't think this is what happened in his fantasies."

Just then, a man in his sixties, tired and slogging a contractor bag, came through the door.

Sumata waved a backhand toward the two of us. "Mr. Duchaj, these women are here from St. Mary's to ask for a donation for their silent auction."

"It's part of the Fall Festival. It's very popular. Your company can be in the program," I said.

He was confused. "We're a siding company."

"Construction donations are among our most popular items to bid on," Cheryl said. "If you donate now, we can have a video made and play it on the website."

"We do vinyl and aluminum siding. You can't just donate a couple boxes. They have to be installed." He shook his head like he couldn't understand the chasm in understanding.

"Exactly! The bidders can call you later!" I said.

"Or somebody else. No, thanks." He began to leave.

"Do you want to sponsor a table?" Cheryl said.

"No." He exited to an office.

"Thanks for your help anyway," I said to Sumata. "Let us know if you want tickets to the Festival."

"Yeah, I don't need construction supplies." She went back to her computer.

Cheryl and I sat in the front seat of my Ford Escape outside the siding office.

"I can't even drive past the back parking lot now," I said. "What do you want to do? I think we used up all the information available to us."

"No, we didn't." She pulled out the crumpled business card from the purse. "There's still 'Your Friend When You Need a Friend.' Maybe Stella needed a friend."

"Do you think he'd remember her?"

"If she paid. Friendship doesn't come cheap, especially when there's business cards."

We called the number on Leonard Diederman's business card. That is how we discovered he was a private investigator.

"I wonder if you can tell me whether Stella Nordler was a client of yours," I asked Mr. Diederman, who sounded asthmatic through my receiver. "She died several years ago; I'm just following up on some issues."

"What kind of issues?" he said.

"I recently came into possession of her purse. It sparked some curiosity on my part, which you might understand if you remember her."

"Of course, I remember her. Murdered, right? That happens less than you might expect in the PI business."

I couldn't envision a local business where it might be rampant, but that was for another call.

"Was she your client?"

"Yes."

"Can you tell me what she needed your services for?"

"She left a bill. If you want to pay it, you can have a copy of the file."

"How big is the bill?" I asked.

"Almost $300, but since she's dead, I'll drop it to $250."

"She's been dead for years. I can't believe you haven't already written it off as a business expense."

"Maybe I have. But it's still $250. Since you have her purse."

"I'll call you back in a minute."

"I can't rationalize spending $250 on Stella Nordler's private investigator," I said to Cheryl. "And no way am I putting something like that on a credit card."

"I have some cash on me," said Cheryl. "Let's pool what we've got."

"Wait," I said. And I dialed Diederman.

"Here's my counteroffer. You may understand that I don't have $250 to spend just to satisfy my curiosity. But I am willing to trade three expensive purses, previously owned but designer and very valuable. If you sell them on eBay, I would expect you to net nearly $500."

"Two-fifty or I hang up."

"Nobody's been interested in that file for years. This is your chance to make some cash. Take it or leave it," I said.

Cheryl nodded.

"What kind of purses?" Diederman said.

"A Coach Charter backpack, a Tory Burch Mercer crescent bag, and a Kate Spade zip top tote."

"I don't know some of those names."

"Trust me, they cost money. Are you in or out?"

"Okay, bring them by my office, and I'll have a look."

"You can start looking up the names now. I don't want to hang around. Have the file ready." I hung up and took a breath.

"Great negotiation," Cheryl said. "You sounded like you could be chewing a cigar."

"We need to get these out of the condo before Dave comes home and wonders what I'm up to." So, we raced back to Clearwater and began digging through the closet and under the bed to find the three purses. They were in a plastic tub on the top shelf.

"I'm going to be sorry to see these go," I said. "I was saving them for a future granddaughter someday since my daughters aren't that interested."

"They'll be much more interested if you solve a murder," Cheryl said.

"Let's go." And we headed to Leonard Diederman for the handoff.

Diederman's office was in a strange strip mall with a tattoo shop, a marijuana dispensary, and a store selling propane tanks, large and small. In front of the propane store, a selection of colorful young men were welding equipment to propane tanks in fabric harnesses.

"They're building flamethrowers," Cheryl said. "I wonder if that's legal."

"I wonder if it's the team from the pot shop," I said. "If they use them to light up marijuana, the whole neighborhood will be at the 7-11 looking for Slurpees and Three Musketeers."

The smallest of signs identified Diederman's office, its darkened front window uninviting. A bell rang when we opened the door.

A man of waxy complexion in a red shirt with a purple tie sat behind a desk. He didn't ask who we were.

"Are those my purses?" He pointed at the stuffed shopping bag.

"Do you have my file?"

Cautiously, Cheryl and I approached his desk and put the shopping bag on top of a giant desk calendar. There was nothing on it but a Chinese take-out flyer stuck in a vinyl corner.

"The file." I put out my hand.

He handed over a manila folder. Inside there were copies of notes and photographs from the Acme Siding parking lot, ground level.

I thought he should have asked Sumata to save a seat at the window. The results would have been better.

Several pictures were of Nordler and Kransky coming out of the van. Sometimes packs of siding could be seen inside.

"These better be as good as you say," Diederman said of the purses.

"That's primo stuff," I started to sound like a drug dealer. Maybe fumes were leaking in from the parking lot.

"What did you report to Stella Nordler?" Cheryl asked.

"Interpretation is extra. You just get the file."

"The file it is then." We headed back out into the light, where we were met by a shrieking Taylor Kransky.

She screamed at us, "What do you two lying bitches think you're doing?" And as a side note, she could really scream.

"We are visiting Mr. Diederman. What are you doing here?"

"Diederman called Stan and told him some women were snooping around and asking about Stella. Stan had to pay him $750 to get her file to see what you were looking for."

"I only had to trade him three previously owned purses for the file. Ours was a better deal," I said.

"The value of a college education," Cheryl said.

"You think you're both some kind of sleuths, like on television or something. You're just sad old women."

"Well, you know what they say about the three ages of women—Youth, middle age, and village detective. We think we have enough here to have the police reopen the case."

"You'll be sorry. I will kill you!" She screamed again, but she was getting hoarse.

"Get in the car," I said to Cheryl. "For some people, 'kill you' may be a figure of speech but…"

"I'm in," Cheryl said. "Time to leave."

We turned off and headed toward the causeway bridge and toward home. I kept checking the rearview mirror. "I think we lost her."

Cheryl was paging through the file. "Stella was on to Nordler and Kransky. This file goes back eighteen months before her death. She was looking into Nordler's expenses. I bet she was planning to file for a divorce."

"That would cut into Taylor Kransky's glamorous living fund." I saw a silver Ford Mustang convertible in my rearview mirror.

"She's coming," I said.

"Keep driving. Head for the police station on Pierce Street,"

But Taylor Kransky sped up and whacked the rear end of my car. I didn't stop.

"Check your phone for a shorter route." I pressed harder on the accelerator.

"On it." Cheryl punched buttons on her phone.

Kransky tried to pass on the left where there was no lane, driving over the yellow line and attempting to force me into the causeway railing. I slowed. She slowed, which gave me a chance to speed up.

Then she crashed into the side of my car, spinning it forty-five degrees.

Then she got out of the car. She was carrying one of the flamethrowers.

"How did she get that?" Cheryl asked.

Cars didn't stop but drove around me. Well, you know, traffic.

"Suggestions?" she said.

"Get out on your side, get to the back of the car, and start filming her on your phone in the middle of the road without her firing that thing at you. If people see you filming, they'll stop and film, too. Then the tweeting will start, and the police will come."

"Or I could just call the police," Cheryl said.

"Good idea." Cheryl got out, and I stayed in the car while Taylor Kransky made her next move which was trying to find out how the flamethrower worked.

Apparently, it was just a squeeze of a nozzle. She fired on my car. I scrambled to climb over the console and glove box to dive out Cheryl's door and run to the rear, missing incineration. I remembered to bring the file and my pink Kate Spade Market bag, which I got on their annual sale at seventy-five percent off. And I ran into the road, missing cars that sped around me. Then I began to film Taylor Kransky myself.

Having my car on fire with a screaming woman shooting at me with a flamethrower proved the incentive to have more cars stop and immortalize the situation on their phones. Taylor pumped the nozzle and fired again, but only a short flame spurted in my direction, perhaps enough to grill hamburgers. A Ford 150 drove around me, halfway into the opposing lane toward Kransky.

The passenger window rolled down, and a tattooed arm reached out and swung a small lunch-sized Igloo cooler, smacking Taylor Kransky in the head and knocking her out cold to the ground. The truck continued driving to the other side of the bridge.

I waved to the truck. An arm out the window waved back.

Cheryl ran and grabbed the flamethrower. The police arrived and collected Kransky. Cheryl and I had to give our evidence about the purse, the film, the internet identification, the file, and the meetings with Nordler and Kransky. We were on the news that night, as so many people had stopped to film flame throwing on the causeway bridge on their phones.

Stan Nordler and Taylor Kransky were arrested for the murder of Stella Nordler.

We used the publicity to advertise the Fall Festival Dinner Dance and Silent Auction, where tickets were only thirty-five dollars a couple.

THANK YOU TO OUR JUDGES

We could not have produced *Paradise is Deadly* without the generous and valued input and support from our panel of award-winning judges, who took the time to read the stories and provide input. A special thanks to Lisa Black, who read all of the stories and wrote the Introduction.

Colette Bancroft

I was the kid whose mother said, "Put down that book, go outside, and play." I grew up in Tampa, earned degrees in English at the University of South Florida and the University of Florida, and taught literature and writing for over a decade. Then I switched to journalism, working for the *Arizona Daily Star* and, since 1997, for the *Tampa Bay Times* as an editor, reporter, and critic. In 2007, I became the Times' book editor, writing reviews, interviewing authors, and helping to direct the annual Times Festival of Reading. In 2020 I edited the anthology *Tampa Bay Noir*, and the story I wrote for it, "The Bite," received the Mystery Writers of America's Robert L. Fish Memorial Award. I'm currently serving my fourth term on the board of the National Book Critics Circle. I live in St. Petersburg with my dog, Marlowe.

Lisa Black

Lisa Black is the New York Times bestselling author of 16 suspense novels, including the *Gardiner & Renner* series and the *Locard Institute* series. Her works have been translated into six languages, optioned for film, and shortlisted for the inaugural Sue Grafton Memorial Award. She is also a full-time Certified Latent Print Examiner and a Certified Crime Scene Analyst, beginning her forensics career at the Coroner's office in Cleveland, Ohio, and then the police department in Cape Coral, Florida. She has spoken to readers and writers at numerous conferences, been a consultant for *CourtTV*, and was a Guest of Honor at 2021 Killer Nashville.

Alan Orloff

Alan Orloff has published ten novels and more than forty short stories. His work has won an Anthony, an Agatha, a Derringer, and two ITW Thriller Awards. He loves cake and arugula, but not together. Never together. He lives and writes in South Florida, where the examples of hijinks are endless. www.alanorloff.com

Susan Thibadeau

You can find Susan Thibadeau's short stories published in *Alfred Hitchcock's Mystery Magazine*. She has also been published in Malice Domestic's anthology, *Mystery Most Geographical*, and the *Lucky Charms: 12 Crime Tales* anthology. Susan is a recipient of the Black Orchid Novella Award. She has an MFA from Chatham University and is a member of the Association of Writers & Writing Programs, Mystery Writers of America, Pennwriters, and Sisters in Crime.

THE CONTRIBUTORS

Tracy Ann
"A Sarasota Legacy Tail"

Tracy Ann lives in sunny Sarasota, Florida. She is an active member of the Florida Gulf Coast Chapter of Sisters in Crime. When not writing, she spends her time exploring the local nature parks, walking the beaches, sailing the coastline, and riding the Legacy Trail.

Mary Ball
"Roses and Oleanders: A Gardening Tale"

Mary Ball is a former computer scientist who had written a cozy mystery and was in the final editing stage when she became a full-time caregiver for her mother and father-in-law. That was five years ago, and she is just now getting back to writing. Her goal is to finish editing the cozy mystery while creating new stories. Getting back into a writing routine after five years is challenging, but she's getting there with the help of the wonderful critique partners of Florida Gulf Coast Sisters in Crime.

Anne Carter
"No Way Out"

Anne Carter is a writer, a motivational speaker, and according to her husband of twenty-five years, a very funny lady. Her many heartfelt stories in *Chicken Soup for the Soul* and *A Cup of Comfort Anthologies* have enchanted readers throughout the years. Born in New York City, Anne began a career as a reading consultant, introducing youngsters to the joy of the written word, via her unique teaching ability. A Florida transplant, she now resides in sunny Venice, Florida, and writes something new every day (grocery lists do count). A lover of mystery, Anne enjoys writing in the cozy genre and recently penned her first full-length novel (agents take note).

A member of the Florida Gulf Coast Sisters in Crime, she is delighted to have her newest short story appear in their outstanding anthology, *Paradise Is Deadly*. Contact Anne at anneanddickcarter@gmail.com

Wendy Dingwall
"Murder in Myakka Park"

Wendy Dingwall writes the award-winning *Yvonne Suarez Travel Mysteries*. She is the founder of the Florida Gulf Coast Chapter of Sisters in Crime and a member of Mystery Writers of America. Sold in 2020, Wendy is the former owner/publisher of Canterbury House Publishing and currently enjoys retired life by pursuing her writing and other varied interests.

In an earlier career as the owner of a travel agency, Wendy was inspired to write a mystery featuring an unusual travel agent protagonist. Enter Yvonne, raised in Miami, Florida. The daughter of a cool, collected British mother and a hot-blooded Cuban father, she is the blending of cultural differences emanating in her unique personality.

Reviewers have said about her mysteries, "They allow readers to experience the legends, lore, sights, and culture of the locations woven into each mystery, as if they are right there on the journey with her characters, watching the mystery unfold."

<h2 style="text-align:center">Mary Dutta
"Deceit by Design"</h2>

Mary Dutta is the winner of the New England Crime Bake Al Blanchard Award for her short story "The Wonderworker," which appears in *Masthead: Best New England Crime Stories*. Her work can also be found in numerous anthologies including *Land of 10,000 Thrills: Bouchercon Anthology 2022* and *Malice Domestic 16: Mystery Most Diabolical*. She is a member of Sisters in Crime and the Short Mystery Fiction Society. Visit her at marydutta.com and enjoy her blog at *Writers Who Kill*.

Harold Emanuel
"A Question of Time"

Harold Emanuel is the author of the *Lionel Trevor/Tech Squad* mystery series. Professor Lionel Trevor leads a Forensic Technology workshop at a local community college. The professor and his students use forensic technology to solve murders.

Harold Emanuel spent his career working in information technology. When he retired, he moved to Sun City Center, a Florida community much like his fictional Sun Coast Shores. He lives with his wife Katherine and teaches Information Technology at Hillsborough Community College.

Sarah Glenn
"Bolita and Blues"

Sarah E. Glenn, a Jane-of-all-trades, has a B.S. in Journalism. She loves reading and writing mystery and horror stories, often with a sidecar of funny. Several have appeared in mystery and paranormal anthologies, including G.W. Thomas' Ghostbreakers series, *Futures Mysterious Anthology Magazine*, and *Fish Tales: The Guppy Anthology*. She belongs to Sisters in Crime, SinC Guppies, and the Short Mystery Fiction Society. Sarah edited two different local newsletters in Lexington, Kentucky, and was a first-round judge in *Futures Mysterious Anthology Magazine's* 2003 'Slesar's Twist Contest'. Later, she was a judge for the 2011 and 2012 Derringers. Since 2013, she has overseen multiple anthologies and story collections for Mystery and Horror, LLC. Interesting fact: Sarah worked the Reports Desk for her local police department, and criminals are dumb.

Tanya Goodwin
"The Fun House"

Tanya Goodwin writes suspense, police procedurals, and crime fiction. Her experiences as a physician are reflected in her characters and in her stories, and her life as a doctor allows her to switch from stethoscope to keyboard. A former New Yorker, she now resides in Florida. Tanya is a member of Sisters in Crime and Mystery Writers of America. You can visit her at her website http://www.tanyagoodwin.com.

Margo Hammond
"How to Get Away with Murder in Florida"

Things to Know About Margo Hammond:
1. Born in Kenosha, Wisconsin.
2. Founded the Times Festival of Reading during her 16-year stint as the book editor at the *St. Petersburg Times.*
3. Co-authored *Between the Covers: The Book Babes Guide to a Woman's Reading Pleasures* (DaCapo Press).
4. Married her husband on his 50th birthday so he would remember their anniversary
5. Writes on literature and art for Creative Pinellas' *Arts Coast Magazine.*
6. Blogs at *Creative Late Bloomers,* launched to honor her mom who began writing a newspaper column at 86.
7. Regularly gives talks at the Dalí Museum and the Osher Lifelong Living Institute at Eckerd College. Most popular: Surrealism and Crime.
8. Is working on a mystery set at the Dalí Museum.
9. Loves to make lists.

10. Current favorite mysteries: Richard Osman's Thursday Murder Club series.
11. Current favorite mystery character: Maud, the septuagenarian psychopath in Helene Tursten's *An Elderly Lady Is Up to No Good.*

Cynthia Harrison
"Madder"

Cynthia Harrison writes crime fiction, in a category she calls "edgy cozy." She has been published in print, audio, and e-book by the Wild Rose Press since 2012. Before that, she self-published a creative writing manual for classes she taught at her local community college. Cindy has been blogging since 2002 on www.cynthiaharrison.com. Her latest novel, *Jane in St. Pete*, is available on Amazon, iPhone, and Nook. Cindy has two grown sons and three grandchildren. She and her husband live in Florida.

Jenna Kernan
"Small Craft Advisory"

Publishers' Weekly bestselling author, Jenna Kernan, writes domestic thrillers and fast-paced crime thrillers described by readers as "jaw-dropping," "riveting," and "gritty." In 2021, she received a Silver Falchion award nomination from Killer Nashville and a bronze medal from the Florida Book Awards in the Popular Fiction category for her debut thriller, *A Killer's Daughter*. Living on Florida's Gulf Coast with her husband, Jenna is a genre-jumper with roots in romantic suspense, who has written over forty books. Look for her latest domestic thrillers, *The Adoption* and *The Ex-wives* available now. Jenna enjoys kayaking, fishing, scuba diving, and clearing a room with her banjo ukulele. A natural redhead, she has increased her sunblock to SPF 50. For a FREE book, join her newsletter and visit her at jennakernan.com.

Cindy Martin
"The Malice Challenge"

Cindy Martin spent 20 years chasing down fugitives. As a producer for the *America's Most Wanted* TV show, she travelled throughout the U.S. and abroad interviewing law enforcement, victims' families, and wrote and edited hundreds of crime segments. Cindy has received three TELLYs and two Cinema In Industry awards for her research and documentary programs. In 2022, she was a finalist in the thriller category of the Six-Word Mystery Contest sponsored by the Rocky Mountain Chapter of Mystery Writers of America. Cindy is a member of National Sisters in Crime, the Florida Gulf Coast Chapter of SinC, Guppies, National Mystery Writers of America, and the Florida Chapter of MWA. Currently, Cindy is writing her debut thriller novel. Aside from reading and writing, Cindy is a fitness instructor. She lives in South Florida with her husband, three daughters, two cats and two dogs.

Gwen Mayo
"Bolita and Blues"

Gwen Mayo is passionate about blending the colorful history of her native Kentucky with her love for mystery fiction. She currently lives and writes in Safety Harbor, Florida, but grew up in a large Irish family in the hills of Eastern Kentucky. Her stories have appeared in anthologies, at online short fiction sites, and in micro-fiction collections. She belongs to Sisters in Crime, SinC Guppies, the Short Mystery Fiction Society, and the Independent Book Publishers Association.

Gwen attended the University of Kentucky on a poetry scholarship but has an associate degree in business and a bachelor's degree in political science. She was a judge for the 2012 Derringers, and the coordinator for the 2011 Derringers.

Interesting fact: Gwen was a brakeman and railroad engineer from 1983 - 1987.

Teresa Michael
"Big Feet"

Teresa Michael is an award-winning mystery author. The first book in the *Mariposa Café* Mystery Series, "Murder in Mariposa Beach," received the Firebird Book Award in the mystery category. Teresa enjoys reading, writing, chocolate chip cookies, a great cappuccino, good food, great wine, and traveling with friends and family. She was the Team Manager for US Archery at the 1996 and 2000 Olympic Games and has visited 49 states and many foreign countries. She is a member of Florida Writers Association,

Florida Chapter of Mystery Writers of America, Southwest Florida Fiction Writers, Women Fiction Writers Association, and is a past president of Florida Gulf Coast Sisters in Crime.

Teresa lives in Sarasota, FL with her husband and two cats and hopes to someday visit that 50th state. Visit her website at https://teresamichaelwrites.pubsitepro.com for more information.

Monica Faeth Myers
"The Purse Detective"

For over twenty years, as a contractor at NASA's Goddard Space Flight Center, Monica Faeth Myers led an international team based at Oxford that used remote sensing satellite data to develop global risk maps of infectious diseases. In 2022, she moved from Bethesda, MD back to Florida where she went to high school and college, abandoning over 110 tea party places from her annual holiday throwback event as well as self-help projects that failed to deliver. She now resides in Clearwater Beach with her husband and dog. Her three adult children are in the world and doing well.

Stephanie Palmarosa
"Buried Secrets of Spanish Point"

A career as a paralegal in family law introduced Stephanie to a broad swath of society inspiring her creation of colorful characters with humor and humanity. She is hard at work on her *Judge Kari* cozy mystery series including *Judge or Not to Judge, Judge Me Tender,* and a third book in progress. She is a member of the Florida Gulf Coast and Guppy Chapters of the Sisters in Crime organization. Stephanie has three adult children and lives in Sarasota, Florida with her law enforcement husband, dog, and cats. Follow her on Instagram @stephaniepalmarosa or visit www.stephaniepalmarosa.com.

Jenny Ramaley
"A Long-Term Plan"

Drawing on her communications experience with engineering, safety, and cybersecurity companies, Jenny Ramaley creates contemporary thrillers and mysteries for teens and adults. Jenny was a Rutgers One-on-One mentee, and her work placed in the Academy Nicholl Fellowships in Screenwriting and Chesterfield Writer's Film Project competitions. Raised in Ohio with Kentucky roots, she and her better half split their time between Pittsburgh and Florida's Gulf Coast. Nothing makes her happier than tromping through Myakka State Park in turquoise hiking boots, jotting story ideas in a dog-eared Moleskine. Visit Jenny's website at jennyramaley.com.

Martha Reed
"Maddie Tate Built a Tabby Wall"

Martha Reed is a multi-award-winning crime fiction author. Her short story, "The Honor Thief," was included in the Bouchercon 2022 Anthony Award-winning anthology, *This Time For Sure,* edited by Hank Phillippi Ryan. Martha's Crescent City NOLA Mystery, "Love Power" won a 2021 Killer Nashville Silver Falchion Award and features Gigi Pascoe, a transgender sleuth. *The Nature of the Grave,* the second book in her *John and Sarah Jarad Nantucket Mystery*

series, won an Independent Publisher (IPPY) Book Award for Mid-Atlantic Best Regional Fiction. Martha is the Immediate Past President of the Florida Gulf Coast Sisters in Crime and fully supports SinC's mission statement: "to promote the ongoing advancement, recognition, and professional development of women crime writers."

Visit her website www.reedmenow.com for more.

B. W. W. Roark
"Accidents Happen"

The "what-if" seed was planted early in this native Floridian. B. W. W. Roark was born in Saint Augustine; an ancient city filled with mysteries. She spent her childhood hunting for buried treasure along the muddy edge of the Matanzas River, making up lies with a friend about their superhero pets, and listening to her father talk about his work on the newspaper with exciting headlines of murder and mayhem.

To help with college expenses, Roark wrote a weekly article about the school's events. After graduating from the University of South Florida, she moved to the southern end of the state. This is where she met her husband. Creating bedtime stories for their two children, and later for grandkids, reminded her of how much she loved diving into the world of "what-if." Today, her writing focus has returned to murder mysteries, as well as supernatural and paranormal fiction.

Barbara Ryan
"Do You Believe in Monsters?"

Barbara Ryan, Ph.D., is a sociologist who has published books and journal articles on Feminism, The Women's Movement, and Identity Politics. She co-founded and directed a Gender and Women's Studies program, was a book review editor for *Gender & Society*, and was a Fulbright Scholar to India. She presented papers on feminism, family, sex and gender, and social activism at national and international meetings throughout Europe.

She is a Mystery Writers of America, National Sisters in Crime, and Sarasota Fiction Writers member. Currently, she is the President of Florida Gulf Coast Sisters in Crime. Recently, her short story, "Do You Believe in Monsters?" was included in *Paradise is Deadly: Gripping Tales from Florida's Gulf Coast*, an anthology she co-edited. Her murder mystery series, featuring Megan Mahony, PI, is in process, with the first book, *Selective Killings,* set in Philadelphia, and the second, *Escape to Murder*, in Sarasota, Florida.

ACKNOWLEDGEMENTS

Florida Gulf Coast Sisters in Crime membership would like to thank the dedicated members who stepped up to help bring their first Anthology to publication. A huge thank you goes to the committee chair, Teresa Michael, who not only kept committee members on track with regular meetings, marking their progress, but she also organized systems to track all aspects of the process in a professional and easy to follow way. This included the timeline duties to publication, tracking the Judges progress, the authors' and editors' submissions, and much more.

We offer a special thank you to the committee members who took time to Zoom in on many meetings. Those who contributed and collaborated on all points were: Wendy Dingwall, Harold Emanuel, Sarah Glenn (Publisher), Martha Reed and Barbara Ryan.

A big thank you to committee members, Wendy Dingwall, Martha Reed, and Barbara Ryan who also took on the extra task of editing to help each author make their short story shine!

A final shout out to the esteemed judges, Collette Bancroft, Lisa Black, Alan Orloff, and Susan Thibadeau, for taking time out of their busy writing schedules to read and judge the submissions using the point system set out by the Anthology committee. We are eternally grateful for their expertise in judging these stories!

ABOUT FLORIDA GULF COAST SISTERS IN CRIME

From its inception in December 2015, the Florida Gulf Coast chapter of Sisters in Crime has dedicated itself to providing opportunities for novice writers to become published and for published writers to further improve their craft and careers. We have welcomed avid mystery and crime readers, as well as librarians, publishers, booksellers, and those interested in promoting local authors and their books.

Over the years, Florida Gulf Coast Sisters in Crime has invited *New York Times* bestselling authors to speak. Our first meeting in March 2016 featured NYT bestselling author Lisa Black. Since then, we've been honored to present authors such as Mary Anna Evans— awards too numerous to mention; two-time Edgar Award winner Lori Roy; bestselling cozy mystery author Carol J. Perry; award-winning thriller author Tori Eldridge; and others.

We offer monthly programming that helps enhance our members' craft. Topics range from workshops on elements and aspects of writing, such as scene setting, dazzling dialogue, character enrichment, and short story. We've offered publishing panels and programs addressing promotion of the authors and their books. These types of programs are ongoing, and many are now available on our chapter's YouTube channel.

We sponsor booths at local and statewide book fairs and craft festivals featuring our member authors as they promote themselves and sell signed copies of their books.

From our early days of fifteen to twenty members, we've grown to become a dynamic group of over sixty. We are hoping to meet the eighty-member mark in 2023. For more information or to join Florida Gulf Coast Sisters in Crime, visit: http://flgcsinc.com.

9 781949 281248